LAWYERS IN GRAY

JOHN ELLSWORTH

vinci
BOOKS

By John Ellsworth

Michael Gresham Legal Thrillers

The Lawyer
The Defendant's Father
The Law Partners
Carlos the Ant
Sakharov the Bear
Annie's Verdict
Dead Lawyer on Aisle 11
30 Days of Justis
The Fifth Justice
Girl, Under Oath
Lawyers in Gray

Vinci Books

vinci-books.com

Published by Vinci Books Ltd in 2025

1

Copyright © John Ellsworth 2022

The author has asserted their moral right to be identified as the author of this work in accordance with the Copyright, Designs and Patents Act 1988.

This work is a work of fiction. Names, characters, places and incidents are the product of the author's imagination or are used fictitiously. Any resemblance to actual persons, living or dead, places and incidents is entirely coincidental.

All rights reserved. No part of this publication may be copied, reproduced, distributed, stored in any retrieval system, or transmitted in any form or by any means, including photocopying, recording, or other electronic or mechanical methods, nor used as a source for any form of machine learning including AI datasets, without the prior written permission of the publisher.

The publisher and the author have made every effort to obtain permissions for any third party material used in this book and to comply with copyright law. Any queries in this respect should be brought to the attention of the publisher and any omissions will be corrected in future editions.

A CIP catalogue record for this book is available from the British Library.

Paperback ISBN: 9781036704636

The EU GPSR authorised representative is Logos Europe, 9 rue Nicolas Poussion, 17000 La Rochelle, France contact@logoseurope.eu

Printed and bound in Great Britain by Clays Ltd, Elcograf S.p.A.

Chapter One

FRANK HEMET

On Monday morning, Frank Hemet drove down 6th Street to Indiana Avenue and the Gray law building in Washington, DC. He had made it in plenty of time for his interview at Gray, Soledad, Wilmar, and Bendix.

After circling the block twice, Hemet spotted an opening, cut the car sharply right, and slid into a parking spot on Indiana Avenue NW. He stepped from his Porsche into ankle-deep snow and began the trudge. Up the curb at the corner, then four doors down.

Upstairs, the Hiring Committee was taking a final look at his application. Printed crisply on linen paper, his resume made him out to be the kind of lawyer they were looking for: University of Michigan law, number two in his class, a clerkship in the Seventh Circuit for a year, a mother who'd recently gone into assisted living in Arlington and now her devoted son was returning to DC to look after her. A family man and that meant everything to a law firm that prided itself on its family values. It all looked good.

Except Frank Hemet's resume was a lie.

They had thoroughly prepared him. His leather Lauren topcoat shed the gently falling snow, while underneath, his two-button Dior suit of navy virgin wool looked rich and capable. They knew that the hiring committee would ask him about federal trials, so he'd been rigorously prepared. He'd watched several trials in US District Court while his assigned federal prosecutor explained what was happening and how Hemet might copy and use it when the time came. They quizzed him every day. They were dead serious about federal trial practice.

He adjusted his half-Windsor in the plate glass door, stood up a little straighter, and approached building security just inside.

"Frank Hemet here for Gray, Soledad, Wilmar, and Bendix."

The older man scanned his screen. "Here you are, Mr. Hemet. Take the visitors' tag and the middle elevator to seven. Get off and go right to reception. They're expecting you in five minutes."

"Thank you, Mr. Duncan."

He did as told, appearing nervous when the elevator doors whooshed open on seven—the more anxious, the more realistic.

They greeted him with an outer office silent as the moon and a staff-free zone at the cherry reception desk. He gave it several minutes, thinking someone must have just stepped away and would be right back. But then the clock turned over, and it was 8:04. What the hell?

He walked beyond reception and peered down the hallway. A small knot of suits gathered at a corner office. He headed straight for them.

It was an anxious group outside the office, and nobody bothered to ask who he was. An older woman whispered to

Hemet that Tommy Gray wouldn't answer his home phone, his mobile phone went to mail, and his office phone kicked over to after-hours routing, even though it was after eight o'clock in the morning. Everyone knew that he never arrived after seven for work. His arrival time was mythical, as constant as the sunrise.

Lanny Jones from Security produced a keyring. He pushed through the crowd.

"It damn sure isn't like him," said Jones as the key turned. The door opened in, and Hemet let the flow of lawyers carry him inside. The next part was a startling death scene.

Sprawled back in his blue leather executive chair was Tommy Gray. Hemet's stomach spasmed: half of Gray's head was pasted to the wall behind him. The 12-gauge shotgun lay on the floor to Gray's right.

A blond man with a transparent lock of hair centered on his scalp entered the room, spun around, taking it all in, and exclaimed, "I have dibs on this office."

"Arnie, give it a rest," said a woman who looked older than the others—Hemet's quick assessment after looking into the most intelligent eyes he'd ever come across. She wore a pencil skirt and a yellow silk blouse. He memorized how her fingers were perfectly manicured, and her eyes were of Elizabeth Taylor violet.

She continued castigating Arnie. "Law firm by-laws hand out office suites. Not your dumb-ass dibs. Who even does dibs anymore?"

When he heard Arnie's claim on the office, Hemet's face tightened, and he said, "Show some respect! He's still warm!"

Arnie responded by touching the dead man's arm. He shook his head. "Not warm at all. Cool as a Safeway ham."

Hemet was upset beyond just the man's idiocy. When he had met with Tommy Gray last Friday at headquarters, Gray had made the offer, and Hemet had accepted. But what happened now that the Chairman was dead?

Two men came forward and had a look. Others turned away in tears, while some tried to remain strong, betrayed by faces that spelled shock. As for Hemet, he had seen so many death scenes he felt nothing either way. But with Gray dead, he knew he needed to improvise, starting right then if he would be hired. He thought he saw an opening in his favor with this group: they needed him. He immediately became indispensable.

He jumped forward and restrained Arnie as he was about to compromise the crime scene by moving the shotgun. "It's a potential crime scene," he said as Arnie twisted violently away from him. "Don't touch or move a thing unless you want your fingerprints on the evidence the police will be examining. And you don't want your fingerprints on that 12-gauge you're about to move."

"Well, look at this, everyone," said Arnie sarcastically. "This has got to be the new criminal lawyer we haven't hired yet." he stuck out his hand and smiled a porcelain smile. "Arnie Truckee, Frank. See? I already know your name. My old man always said never forget a man's name. It's his most important possession. Is your name your best asset, Frank?"

Hemet ignored Truckee. "Listen, everyone, touch nothing. We might be standing inside a crime scene, and that's how we should treat it for the moment. We should all leave the office and wait for the police elsewhere. Has someone called them?"

Inga Kopovsky, the lawyer with the intelligent eyes, held

her phone out to Hemet. "Done, dialed 911 as soon as we came through the door."

"Well done," he said. "All right, everyone, let's go into the main conference room. Inga has the police on the way. We want to present a calm front ready to cooperate without a hair out of place. Inga, please lead the way."

"Hey, I like this take-charge guy," Arnie cried. "I feel innocent already!"

They made their way into the firm's swank meet-and-greet room—cut from the same pattern as 10,000 others in Washington, DC—and painted in the same Pantone gray as the building's exterior.

The partners gathered around, selected chairs, poured water out of crystal pitchers into crystal glasses, and made anxious chatter. Once everyone was seated, Hemet spoke up again. "Let me just suggest that we try to figure out who spoke last to Mr. Gray. The police will want to know who was last with him, so let's work that out before they get here. We don't need any slip-ups in the story we're going to tell them."

Tissues were balled up and sent to the trash, and handkerchiefs folded and put away—no more tears, time for strategy—precisely what lawyers love best.

Said the partner Hemet would learn was Mergers and Acquisitions, "He spoke with me last night about eight o'clock as I passed his office as I was leaving for home. He called me, and I stuck my head in the door. He wanted to know how many new cases I'd opened this month."

"Typical," snorted Truckee. "I'd expect nothing less from the money-grubbing senior."

"Arnie! For fuck's sake!" Inga drew a deep breath and stopped. "Pardon me."

"It sounds like he was compos mentis," offered Sylvester

Clemens, the partner heading up the Trusts and Estates practice, where every case asked the same questions about mental competency. "Asking about new business—that's a good sign he was all there," Clemens continued with a knowing smile and pointed at his head.

"I was in Tommy's office, using the en suite bathroom when Alfred passed by," said Inga, giving a name to the M and A man. "I could hear Tommy call to him."

"You were?" asked Truckee suspiciously. "In his office doing what?"

Inga sniffed and tossed her head. "That, dear Arnie, will be a confidential matter between the detectives and me. That's all I have to say about it to you."

"So you were the last one to see him alive?" guessed Truckee. "This is getting a little funky. Everyone knows he had an eye for you. Are you listed in his last will and testament by any chance?"

Inga ignored the comment. "It looks like our board of directors is all here. I'm calling an emergency meeting. I think we need to appoint Frank Hemet here as our representative with the police. And we need to hire him to do that. Not how we usually do things, but this could blow up in our faces. All in favor?"

Six hands went up. Arnie played tricks, raising then lowering his hand several times. Inga said, "Motion passed. Frank Hemet, welcome to Gray. Can we take it you have accepted our offer?"

"What is the offer?"

Roman Challis, who had automatically become Gray's next Chairman and managing partner, spoke up. "Here's the offer: two-fifty a year guaranteed against actual earnings. Retirement fully funded, health and dental 100%, Wizards tickets, and biannual bonuses. What say you?"

"Yes, I accept the offer. Why don't we move beyond that quickly, and let's plan our meeting with the police? I want to talk to them as the firm rep for openers."

"Question," said Arnie, raising his hand to be called upon. "The police will want to speak with all of us. Should we have our separate lawyers with us? That would get expensive fast."

"That's an excellent question, Arnie," Hemet replied. "For safety's sake, if you were around the office between four p.m. yesterday and seven a.m. this morning, it would be advisable to have an attorney. We're talking about deniability here and the ability to prove your innocence."

"What about me?" said Mergers and Acquisitions.

"Yes, sir?" he said. "What is your name?"

"Alfred Falsgraf. I do M and A. I was with Tommy Gray last night about five-thirty and again at eight as we talked about the firm's most vital M and A case. We were together for maybe fifteen minutes. Do I need counsel?"

"I think you do," Hemet said without hesitation. "Incidentally," he tacked on, "Does anybody know whether Mr. Gray was right- or left-handed?"

"Left-handed," Inga immediately said.

"Left," said Falsgraf. "He always sat beside me at Thursday lunch. It was an effort banging elbows as we ate. I'm right-handed. We fought it out every week," he added with a sad smile. "God, I miss Tommy already."

"Well," Frank said, "his being left-handed is interesting. I say this because the gun in his office is beneath his right hand. If he shot himself, he did it using his right hand."

"Jesus!" said Arnie. "Man, I'm so glad you're on our side, Hemet."

Hemet looked from face to face. "Any ideas about that?"

"Strange," they all agreed. "Unexplainable. Makes little sense."

Inga pursed her lips and blew a stream of air. "Wow."

Hemet said, "It wouldn't be unheard of for someone to shoot themself with their weak hand, but it would be awkward. People who commit suicide almost always make double sure they don't survive and go to extra lengths to make sure the manner of death is foolproof. That's why it bothers me he used his weak hand to shoot himself. We'll leave that one for the police to figure out."

"Now, I want my own lawyer," Arnie said. "Mr. Hemet, you can go home now. You just earned your salary for a year."

"You're suggesting there's a killer loose among us?" Falsgraf said with a slight lisp. "I dislike this, period. Was I the last one with him last night? Oh, my God."

"Don't panic," Hemet said. "My observation is probably easily explained away. Maybe he ate left-handed and did other things with his right. It happens."

Falsgraf said to Arnie, "I'm with you. I'm lawyering up. Wait, Mr. Hemet—"

"—Frank, please."

"Frank, please answer this. Why can't you act as the criminal lawyer for everyone in the firm? Wouldn't that work?"

"No," Hemet said. "There will be conflicts among you all."

"And a lawyer cannot represent clients with conflicting interests. Got it."

"Three bonus points for you," Arnie said with a yawn he did not cover. "You're a lawyer, Falstaff—"—purposely calling him by the name of a once-popular beer. "You should know these things without stopping to think about it."

"Given the right hand, left-hand question," Hemet said, "it would likely be a good idea for us all to return to our offices and start calling criminal lawyers—just to be safe. And Mr. Challis, leave the building. Go somewhere they can't locate you because I don't want you giving a statement just yet. You're a political representative of Gray, and whatever you say will impact the firm's contract with DOJ. So you disappear. Inga and I will hunt down the lead detective and give an official firm statement. They'll be after that any minute, anyway. So the rest of you should head on out. Now."

Inga Kopovsky stood aside while the group rose and headed for the door with Roman Challis in the lead. When they were gone, and it was just the two of them, she sat down. They could hear the police calling to each other in the hallway outside. He held a finger to his lips. She crossed her legs and pulled a cigarette out of her jacket pocket. She lit up and blew smoke at the wall and said in a whisper, "If they swab his penis," she said slowly and judiciously, "they'll find my DNA on him."

"So, you were lovers."

"Sometimes yes, sometimes no. We fought like cats and dogs."

"Who all knows you fought?"

She took a deep drag and held it down. Then, in a long exhale, she said, smoke creeping out from beneath her shiny white teeth, "Our computers know. We fought by email."

"They'll have his computer locked away already," Hemet said, picturing the police he knew were already at work in Gray's office.

"I know. I'm sunk."

"Without giving me details, when was the last time you fought?"

"Last night. When I left him, I was in a fury, and so was he. 'You deserve to have someone just step up and shoot you,' were my parting words to him. Jesus, Joseph, and Mary."

"Indeed. Not good at all because it's on the CCTV video. What did you fight about?"

"Top-secret documents."

"What about them?"

"I was afraid they were going to be disclosed."

"Disclosed? By Tommy?"

"That's right."

Hemet moved on without following up. There was more, but he didn't want to know it just then. "When was the last email you received from Gray?"

"Midnight. Tommy said he should just shoot himself if I felt that way. Something to that effect."

"Oh. Not good, Inga."

"You will be my lawyer."

"I will?"

"I'm speaking as the second chairman. You now represent me. Don't worry. I'll pay your usual fee."

"Let's talk about it."

She shook her head and tapped ash into her cupped hand. "No need to talk. You're my guy."

Hemet had to ask. "Inga, if I may, how old are you?"

"Fifty-two. I practice tax law and have for nearly thirty years."

"And Tommy Gray was seventy?"

"Yes. Just."

She cocked her head and looked at him. Then a smile crossed her face. "Oh, come on, say it."

"What? No, I wasn't—"

"Yes, you were. What are two old coots thinking, doing it on the desk at fifty-two and seventy."

"I wasn't thinking exactly that," Hemet said, and he felt somewhat outsmarted, for she had got the truth out of him. That couldn't happen again, he thought, with a newfound respect for Inga Kopovsky.

"We had makeup sex, if you must know."

"When?"

She smiled and stubbed her cigarette out in a cut crystal glass.

"This morning at five in his office. Yes, he was as alive as he ever got when we screwed. I can attest to that."

"What happened after that?"

"I went home to change for work."

"And you came back, and he was dead?"

"Pretty much. Does that make me a suspect?"

Hemet's forehead furrowed as he gave it his best thinking.

"Maybe the strongest suspect." He at last said.

"So, what do I do?"

"Get yourself a real lawyer and don't talk to the police. Ever."

"I said you were my lawyer."

"You don't want me. I'm not that kind of lawyer."

"What kind are you then?"

"Not that kind."

There was a knock on the door. Hemet answered and found himself face to face with two suited-up detectives, badge lanyards around their necks, notepads at the ready. Hemet blocked the door.

"We've got a problem right outta the gate," said the deeply tanned detective just returned from Cabo. "The serial number on the Mossberg shotgun is filed off. So we're looking for a metal file with filings to match the gun's metal. Where do we start?"

Hemet said, "I suggest you start with a search warrant. After you have probable cause, which you don't."

The detectives traded a look. "So that's how you wanna play this?" said the detective with no tan.

"Is there any other way?" stated Hemet. He smiled at the detectives. "You are on notice that I represent all attorneys and staff in this law firm. You are on notice you are not to speak to any of them outside my presence. Now leave our building and don't come back without a search warrant," he finished and shut the door on them.

"You lied," said Inga, "you *are* that kind of lawyer."

"Suppose you show me to my new office."

Chapter Two

MILES STANDISH

My name is Miles Standish, and I was once the managing partner at Frank Hemet's new employer, Gray law. Top secret documents had walked out of Gray while I headed up the 700-lawyer firm. The papers had surfaced inside the files of our adversary, a group of Russians who were fracking American oil and gas deposits.

The mess was blamed on me, as it happened on my watch. I had no idea who the guilty party was, and I had no idea how to catch them. I wasn't a spy and didn't know the first thing about spying. That was all about to change.

I was fired, and Tommy Gray took over until his death. His time at the helm was about three months, give or take. During that time, I fumed and fought back feelings that threatened to load my gun and send me back to the law firm and start shooting. As an Afghanistan combat veteran, I was pretty capable of gunning down those who had voted me out.

The week after Tommy's death, the US Attorney hit me with a grand jury subpoena. So I waited for my day, then drove downtown and parked in witness parking at the US District Court building on Constitution Avenue.

The time was 8:57 when I arrived outside the grand jury room. I was escorted inside by an overweight US Marshal who kept his hand on his gun the whole time he steered me to the witness chair as if I were incapable of finding it on my own. I was sure the grand jury noticed.

The Assistant US Attorney with the shaved head drank down his cold coffee and wiped his mouth on his navy coat sleeve. His name was Llewelyn Jewel, and he projected the unbelieving voice all feds were taught to use, and said to me, "Your name is Miles Standish?"

"Correct," I answered, steadying my voice.

"Narrowing down, now. While you were the managing partner at Gray law, top-secret government documents entrusted to your firm wound up in Russian hands, is that correct?"

"Correct."

"Suppose you tell the grand jury how that happened."

"I don't know how it happened."

"Suppose you tell the grand jury how you sold those documents to the Russians."

"I did not."

"I believe you're lying. Let me tell you why."

"Well, that's fair-minded," I said sarcastically. I was there for target practice, I realized.

He dropped his cheaters over his gray eyes. "I have examined your 2018 tax return, Mr. Standish. The return includes what the IRS calls a LUQ—a large, unexplained, questionable deposit. Your deposit is November 17, 2018, for $225,000. Does that ring a bell?"

"It does."

"What is that deposit about?"

"I did off-site work for a client."

"Off-site?"

"On my own time. Gray law allowed us 100 hours of off-site work a year. What we earned, we kept."

"Client name?"

"Privileged. I can't tell you that."

"Would it be Western Energy Reserves?" That was the Russian fracking group using a common American-style name.

"Same answer."

"Could it have been payment for top-secret documents you sold?" He looked at the jury, telling them here came the key point.

"No."

"Isn't it true you were fired from Gray law because you were thought to be guilty of selling documents?"

"I've heard that rumor. But I don't know the exact reason I was let go."

"Come now. Are we sure about that?"

"Yes."

"A little background into your job at Gray law. Tell the jury your version of the Russian invasion, as you've been known to call it, Mr. Standish. The jury wants to hear more about the Russians."

"Well, Russian wildcatters came to the US in 2014. They were a flood of locusts. They managed to toxify an Oklahoma lake and my firm was hired by the DOJ to help stop them. We received Top Secret government records. Long story short, these records turned up in the Russian files. We had leaked."

"So you admit they came from your law firm, Mr. Standish. Would I be right?"

"So it would seem."

"And what did DHS do when it found out its documents were leaked? What did the EPA do?"

"The EPA panicked over the leak. They called me in and told me they would sever all ties with Gray law unless the firm took significant security measures. I returned to Gray and called an emergency board meeting. The board's immediate response was it needed to take decisive action to show the EPA we were cleaning up our law firm. They decided I would be the burnt offering and voted me out 3-2. Then they voted in Tommy Gray as the new Chairman. Tommy had served ten years in Army Intelligence in Iraq. The board rallied around Tommy, the son of the founder of Gray law. The board could trust Tommy to turn the ship around. The irony was, so could I."

"How close were they to exposing you? Isn't it true you were the one selling documents?"

"No."

"Did you have any off-shore bank accounts in 2018?"

"None."

"Have you had any since?"

"None."

"I'm ready to eat lunch. We're going to lunch now. You're excused now, Mr. Standish. We will contact you for fingerprinting and DNA samples and a mug shot."

"Am I being arrested?"

"I can't say. Have a nice lunch."

Just like that, the grand jury had departed, and Llewelyn Jewel turned away, leaving me sitting in the witness chair, looking half guilty just because I was a lawyer. I was a target, a person who might be indicted at any minute.

I gathered my things and thought back to the day I was

let go from Gray law. It was pretty damn demeaning. The memory is painful, but it came to mind whenever I was trying to switch gears and think about something pleasant, like my greenhouse plants.

After they fired me, my secretary loaded my junk drawer and ego wall in a cardboard box that said *Amazon* on the side. We hugged goodbye. She cried and told me I'd be back. Then, I was climbing into my Mercedes in the basement. I pressed the starter button on the dashboard and let out a long sigh. 'Well, this sucks,' I said. I was forty-four, unemployed, and in a marriage that was dying a slow death.

I headed home.

I was days away from becoming a spy but I had no clue.

Chapter Three

BENJI

I left the courthouse feeling sick to my stomach and confused about how I'd come across. Did I look like the ordinary spy trading US secrets for Russian rubles? How did the grand jury perceive me? They must have noticed my trembling hands and fluttery voice—which would make me look guilty as hell.

Driving along Constitution Avenue, I switched on my blinker for Pennsylvania Avenue when my phone chimed. A new text. Ordinarily, I would never have looked at it while I was driving, but there was always the off-chance it was Benji, so I tapped the screen for text messages.

Sure enough, a message from Benji. He was my ten-year-old Little Brother, and his texts and calls got top priority. Especially since Immanuel Rayito had moved back into Benji's house. He was a thug Benji's mother kept around for God only knows what. Big Brother Big Sisters had existed in DC since I was a young lawyer learning how to patty-cake. A community mentoring program matched kids from low-income, single-parent households with adult volunteer mentors. Most mentors were in their twenties. I had stuck around longer than that because there were never enough Big Brother men to go around and because Deonna couldn't have kids, so I got my fathering with Big Brother. But the real reason: I'd once had a Big Brother, and he'd changed my life.

So I pulled over and texted Benji back. Do you want to meet? I asked him. Almost immediately, the text came back, "roger." We had a spot near his low-income housing, our special meeting place. We never varied. We always went to Smitty's Cafe.

His home was Carver Terrace on Maryland NE. Twenty minutes later, I pulled into the lot at Smitty's, parked, and went inside. Smells of fried, fatty hamburger, scalded coffee, Lysol, and greasy menus. I would have to send the clothes I wore to the cleaners after the visit, for they wouldn't be fit to wear again.

It didn't take me long to find him standing slumped on his right hip at the jukebox, feeding quarters (where was he getting quarters?), bringing up Kanye and Jay-Z and Snoop. Hey, it was his quarter, so why would I tell him his sounds sucked? I came up behind him and grabbed his shoulders. He turned his head and smiled. "You came."

"I always come. One of these years, you'll get that. There's a table by the kitchen door. Let's grab it."

We did, and soon we had coffee, pie, and cherry Cokes on the way. I gave him space, letting him talk about his text when he was ready. First, we did the Wizards. I followed them religiously for Benji. Then we decided on the next movie we'd catch. Then a long discussion about why he couldn't put on weight and try out for football in September. He was very undersized for his age group (50th percentile) but determined he'd be 90th by August. His regimen consisted of protein shakes, malts, and weight-lifting to build muscle. But those things cost money, and he had none. I looked at his undersized frame and was filled with despair and a great tenderness for my boy. He just didn't get it. He had suffered malnutrition at a younger age, and his growth had stopped. I'd already had him to a nutritionist and a physical therapist for guidance in athletic training. But his damaged body just wouldn't jump back into the growth spurts enjoyed by healthy ten-year-olds. So we kept searching for answers.

"So, Immanuel kicked my ass last night." He looked away, maybe to avoid the rise he knew this would get. His mahogany skin, short braids, and flawless face made him look even younger than his ten years. It was all I could do to keep myself from swooping him up and taking him away from his worthless mother, and raising him myself. He needed it. Maybe I did, too.

"Did he break anything? Are you pissing blood? Do we need to go to the ER?"

"It wasn't like that. He used his belt." Benji turned in the booth and pulled up his shirt, showing me his back. Long, angry striations ran vertically and horizontally on his skin. Someone had played tic-tac-toe on my boy's back. I was instantly enraged. The soldier inside of me, the one who'd done two combat tours in Afghanistan, boiled up. I would kill the stepfather who came and went in Benji's household.

"Get up. We're going to talk to him."

"No, bro, he'll kill me for telling you."

"No, he won't. I'm going to put the fear in him."

"Like what, dude?"

"Like a gun up his ass."

"Wow. Now I want to be there."

"Drink up your Coke, and let's go."

I stood and tossed a twenty on the table and headed for the door. Benji caught up. We climbed into my Mercedes and headed off for the Carver Terrace on Maryland Avenue.

We didn't talk as we weaved in and out of rush hour traffic. Finally, we pulled into the parking lot for the paper-bag-brown Carver Towers and parked. Benji reached over and touched my arm. "You really carrying?"

"No."

"Immanuel be carrying a razor. He'll cut you, Mr. Standish."

"We'll see about that." I went around my car, popped the trunk, and grabbed the tire iron. "We'll see about him and his razor. Take me to your number."

We climbed concrete and steel stairs up to the fourth floor—the elevators had been out for weeks. Benji slipped his key in the knob, and in we went.

Sure enough, Immanuel was lying back on the couch reading the sports page and listening to ESPN. He was no sports enthusiast. He was a gambler—betting twenties on sporting events.

He turned his head. "What's this, Ben? You bring the man wit choo?"

"I'm not the man. I'm the Big Brother. And if you ever touch this boy again, I'm coming back, and I'm going to bash your fucking head in. You feel me?"

"I feel you, dog, but that's fucked up." He climbed up from the couch and came around to get in my space. My hand tightened on my tire iron. Just try it, I thought. Come on, come on.

He flicked his wrist, and an eight-inch switchblade flashed between us. "So. You got the tire tool. I got the blade. Who goes first, honky?"

"That would be me. I'm going to hit you once and knock your fucking brains out of your ugly fucking head, so you never touch Benji again. Get it?"

He leaned away when he saw my anger. "It not like that, dog. The boy had it coming."

"Why did a ten-year-old boy have an assault and battery coming from a prick like you?"

"He lifted five dollar out my wallet."

"Like hell he did. Benji's no petty thief like you."

"Watch that mouth, honky."

"Do something. Do anything. Come on." I was so ready to beat him bloody. Just come on! My mind was screaming. I raised the tire iron, and he stepped back two steps.

"You crazy, nigger."

"I am crazy. I love this kid, and I hate child abusers. Next time, I bring a gun, and you're going down. That's a promise, dog."

"Try me, dude."

"When I leave, if I ever hear again you've touched Benji—or his mother, I'm coming back for you, and I'm going to hurt you, fuckhead. Now get out of my sight."

He was caught between wanting to attack me and wanting me to go away. So he stepped back and went back to his newspaper."

I headed for the entrance, where I stopped and shook hands with Benji. We always shook hands now. He'd let me know when we'd outgrown hugs over a year ago. Now it was handshakes and a look into the other guy's eyes, just like I taught him.

"Call me," was all I said.

"Good on you, bro," he whispered back.

"Call me."

I went home and made some calls. For one, I had my

investigator from my old firm take on the investigation of Philomena Rashad, Benji's mother. I told him I wanted her watched for a month. All the time she spent at home; all the time she spent away or flat didn't come home at night. Photos of everyone coming and going, especially men. Track her at her work. Does she have a real job? Is she someone who's leaving for work in the morning but diverting to the underworld, the world of hard women and even harder drugs? Why was I doing all this? Because I wanted Benji, and the time would come when I'd need this information about her.

Two hours later, I called Benji's cell.

"How's it going over there?"

"I'm trying to do my math problems. Immanuel left right after you. He didn't say where he was going."

"Do you have food?"

"Not really. There are some spaghetti noodles. I eat those with salt and ketchup sometimes."

"Jesus. I'm on my way. I'll text you when I'm downstairs."

"Where we going?"

"We're going to get you something to eat. I'm thinking Safeway, and I'm thinking of a week of food. Stuff you can prepare."

"I don't know if I can wait that long, honest, Mr. Standish."

"Miles, Benji. I'm Miles to you. And if you can't wait, we'll hit a drive-through and get whatever you like. Then the grocery store. Then we can take a look at your math problems."

"Wow. Okay."

"Have you heard from mama?"

"Not since last Wednesday. Over a week ago. I'm shitting bricks they're gonna come tell me she's dead. Every time I hear someone out in the hallway, I say a prayer. The same prayer every time, and so far it's working."

"Do you think we should call children's social services? I'm leaning that way."

"No! They'll put me in foster care that's worse than here. You promised you'd never do that to me. Don't forget."

"I did make that promise. But I'm wondering if we should reconsider."

"That sounds like lawyer talk, Miles, that reconsider. A deal's a deal. There is no reconsider to real people."

"You're right, Benji. So I'm at Rochester and Grand. I'll be at your place in ten minutes. Look for a text and come right down."

I didn't tell him I hated his neighborhood at night, that it scared me. But he probably already had that figured out-- Benji was wise way beyond his years.

"I'll come right down. Goodbye."

We shopped Giant that night, then hit Jack in the Box and picked up ten tacos and drinks, then back to Benji's, where we escaped the porch sitters and made it upstairs. The math book took up the rest of our time that night. I left for home at ten.

Benji was admiring his stuffed cabinets in the kitchen as I closed the door behind me.

Good for him.

Chapter Four

MILES STANDISH

I remember none of the drive home from Benji's. I was in a rage. I tore off my clothes and pulled on my sweatpants and sweatshirt. Then I went downstairs to my gym and lifted and ran on my blade prosthesis until I was drained, followed by a protein drink and thirty minutes of meditation. The blade prosthesis was the gift Afghanistan gave me in 2004 when my Humvee hit an IED. Below-the-knee amputation, but I didn't let it slow me down and ran five miles a day on my treadmill.

When I came back upstairs, there was a message on my cell phone. My wife, Deonna, had left directions for watering her plants out back in the greenhouse. It seemed Max didn't want her coming here anymore without him to look after her.

Suddenly, I had the urge to maul Max Jennings. Max was the Gray lawyer Deonna left me over. When they had sacked me, he was the first to raise his hand to fire me. Deonna, now shacked up with Max and looked extraordinarily happy at our divorce mediations.

It was time to make coffee and talk myself down. The counselors at the VA were all about vets learning to talk themselves down from violent thoughts. So, I did that, made some coffee, and checked my impulses at the door. I focused my mind on Deonna calling me that morning and telling me to water her plants in the greenhouse. Everyone would return in one piece from that mission.

Chapter Five

My name is Michael Gresham, and I was once the managing partner at Frank Hemet's new employer, Gray law. Top secret documents had walked out of Gray while I headed up the 700-lawyer firm. The papers had surfaced inside the files of our adversary, a group of Russians who were fracking American oil and gas deposits.

The mess was blamed on me, as it happened on my watch. I had no idea who the guilty party was, and I had no idea how to catch them. I wasn't a spy and didn't know the first thing about spying. That was all about to change.

I was fired, and Tommy Gray took over until his death. His time at the helm was about three months, give or take. During that time, I fumed and fought back feelings that threatened to load my gun and send me back to the law firm and start shooting. As an Afghanistan combat veteran, I was pretty capable of gunning down those who had voted me out.

The week after Tommy's death, the US Attorney hit me with a grand jury subpoena. So I waited for my day, then drove downtown and parked in witness parking at the US District Court building on Constitution Avenue.

The time was 8:57 when I arrived outside the grand jury room. I was escorted inside by an overweight US Marshal who kept his hand on his gun the whole time he steered me to the witness chair as if I were incapable of finding it on my own. I was sure the grand jury noticed.

The Assistant US Attorney with the shaved head drank down his cold coffee and wiped his mouth on his navy coat sleeve. His name was Llewelyn Jewel, and he projected the unbelieving voice all feds were taught to use, and said to me, "Your name is Michael Gresham?"

"Correct," I answered, steadying my voice.

"Narrowing down, now. While you were the managing partner at Gray law, top-secret government documents entrusted to your firm wound up in Russian hands, is that correct?"

"Correct."

"Suppose you tell the grand jury how that happened."

"I don't know how it happened."

"Suppose you tell the grand jury how you sold those documents to the Russians."

"I did not."

"I believe you're lying. Let me tell you why."

"Well, that's fair-minded," I said sarcastically. I was there for target practice, I realized.

He dropped his cheaters over his gray eyes. "I have examined your 2018 tax return, Mr. Standish. The return includes what the IRS calls a LUQ—a large, unexplained, questionable deposit. Your deposit is November 17, 2018, for $225,000. Does that ring a bell?"

"It does."

"What is that deposit about?"

"I did off-site work for a client."

"Off-site?"

"On my own time. Gray law allowed us 100 hours of off-site work a year. What we earned, we kept."

"Client name?"

"Privileged. I can't tell you that."

"Would it be Western Energy Reserves?" That was the Russian fracking group using a common American-style name.

"Same answer."

"Could it have been payment for top-secret documents you sold?" He looked at the jury, telling them here came the key point.

"No."

"Isn't it true you were fired from Gray law because you were thought to be guilty of selling documents?"

"I've heard that rumor. But I don't know the exact reason I was let go."

"Come now. Are we sure about that?"

"Yes."

"A little background into your job at Gray law. Tell the jury your version of the Russian invasion, as you've been known to call it, Mr. Standish. The jury wants to hear more about the Russians."

"Well, Russian wildcatters came to the US in 2014. They were a flood of locusts. They managed to toxify an Oklahoma lake and my firm was hired by the DOJ to help stop them. We received Top Secret government records. Long story short, these records turned up in the Russian files. We had leaked."

"So you admit they came from your law firm, Mr. Standish. Would I be right?"

"So it would seem."

"And what did DHS do when it found out its documents were leaked? What did the EPA do?"

"The EPA panicked over the leak. They called me in and told me they would sever all ties with Gray law unless the firm took significant security measures. I returned to Gray and called an emergency board meeting. The board's immediate response was it needed to take decisive action to show the EPA we were cleaning up our law firm. They decided I would be the burnt offering and voted me out 3-2. Then they voted in Tommy Gray as the new Chairman. Tommy had served ten years in Army Intelligence in Iraq. The board rallied around Tommy, the son of the founder of Gray law. The board could trust Tommy to turn the ship around. The irony was, so could I."

"How close were they to exposing you? Isn't it true you were the one selling documents?"

"No."

"Did you have any off-shore bank accounts in 2018?"

"None."

"Have you had any since?"

"None."

"I'm ready to eat lunch. We're going to lunch now. You're excused now, Mr. Standish. We will contact you for fingerprinting and DNA samples and a mug shot."

"Am I being arrested?"

"I can't say. Have a nice lunch."

Just like that, the grand jury had departed, and Llewelyn Jewel turned away, leaving me sitting in the witness chair, looking half guilty just because I was a lawyer. I was a target, a person who might be indicted at any minute.

I gathered my things and thought back to the day I was let go from Gray law. It was pretty damn demeaning. The memory is painful, but it came to mind whenever I was trying to switch gears and think about something pleasant, like my greenhouse plants.

After they fired me, my secretary loaded my junk drawer and ego wall in a cardboard box that said *Amazon* on the side. We hugged goodbye. She cried and told me I'd be back. Then, I was climbing into my Mercedes in the basement. I pressed the starter button on the dashboard and let out a long sigh. 'Well, this sucks,' I said. I was forty-four, unemployed, and in a marriage that was dying a slow death.

I headed home.

I was days away from becoming a spy but I had no clue.

Chapter Six

TWO FBI AGENTS

Two FBI agents took custody of Joshua Winehouse at the Canadian border. The RCMP had arrested him in Quebec City, trying to flee after robbing a bank. Now they were turning him over to the US, where the charges against him trumped the Canadians' charges.

While the Canucks watched at the border exchange, the two FBI agents belted Winehouse in the backseat of their black Dodge Charger. They were very gentle with him.

They drove back across the Rainbow International Bridge. Three miles south, they suddenly nosed off into the woods. An exchange took place. Winehouse was moved at gunpoint into the trunk of the FBI undercover vehicle. His mouth was taped shut with silver tape. While they were at it, they taped his eyes and ears closed, too.

"Can't be too careful," said Marshal Lakin, the agent in charge. "I'd tape his asshole shut for two cents."

The man had murdered a three-year-old girl in Washington DC, the daughter of a US Senator's Chief of Staff. Marshal Lakin, the head of the Washington, DC,

FBI, had taken the arrest because the case was a newsmaker.

"Why do we even bother?" said Frank Hemet, the newest hire at Gray law, who was best friends with the Senator's Chief of Staff. Hemet had promised the Chief of Staff to transport the killer personally. He looked up from the bloated, white body of the criminal whose belly was exposed where he lay on his side in the trunk. Hemet said, "Why not just shoot him in the head and leave him for the animals?"

"Good point," said Lakin. He stood staring at the man in the trunk as he said this. The whole process passed before the older Special Agent's eyes jaded by all the court failures to punish adequately. He saw Winehouse's future: bail hearing, DNA evidence proving the semen in the little girl's body was that of the man in the trunk. A plea deal. Twenty years in prison. He would then be released into society prematurely, while his three-year-old victim was gone forever.

Lakin, a tall, muscular man who lifted every day, suddenly bent and lifted the prisoner out and let him fall handcuffed onto his face. He dragged him and propped him up against a pine tree. Then painstakingly removed all tape. He stood before the man and pulled his Glock from his waistband holster. He turned it in his hands, examining it for specks of dirt. Then he turned his attention back to Winehouse. He pointed the gun's 9 mm muzzle at his face and ever so slowly approached him until the gun touched the man's lips.

"Open," said Lakin.

Teeth chattering.

"Scared, are we?"

Hemet's hatred took a twist, and he was worried. "The RCMP arrested him just as he was boarding a ship for

Iceland. They knew why we wanted him. They still know. And we're not over five miles from the border."

"But they know the rules." The gun was still resting in the prisoner's mouth.

"True."

Lakin turned back to the prisoner and looked down. He had wet himself. "Well, that's rude," said Lakin, and he pulled the trigger twice. The Glock erupted in the quiet forest. He removed his gun from the empty skull and pulled a small bottle of clear liquid from his side pocket. With the aid of his handkerchief, he wiped down his weapon, taking special care around the muzzle where it had touched the rapist named Winehouse. Then he gathered the silver tape and made a ball.

Lakin looked up at Hemet.

"Call the next case."

Lakin then called the county sheriff and reported a shooting. A prisoner had made a break when they stopped to urinate at the roadside. Call the coroner, he ordered the sheriff. The sheriff jotted down the location and said he was on it. Lakin thanked him and said to look him up in DC that he owed lunch.

At Salamanca, they pulled into a diner for breakfast.

Five minutes later, Lakin set his menu aside. "A good shooting always makes me hungry for eggs and bacon. How about you, Hemet?"

"I think just toast and coffee for me, Sir. It messed with my appetite."

"You weren't in the wars, then."

"Thirty days in Iraq, then my shoulder was taken out by a Kalashnikov 7.62 round."

"Ouch."

"Back to the States. A year of surgeries and rehab. Then they offered me a federal job. I chose the FBI."

"Good choice."

"I still think so. The Bureau's been fair to me."

"And now we've snuck you into Gray law," said Lakin.

"I'm thinking about the Gray law business. The missing documents. Do you know this Miles Standish? Maybe I've been up against him in court a time or two. He's one of those lawyers who comes prepared. He always has a better grasp of the law and facts than even the judge."

Lakin scowled. "I want him on my team. The US Attorney thinks he's their traitor. Fuck the US Attorney. Standish is a war veteran. Lost a leg in Afghanistan. A patriot like that doesn't go bad and sell secrets to the Russians. I'm calling the US Attorney off."

"How so?"

"Tell them I won't support their case. Then they have no witnesses, and that means they have no case. I want Standish on my side because I have an idea."

"With Miles Standish?"

Lakin nodded but didn't say anymore as his breakfast had arrived. He noisily chewed his bacon and hungrily mopped yolk with toast. When Lakin was finished, there was a moment to sit back and grind away at his mouth and mustache with napkins until sure his mustache was cleared of detritus. Then he said, "I want Miles Standish to head up a team I'm putting together. I'm getting huge pressure from HQ to solve the Gray leaks without delay. Standish knows the firm, knows the players, and I like what I see in his file. He belongs to me."

"How can I help, Sir?"

"When we get back tomorrow afternoon, there's a meeting."

"All right."

Hemet waited for more, but there was nothing more forthcoming. Outside at the car, they traded places. It was Hemet's turn to drive and Lakin's turn to doze off.

Then they were headed for Washington, DC, comforted by the great justice they pulled off that morning in the woods.

Lakin patted the phone in his pocket just as he was drifting off. He had snapped a photo of the dead man's face.

The Chief of Staff would thank him with tears.

They always did.

Chapter Seven

MILES STANDISH

The day had started sunny and 31 degrees, but the morning sky was heavy with storm clouds by ten o'clock. I looked up through the greenhouse glass and knew it would soon snow. I decided on a trip to Gardiner's bookstore and the collected writings of Justice Benjamin Cardozo. He always settled me down.

I found my Cardozo at Gardiner's and was waiting to pay when someone clasped my shoulder from behind and roared, "Standish in retirement reads... Who is it, Miles? Let me see."

He reached around me and turned the book to read its cover. "Reading Benjamin Cardozo! Comeback in the works, Miles?" crowed Renz Aldrich.

My heart fell. The last person I wanted to see that day was the gossip of the nether world, Renz Aldrich himself. I forced a half-smile at a man I had once commanded from my seat as chairman.

"Hello, Aldrich. How are you getting along?"

Aldrich's Cheshire smile said I had just entered an inner

circle in conversing with him. He sounded conspiratorial, saying, "Here he is, the great man himself. All Gray would say was that you wanted more time with the family and wanted to write. How is that great memoir coming, my leader?

"You've heard wrong," said I in a subdued voice.

"Then what about lunch? Surely, you'd like to catch up on the view from twenty-thousand leagues under the seventh floor? My treat?"

I knew I had nothing else going on, plus I would've done just about anything to shut up the blathering idiot. So, I agreed to the invite. "Please. Run along to Bushnell's Inn and reserve us a table. I'll be along shortly."

"At your service, Miles. I'm on my way. Oh, here, would you mind paying for my book for me? I'll pay you back at lunch." Handing over a fat book with a bright cover and a title indicating the owner would learn how to fix common problems around the house, Aldrich backed away, throwing off a salute as he went.

Thirty minutes later, we were eating. Aldrich did all the talking. That would never change.

He buttered his bread and leaned into the table like we were conspiring.

"Terrible loss to all of us when poor Tommy was murdered. Are you on the trail of the monster who did this?"

"Only what I read in the papers. I need more water."

He ignored me.

"How's the stew?" I asked. "I hear it's a real man's dish."

"Everything you've heard. What about the pastrami sand?"

"Rubbery and not the quality of most Jewish delis, but it will do. I'm not disappointed."

"Hear that, everyone?" Aldrich announced just a little too loudly for my comfort.

"Renz, I—I—How's Max Jennings doing?"

"J-Jennings?" said Aldrich, pretending to stumble. "Do you mean what have I heard about his tryst with the beautiful Deonna?"

"No, I mean is Max still running the Western Energy Reserves cases?"

"Your old cases, captain. He runs every inch now. We're about to lose Colorado, Miles. It's about to all come tumbling down, and an enormous loss of other states, other skittish judges with it. Bad news all around, Miles. Duty calls. Do you hear its voice?"

"Sorry to hear about that, but Gray law was the one who banished me. Accused me of leaking documents to the Reds. What kind of report walked off this time?"

"Our expert's fracking report. He just mentioned that he wouldn't be surprised if half of Colorado caved in when Western Energy Reserves was done fracking there. But here is the bad part: It said Colorado's mess would've happened anyway because the aquifers are being polluted upstream by the farmers and cities. Someone released it, and now the Russians have it and are crowing."

"Damn poor job, how that was handled," I said. I'd read the report, and the guy studied surface water only. The whole point that fracking poisons underground water couldn't be raised because our trial team didn't have an expert witness in the wings to make the point and blow the report apart. So much for trial by surprise.

"And Singer, is he still in charge of the black arts?"

"John Singer's black arts will tumble to our new criminal lawyer, Frank Hemet."

The black arts were dirty, but every law firm needed a fixer. Much of it was ugly.

The check arrived after coffee. Aldrich snatched it up and produced an Amex platinum. Just as he would, I thought, just as he would.

"I'll take my book now, old chum," Renz said. I had all but forgotten about his book on home repairs. I'd left it in my car. Which meant another five minutes in Renz's presence while we hiked to my car.

"Tell you what, I ran home to change clothes and left both books there. I'll drop it by Monday if that's soon enough."

"Fine, fine, be good to see you back on Gray's soil."

"It's been nice, Aldrich," I said on the way out.

"So it has," said Aldrich. "Kisses to Deonna."

I gave a toss of my head and pushed on outside.

Now it was snowing to beat hell, and me with rear-wheel drive. What was I thinking? When would I go to AWD like everyone else? Maybe never. The roads would be salted. I'd take care. The coffee had leached out the wine.

I could just make it home in time for my nap.

Then I remembered—$49.95. My lunch had been under $30.00. Aldrich had just made $19.95 and could fix any leaky sink in the house. Assuming I ever bothered to drop off his book.

"Damn poor business," I scolded myself. "You slipping?" I taunted.

The Mercedes lost it a block from home and got stuck in the snow. My below-the-knee amputation was good for slipping and sliding in the snow. But I had no choice and set out to walk the rest of the way, planning to retrieve the useless car only when the great thaw came. In the meantime, I'd Uber.

Then, just as I dropped my chin into my chest and leaned into the blowing snow, a car pulled up beside me, slid to a stop, and the passenger door flew open. I half-turned, curious.

"Miles, my God man, you'll catch pneumonia out here. Climb on in!"

I considered. I was still a block from home and had snow in my shoes and down my gloves. My hat was wet—wool blend advertised waterproof—and moisture would any minute reach my head. I bent down and peered inside. Leaning across the passenger seat and smiling was none other than Frank Hemet. We knew each other from way back. But it was highly unusual he would stop to ask me to hop in. Was I about to be arrested?

I stepped off the sidewalk and waded through the water running along the curb, stepping through the slush and ice, and turned to enter the car butt first.

"Frank. Your timing has never been better."

"Buckle up, Miles. We've got a trip to make."

"We do?"

"I'm working at Gray. People who aren't part of Gray are having a meeting, and I was told to come to get you and take you there."

"But I'm about to be indicted."

"Things change, Miles. You have some people in high places who still believe in you. That's why you're walking around free today. If I'd had my way, I'd have thrown your ass in jail after the grand jury. You're a lucky man to be getting a second chance."

I leaned back without comment.

Hemet was someone I'd never share a word with again.

But now he had me inside his car and was taking me God only knew where. Maybe to the river to shoot me and float me away. Or maybe to the same garbage dump in Jersey where Jimmy Hoffa's buried.

I broke out in a sweat and looked out the window. That was as close as I'd ever be to Frank Hemet.

Or his FBI.

Chapter Eight

MILES STANDISH

"Take me where?" I asked. "What's this about, Frank? I'm headed home if you'll only drop me."

"No can do, Miles. You're needed for an outside thing."

"What kind of outside thing are you talking about?"

"Patience, Miles, patience. I'm not even sure how to answer. The meeting we're headed off to has to do with your old friend, Roman Challis, I believe."

"Why Roman?"

"Because of Tommy Gray's death. Suicide? Or maybe someone inside Gray killed him. Or maybe the Russians? We need someone smarter than us to figure it out."

I stopped to consider. I still didn't see what any of it had to do with me. But I am a curious type. Renz Aldrich had just finished telling me that Frank Hemet now handled Gray's black arts. It caught my interest.

Hemet drove as if the snow weren't there. We were swaying around corners, fishtailing at the lights and stop signs, sliding to stoplights. I immediately felt we were late or the meeting was urgent.

We drove through Arlington and then Falls Church while Hemet kept his gaze straight ahead on the road, picking his way through the slow-moving traffic.

"You've still got friends at Gray law," Hemet said out of the blue, perhaps thinking aloud.

"That's random."

"But it's true. You have plenty of friends yet at Gray."

"How could anyone loyal to me during that time still be working at Gray?" I asked.

"Don't know how to answer that, Miles. But I've asked around. I think it was because they kept their heads down and made themselves scarce during the purge. Everyone seemed to forget those who supported you, especially your Environmental team. I think it's because they had so much information about EPA cases in their institutional memory, the firm couldn't afford to lose them. That's my best answer. Institutional knowledge can neither be passed along nor inherited. Many are there because their usefulness outweighed their Miles Standish loyalties. Short answer, they had no choice. They had to keep them."

We had run out of streetlights and had turned onto a gravel road, which we followed by headlights only in the failing light. Brick walls lined either side of the road and the occasional gate large enough for a motor vehicle to enter. Everything seemed so familiar.

Just as the sun slipped out of the clouds for a moment, I glimpsed a large red brick house just ahead. It was a classic Nineteenth-Century plantation, giant white columns out front, paved drive, carriage house off to the side, impeccably painted and trimmed, evergreen trees everywhere. Then we were motoring up around its circle drive and pulling up to the front door, where Hemet turned off the key and told me to please follow him inside.

My guess was confirmed when I saw the porch, the red front door, and the straw wreath.

I'd been there before.

Chapter Nine

MILES STANDISH

I'd been there several years ago for an organizational meeting. A placard on a stand just inside the front door announced a conference of Western Energy Reserves back in 2014.

Hemet and I were patted down at the front door. They searched us for weapons, which meant they expected weapons. It wasn't the Boy Scouts.

We walked inside, and my eyes adjusted to the dim light. Into the high-ceilinged living room we walked and found a semicircle of chairs and perhaps a dozen men gathered in small groups, talking over outbursts of laughter. They paid little notice to me, and I did not attempt eye contact or greetings. Tit for tat, I thought.

There it all was, just as I remembered: the grand piano, its top closed down as if the pianist had permanently left the building; six-foot portraits of men wearing extremely well-pressed suits and women wearing evening gowns, peering down from the room's sweeping staircase as if they were forty-year-old debutantes making their coming-out; a floor-to-ceiling stone fireplace with its gas log blazing and looking as efficient as a candle in a warehouse.

"Here comes the retiree in from the greenhouse, the man of the hour, Miles Standish!" cried Marshall Lakin loudly enough to settle the smaller conversations around the ring and engage all eyes on me. "Miles, I hope you're ready again for the boxing match, my friend. We're here to plead with you to find Tommy's killer. There's our secret."

Lakin was lanky with the full Hollywood hair of the Netflix stars. He was muscular and wore his three-piece suit loose as if there were no strangers to impress. Then there was the long, thin nose, the very definition of the WASPish Harvard man.

"I love retirement," I replied to Lakin. "Not much need for constant crowds and get-togethers. The solitary life suits me to a T. And what about you, Marshall? All's well?"

"Well enough." Lakin silenced the room and asked everyone to find a seat. Hemet stepped back, found a chair with his legs, and lowered himself. I followed and was immediately aware I was seated next to Liam Hunt. He was the administrative assistant of Senator Donovan Hamlish of Illinois, the chairperson of the Senate Foreign Relations Committee. Next to Hunt sat George Maximus Washington, the Assistant Secretary of the Interior, who was balancing a highball glass on his knee and toying with his necktie at his Adam's apple. Beside Assistant Secretary Washington was a man unknown to me but bullish and stout with close-cropped hair and hands too large for his body. I took a stab that he was another FBI agent, the one who would oversee whatever detail developed from the meeting. Several other spies, including a certain Senator Longmire and Paul Worthington with the CIA, a man with a serious demeanor.

Finally, there was Nicki Pitts, a Berliner by birth, as in "Ich komme aus Berlin," and not to be confused with the infamous, "Ich bin ein Berliner," meaning "I am a jelly donut." I knew him from previous dealings with the Berlin office, a man who, like John Singer, had spent a good deal of his career in the black arts.

Why I was there was anyone's guess, I thought, as I was by now swimming in names, faces, and pedigrees. In the end, I was clueless. They wanted me to find Tommy's killer? Had he been serious? Then why all the government heavyweights? There must be more. I waited for someone to break the ice, and I guessed that would be none other than Marshall Lakin.

"Someone get the front door," called Lakin. "Make sure we're locked in." Hemet hopped to it, crossing quickly and disappearing back down the long tile hallway. Everyone could hear the bolt being thrown. Then he returned and took his seat.

"Everyone knows everyone except maybe Nicki Pitts. Nicki joins us from the shadows and brings us some important information. Oh, and we all know Miles Standish, of course, who has kindly agreed to meet with us this afternoon upon last-minute notice. Poor Miles does not know why I've invited him, and I can only beg for his indulgence as Nicki's story unfolds."

"So be it," I responded, nodding. "As long as I'm home in time for the Wizards tip-off."

There was no appreciative laughter. And no one was smiling.

Pitts stood and approached me. He shook my hand and gave me a forced smile—or perhaps an embarrassed smile, I thought upon second glance.

So, I gave a big smile back and a nod, attempting to

commiserate. I guessed Pitts was probably thirty-five. He wore his hair in a bun, complete with a spotty beard, and his eyeglasses appeared purple under the glittering chandelier.

Lakin cut right to the chase, bringing the group an update on Pitts's pedigree as if he weren't sitting right there among us.

Then I listened to the spy.

Chapter Ten

MILES STANDISH

Pitts told us he was raised in Galveston and had served in the US Army Special Forces. Following his honorable discharge, Blackwater had recruited him, the soldier of fortune firm, earning $1 million a day in Iraq as bodyguards for US officials and ranking military.

When he got back to the States, he was loaded to the gills with cash after making $1000 a day in Iraq, but he was wholly ready to let go of military and paramilitary work. Instead, he went back to school and took paralegal studies, the farthest thing he could think of from carrying guns and guarding honchos.

After graduation, Pitts started working in Washington, DC, at Gray law, Pitts soon noticed that the attorney he was assigned to was going out with a young Gray paralegal named Alina. She stole Pitts's heart away at first glance. Then, after she smiled at him while dancing, he was hooked.

One night at closing time, they went for bacon and eggs and coffee. While they were enjoying themselves, Alina said out of the blue, "Did you know that a certain paralegal in the Gray firm is stealing documents and selling them over to opposing counsel? Hasn't anyone noticed the Gucci she wears every day?"

"No," said Pitts as he munched his toast. "Who is doing such a thing?"

"Well," she said as she carefully chose her words, "the main violator shall remain nameless until I get the help I need."

I could feel everyone's attention spike. You could've heard a pin.

Wondering whether DOJ documents were involved compelled Pitts to ask Alina more questions about the paralegal. At first, Alina didn't seem to mind revealing information to her new boyfriend.

But then Pitts began wondering whether Alina was involved and asked her outright. "And what about you, Alina? Has she ever asked you to take secret documents and deliver them to the opposing attorneys?"

"No! I wouldn't have done it even if she'd asked."

"How much do they pay her?"

"Five-thousand dollars for anything they buy."

One thing led to another, and she was still employed at Gray when Tommy Gray died. Then she suddenly disappeared from Pitts's life, leaving no trail, no message, nothing but an empty space in the closet and two dresser drawers.

But there was a single file remaining behind. Pitts took a long drink of water and then looked to Lakin. "Do I talk about the file now?"

"Please do."

Chapter Eleven

MILES STANDISH

"Go ahead, son," said Lakin. "Please tell the group what you told me."

Pitts swallowed hard and stared at the ceiling for several moments, then he began. "When Alina moved out, she left behind a file. Inside that file was a ten-page report from one expert witness in a fracking case. The expert witness had been hired and paid by Gray to give an opinion on Oklahoma's earthquake problem. The report would not be used by Gray because it was adverse."

Lakin spoke up, "Meaning it would ordinarily have been dumped, never to be seen again. Now, Nicki, how is that report so relevant to what we're doing here tonight?"

"Alina knew who was offering the report for sale to the Russians. She left it for me to warn Tommy's replacement. That would be Roman Challis."

"Who else knows about this?" asked Senator Longmire.

"That's the most devious part," said Pitts. "When I found she had left me the report, I immediately took it to

Roman Challis. In fact, I charged through the law firm and barged into the office of Mr. Challis. He didn't know me personally, but only knew me as a name. My first words were, 'You will not believe this, Mr. Challis,' and I plunked the report right down in front of him. He began reading while I explained Alina knew who was trying to sell the report to the Russians. I crossed the line and told him he had to take action at that moment. The sale was that close."

It was my turn to speak up. "What did Roman Challis do when you gave him this information? Did he ask you to produce Alina for the name?"

Pitts rocked his head. "That's just it. I've been expecting the police to come knocking down my door and demand the rest of my files, Alina's files, and demand I lead them to Alina. Instead, Mr. Challis walked me to his door and all but pushed me out of his office. So there I stood. I still had the report because he had shoved it back across the desk at me, and I was standing there bewildered beyond words."

"And did he ever get back to you?" asked Assistant Secretary Washington. "Or is Gray still rocking along as if nothing had happened?"

"He did not. I never heard—not a word from him, even though I had the report and much more. Gentlemen, the sale went through, the Russians used this report in court, and the fracking resumed. This report cost you Oklahoma."

"My God," I uttered. This was the new Gray.

But Pitts wasn't done. "Alina knows the name of the person at Gray who did this, and she wants to stop her. But she cannot afford to be involved in the police investigation. So, she disappeared and left the report with me so that it would find its way here tonight to a group of people committed to catching a killer and a mole."

I was stunned. I shook my head, making sure I was awake and not dreaming these things.

"Gentlemen," Lakin broke in, "the report is real. And it was used in court by the Russians, just like Nicki's told you."

Turning to me, Lakin continued. "Miles, Gray is your legacy. You know it better than anyone. Those of us here tonight are here to ask you to take on this case and find out who killed Tommy—that's number one. Number two is to locate the mole and dispose of them. If the mole was Tommy, we'd have to live with that. That's the purpose of why we're meeting here today. We've been deciding who we can trust. That is you and you alone. It's about loyalty, Miles, and loyalty always came back to you when you were the chairman. It was your trademark. Will you take it on?"

I was watching Nicki Pitts, who sat hunched forward on the edge of his seat. His eyes were glued on me, and his body language showed he was one tick away from jumping into the air with glee.

I swallowed hard. Deceit and trickery were the last things I wanted in my life just then. Hadn't Deonna already brought enough of that into my life? I looked around the room. Everyone there knew about Deonna. And they all knew about how I had been forced out of Gray. Yet they all wanted me, anyway. They said they wanted me for my loyalty. Whether she ever realized that, it was the single trait Deonna had found most appealing in me as well.

"How can I say no?" I said. It felt good beyond anything I'd felt lately—to be wanted again. But most of all, I wanted Tommy's killer.

"Here's the thing," Lakin went on. "If we move in-house, if we give this to Challis or Jennings or Inga or Falsgraf, even Arnie Truckee, we lose control. Any of our Fearless Five could be who we're looking for, and I don't say that lightly. Tonight, all of you have top-secret clearance because these are Justice Department cases outsourced to Gray. I've seen to your clearances before you were invited. You were invited because Standish will need to call on one or all of us for help while he discovers who killed Tommy and tracks down our mole. From this moment on, your allegiance shifts from Gray to Miles Standish. On my orders and the orders of the President."

It sounded good, but I knew the FBI. I wanted to nail it down.

"What about you, may I ask?" I said to Lakin. "Time to get everyone's cards on the table."

The glimmer of a smile he had just worn was quickly quashed. "The FBI does not do local murder investigations. You know that, Standish."

"I do. I was just wondering how 'in' we all are."

"I'm as near as the phone," Lakin replied with a hardness to his voice.

"That's a relief," I said. "I have a direct line to a federal investigative agency, probably the best in the world, who won't help."

"Can't, Standish. You know the drill. Let's move on."

I knew I had pushed it far enough. Lakin wasn't amused at this point. So I dropped it, my point having been made.

I would work alone, and the killer would be mine to find —alone.

"What about the police?" I said to the crowd.

"No problem," said Senator Longmire. "I've already let them know we'll be doing a parallel investigation. Around the Beltway, they're used to that. They've agreed to copy you on all reports."

"Well done," I said. "There's a boost." I wouldn't say I liked the idea of an investigation parallel to the police, which meant each side copied the other side with everything it was finding out. Most often, I would be the one turning over evidence while the police were "forgetting" to reciprocate.

Chapter Twelve

MILES STANDISH

The meeting broke up, leaving me to meet and greet the others in attendance. Soon, Lakin came to me and suggested we walk around the grounds.

It was pitch black outside, and the snow had tapered. We decided on the gravel path leading back to the outer road and set off. "It's beautiful here," I said as if seeing the grounds was the whole predicate for spending time together away from the world.

We heard passenger jets and mail jets landing at Reagan. We could make out dark woods from which no light escaped all around us.

I had checked myself and realized I was the only meeting-goer not wearing a necktie. I had attended in the same wool fiber pants and blue work shirt I had worn when I entered Gardiner's Books. It seemed like days ago but was just hours.

Our shoes crunched the gravel, and the slush of snowmelt recorded our tracks. A thin fog bank parted for us as we walked toward the outer road. Soon, we heard rubber tires rolling down the gravel road, which still lay out of sight. At that point, we turned and headed back, slowing our steps enough to trade words before reaching the plantation house.

"How will you proceed?" asked Lakin. "I know it's probably too soon to ask you, but I'm just wondering about your initial take on things."

I answered in the voice of one strategizing as he went. "First, the cause of death. I'm convinced it wasn't a suicide. Tommy could be rash, but not suicidal. Too much ego there. So I'll concentrate on the murder first."

"Excellent," he said across the freezing air. "Here's why I wanted to get you alone. This is the FBI's thinking. Whoever killed Tommy Gray killed him because he was collaborating with the Russians. Or they killed him because he wouldn't collaborate with the Russians, and they needed him out of the way so it could be done. Either way, it was about the Russians. Now you know our interest in the case."

"I understand what you're saying, and I don't disagree. Now, what about the documents disappearing from Gray's files and turning up in Russian files?"

"Remember, if we go after the mole directly, we've just tipped him off, and all of his efforts will cease. Then we'll never pinpoint him and, eventually, he's turning over documents and strategies again. So we cannot proceed inside of Gray. We have to approach from outside."

"Why isn't the FBI doing that?"

"We already have. Frank Hemet is one of us."

"Of course. But, it's puzzling. FBI now working at Gray?"

"Yes, he's ours, and that's why I sent him to fetch you. Thought you were more likely to go with another lawyer than one of us."

"True."

"You are the one who will find the mole. Frank doesn't have the relationships you have. On the other hand, Frank can get the documents you need."

"This just turned much more elaborate."

"Miles, our national security is in jeopardy. This is our homeland's oil supply, our natural gas supply. We are dead serious."

"What if I fail?"

"You won't fail. You know Gray."

"What about the Russians' lawyers? Are they free from all this?"

"The lawyers fighting us? We have people inside. They will pay. Eventually."

"Do they know who's turning over documents to them?"

"Not yet."

We were fifty feet from the house then, so I plunged ahead with what I had to say. "You'll have my best efforts, then. If that isn't good enough, you've got yourself the wrong detective looking for a killer."

"Nonsense. There is no one else. You know Gray like you know the path to your bathroom in the middle of the night."

"That well? If you say so, Lakin."

I realized I didn't like my new role just then. I was sorry the night had ever happened. I much preferred my horticulture and my Cardozo and Wizards to another round of working on the problems of Gray.

I shivered and then couldn't stop. The temperature had dropped four degrees, said my watch. On the good side, I was wearing my now-dry London Fog coat. I stumbled over an exposed root that had grown through the gravel and almost fell headlong onto the driveway. Lakin reached and caught the back of my coat, then took my arm and brought me upright.

"See? I'm stumbling in the dark already."

"But notice. We are there to catch you. Now, go home, rest up, and we look for an office tomorrow. Wait. Here's a sliver of moonlight." Lakin found a card and held it up with the moon behind it while he made a note on the back, a street address. "Meet me there in the a.m.," he told me. "Eight-thirty on the nose."

Just then, a large pushback against taking on the assignment formed inside. I knew what it was, and I had to clear the decks with Lakin. "One thing. I don't want your FBI all over me. I want my normal life to continue. Keep your men away from me. Keep them out of sight if you can't keep them away. No interference in my life. Can we agree?"

"Within reason. I can certainly keep them out of sight. Yes, it can be done."

"Then do it."

How on earth had this new assignment happened? And so fast! And with such little resistance from me. Then I remembered Frank Hemet waiting inside to take me home, and my pace quickened. "Mustn't keep Frank waiting," I muttered.

"Dear me, forgot about poor Frank. I'll need to apologize."

"Likewise."

Then we were both stepping ahead with the quick rhythm of a couple whose blind date was a maybe.

Chapter Thirteen

MILES STANDISH

We met at the property at 8:30 a.m., and Lakin let us in with his card. "All locks on all our properties use the same card coding. Saves making up a database just for cards, eh?"

He told me the FBI owned the building, but no one would know that. Lakin so much as promised me, "It's rough, almost a loft, but it's a huge space, and if need be, you can fill it wall to wall with whomever you need to catch a mole selling secret government documents. Let me know what you need; it'll be there that same day if it's found within the lower forty-eight states. Worldwide is next day."

"The FBI has a fleet of aircraft? Of course, they would."

"Our fleet rivals Fed-Ex. Just don't tell anyone."

We climbed the stairs to the second floor. Again with the key, again another unlocked door. I pushed it open. Lakin motioned I should enter before him, showing it belonged to me now.

I stepped inside and turned. Lakin beat me to the light

switch I had reached out to flick. Suddenly, the entire ceiling blinked to life, and there was light saturating every surface.

Along the east wall was a bank of floor-to-ceiling windows that looked out on a building beyond the lot, looking right back with its floor-to-ceiling windows.

"We'll have to keep the shades drawn," I said.

"No shades. Articulating metal window covers that can operate manually or electronically. They're set up to work separately or as a bank of shades that close in under ten seconds. FBI standard window covers. Electronic cloaking."

"What about electronic listening devices from the next building?"

"In place. My advice is to keep the metal shades drawn from here on. They're your best security from prying eyes and electronic snoops."

"What else?"

"This is an occupied FBI property from this minute on. You are now under the protection of the FBI's technical countermeasures arm. Here are some guidelines I'll just drop on you. Don't worry, what I'm telling you is inside the welcome package on your desk in your private office. Let me quote from our manual.

"A Technical Security Countermeasures (TSCM) survey, also known as a sweep, is a service provided by highly qualified FBI personnel to detect technical surveillance devices and hazards and to identify technical security weaknesses that could facilitate a technical penetration of this facility. It consists of several parts.

•An electronic search of the radio frequency (RF) spectrum to detect any unauthorized emanations from this floor.

•An electronically enhanced search of walls, ceilings, floors, furnishings, and accessories to look for clandestine microphones, recorders, or transmitters, both active and quiescent.

- A physical examination of the interior and exterior areas, such as the space above false ceilings and heating, air conditioning, plumbing, and ventilation systems, to search for physical evidence of eavesdropping.
- Identification of physical security weaknesses that an eavesdropper could exploit to gain access to place technical surveillance equipment in the target area.

"During the survey, TSCM team members may enter office areas where your employees are working. Employees should be advised in writing that a technical security inspection is being conducted and that they should not discuss it in the office before, during, or after the survey. This goes on every day, seven days a week. Plus, because your work is now top secret, overlook teams will guard the premises twenty-four-seven. Miles, you're good to go. Why don't we begin with your private office?"

"Astonishing," I was able to say.

"Our nation is being killed by a few bad apples, or maybe just one, at Gray. The same technical services are at work in the law firm, given that its records and files are also deemed top secret. But the problem remains, a two-legged creature is passing right through all that. It's excruciating for me to watch. I'm taking steps with new hires. I've recommended that Roman Challis fire every Environmental team member and just start over. He wouldn't hear of it; there are partnership and equity considerations, yadda yadda yadda. Plus, he's right about this. There is a treasure trove of institutional knowledge on the Environmental law team, and that's irreplaceable. He has me there. One step down from there is the same old question, who do you fire first?

It's out of our control, so here you are, doing from outside what can't be done from inside."

"I feel like I'm on overload. Huge responsibility here, Marshall."

"You're as big as the FBI and the DOJ combined. Don't forget that. It's only your footprint that is small. Call for help. There are thousands of us on your team."

We continued into my office, where I sat behind my mahogany desk. It was all there, the desk set, the small desk tools, writing implements, even a box of tissues.

"The computer system is in place?"

"VPN. Nice and tidy. All possible safeguards. It even sends a signal and shuts down if a thumb drive is plugged in. It's all covered."

Which reminded me. "While we have a minute, let me give you this," I said, taking out the envelope delivered through my living room window two hours ago. I handed the envelope to Lakin, who carefully received it from me by holding it only by its edges.

"Prints. DNA. We'll get right on it. Any ideas?"

"Hell no. I have trouble believing it's connected to our meeting last night, but the message says it is. What, we're exposed already?"

"I wouldn't say that. But we'll understand it, and I'll brief you then. Is there a security system at home?"

"The best."

"We'll be replacing it with our own. Do you have a dog?"

"Seriously?"

"A watchdog. A little yapper with a Lhasa Apso's hearing. Or Chihuahua. Except the Mexican dog will drive you nuts with its need to always occupy your lap and have your attention. I'm thinking Lhasa Apso for you, Miles. The

Tibetan monks bred this dog to guard their temple. Let one guard yours."

"I don't think so. It's just me, and I'll be gone all day now. Plus, I don't do temples all that well."

"You'll sleep easier. What about self-defense? Do you keep a firearm?"

"Still have my Marine Corps semi-automatic M1911 Colt. It's forty-five caliber, and I shoot it every month."

"Shoot it several times a week from here on. Get yourself a Sig P365 XL and carry it IWB. Am I making sense?"

"Inside the waistband carry. Let me think about that one."

"Don't think about it: do it. That little nine-millimeter might save your life some night in a parking garage. Or in your yard drinking coffee while you watch the grass grow. Get it and wear it. I'll have one waiting on your kitchen table when you get home. Shoot it three times a week. The address of our gun range is also inside your packet. Go to the one in Virginia. One of our range masters will meet you to go over firearm safety and basic care and carrying techniques, shooting at close range, standing, moving, from on your back, getting up off the floor, anything we can come up with. This package on your desk gives you an account to charge to if you decide to use a closer commercial firing range once you get going. What else? Your car will be swept by our technical people anytime you need to drive it. It's a fast process and only takes a couple of minutes."

"So that's that? It's quite a list."

Lakin leaned across the desk. His hatchet face reminded me of a US military commander I had served under in the army, 10th Mountain Division.

"Quite a list?" he said. "Quite a list? We haven't even started yet. We will provide all foodstuffs at your home.

Why? Because this is the FSK, Putin's replacement for the KGB; he wants you stopped and doesn't care how. Remember the woman in the airport running up to the total stranger and spraying a toxin in his face? He died and died fast. We don't want that for you, so you will be under surveillance from here on out. So will any of your key soldiers—your lawyers and key staff. We will drive you and protect your motor vehicle trips with additional vehicles. Your house will be watched night and day. Who has access to your home besides you?"

"My wife, Deonna. She comes and goes."

"We'll put her on the list of okays. We might even watch her."

"My God, how many people do you have?"

Lakin nodded slowly. "There's no limit. We're everywhere. The Russians are here, and they are everywhere."

"Lakin, why didn't you tell me all this last night?"

"Seriously? Would you have taken the job? Doubtful."

"You're wrong. I would have begged to get this job. What's our goal besides catching a killer and plugging a hole?

"We want you re-installed as chairman at Gray."

"And Challis?"

"He will stumble and fall. Not for you to concern yourself with."

"I don't want that job back."

"Short term, then. Your country needs you in that chairman's chair. That's where the country's brain trust lives. There's no better firm in America for this. We just have some weeding to do, that's all."

"I'm exhausted hearing all this."

"Let's go back to the main area. Look it over and tell me

what you want. I'll record you on my phone. Your needs will be met within twenty-four hours."

"First, I need to think about employees. What do you say we find a coffee shop, get something to bring back here, and put our heads together and talk staffing?"

"Never mind. I'll send a man."

Lakin spoke into his wrist, and orders were placed.

Then it was time to staff. I packed up my briefcase and headed for my car, only to find I now had a driver, and he insisted we use his Cadillac SUV. I climbed in the back, and we headed for the courthouse on 333 Constitution Avenue NW, the District Court, where I'd find many of the lawyers I wanted on my team. Much easier to solicit them away from the Gray Building. No one would ever need to know.

I spoke with six attorneys over the next three hours at the courthouse. Two said they might be interested in an opportunity at a new firm I was building. The rest were noncommittal and seemed to humor me as much as anything. I didn't blame them; I smelled like sour grapes and knew it. So, I headed back to my office. Lakin was to meet me at one o'clock.

I forced myself into a calm place and remembered I wanted to text Benji for an update. I punched his picture on my contacts list and waited. Finally, his distant, small voice said, "Hello, Mr. Standish. Is something wrong?"

"No, no, no, I'm just calling to check on you. How is it going with Immanuel Rayito? Has he hurt you? Or even threatened you?"

"Naw, I think he moved out. When I got up the next morning, his stuff was gone and my mom was crying in the kitchen. I had to tell her what happened."

"Did you show her the lash marks on your back?"

"I did. It made her cry."

"It did me, too. More of that stuff. Now, what about mom's income? Do you know if she can make it without Rayito's paycheck?"

"No. She says she's now $500 short every month. And she acts like it's my fault."

"Give me your mailing address, Benji."

He gave the address while I took it down, then asked, "Why do you need my address? You know how to find me,"

"I'm sending something to your mom. It's no concern of yours."

"She'll tell me. I'm like the husband she tells everything too."

"Don't worry about it. Call me when you want. Movie on Saturday. I'll be there at noon."

"Great! I want the tub of popcorn and the supreme Coke!"

"Me too. I'm hungry just thinking about it."

We hung up, and I dug my checkbook out of my desk. I wrote a check to Benji's mother, Aretha. It was five hundred dollars. Down at the bottom, I wrote, "Month 1: living assistance for Benji."

It would reach them tomorrow.

Chapter Fourteen

MILES STANDISH

At one o'clock sharp, Lakin arrived at my office. He knew my weaknesses and was producing Starbucks in venti cups. I was impressed and told him so.

"All right, Miles," he said. "Let's see who you want on your staff."

On the first page of a brand-new yellow pad, I wrote the word, "Staff."

"The first person I want is Frank Hemet. He's running black arts at Gray, as well as criminal law. Challis won't start wondering why he's gone so much if it looks like he's away on black arts work, tuning someone up, or stealing records from another law firm. Frank has total access to all Gray records, and I'll need that."

"I'll contact Frank and let him know he's in. I know he wants it."

"Next up, Inga Kopovsky. She's a Gray insider loyal to me. She was screwing Tommy Gray for job security. She said to me, 'Who wants a fifty-two-year-old female tax lawyer who's all dried up? I have to take hormones to stay wet enough for Tommy.'"

"That's honest."

"She's too old to lie to me. We've been friends for fifteen years, and she'll have my back. She's also a voting member of the Gray board. I need that."

"Do you want me to approach her?"

"I'll do it today after work. We'll see where she's at."

"Got it."

"I want Isabel Kipling, a DOJ environmental lawyer. She was one of my go-to's when I was running Gray. She's been at the DOJ doing environmental enforcement for twenty years. Isabel knows as much about American environmental struggles as anyone else on earth. She's a must-have. You do her."

"I'm on it. You want a meeting with everyone when?"

"Tomorrow morning."

"Done."

"Then I want this guy, Marshall Lakin."

Lakin laughed. "FBI is at your service."

"I know—the FBI answers to DOJ. DOJ and I are like that," I said, showing crossed fingers. "Which means I also need Paul Worthington of CIA. He was standoffish last night, by the way. What's his deal?"

"CIA doesn't operate domestically. Except they do—as much or more than the FBI. He probably wasn't comfortable being seen out in the open, operating on a domestic problem."

"Yeah, but it's the Russians."

"Agree. It is the Russians."

"Anything goes," I said and meant it. I despised the Russian government for how I had grown up in school, being made to watch Russian nuclear bomb testing on TV and being told that's why we hide under our desks for practice. "Anything goes," I repeated.

"Well, almost, but not quite."

"What's out of bounds to me?"

"Murder and kidnapping. Anything else, and you're wide open."

"Meaning I can bribe, threaten, pay off, steal, extort—all the stuff the FBI can do, too."

"I wouldn't go that far, Standish."

"Hey, let's be real here. So far it's been working."

"Who else?"

"Daniel Turner."

"The Russian lawyer from Western Energy Reserves who fled and has asylum here? The Russians will murder him if they catch the name change and plastic surgery."

"So protect him. He's a resource who can give me names and cases at Gray. He's a must-have."

"Done. Who else?"

"A dozen paralegals and typists. These will work on segments of the cases we have going. None of them will have the big picture."

"Who else?"

"More will come to me as we start up. I'll keep you in the loop."

"You must, or I can't protect who I don't know about."

"Got you. That's about it, so far."

"So, what's your goal, Standish? Where are you going with this?"

"One, find Tommy's killer. Two, shoot moles. The leaks must stop."

"What about moving back inside Gray and running things again?"

"I told you I don't want that. We can move Frank into that spot or Inga."

"Inga's too old."

"Tommy Gray was seventy."

"That doesn't make it right. No American president should be in his seventies. No Gray chairman should either."

"I can respect that. Remember I'm forty-four."

"That isn't seventy. Don't even go there."

"If we're done here, I'm going to go hunt down Inga. She's a big fish for me to bring into the boat. A huge one, actually. She has enough followers and powers with the board to move the law firm in just about any direction we need. I'll call her and meet at her home."

"You do that. We'll be with you."

"Sure. All right, thanks for everything."

"It's my job."

"The Russians hit a wall starting now."

Lakin dug into his satchel. "Almost forgot. Here's the video of Tommy Gray meeting with Gerry Heinlein. Watch this before doing anything else, please." Lakin passed a thumb drive to me.

"What's it about?" I asked.

"Just watch it."

"Gerry Heinlein of Heinlein, Stahl, and Black?"

"The same. He's going to be a problem for you. Tackle it now."

"Will do.

Chapter Fifteen

MILES STANDISH

Frank Hemet let himself into our new office with his passkey at 2:45, thirty minutes after Lakin departed. I was studying Western Energy Reserves court papers on my computer. I found it fascinating and knew the case momentum had favored the government until the Russians presented the stolen document. I had seen all this before, the study of Russian fracking by a University of Colorado professor of petroleum mining. He had commented that Colorado farmers and ranchers caused Colorado's groundwater pollution, and he doubted Russian fracking in his state had anything to do with it. It was a private report that Gray had buried because no studies disputed or corroborated what he said. Yet it somehow grew legs and walked down the street to the Russian lawyers. From then on, the case momentum shifted in favor of Western Energy Reserves after the study was used in court to bury the EPA on a Colorado fracking case on the Eastern Slope.

Frank called into me as I monitored him on CCTV to see how well the system was.

"Come in, Frank," I called. "I'm reading about where the Russians twisted a case around that they were losing, thanks to a Gray document that ended up in Russian hands."

"Who's the culprit, Miles? What Gray lawyer would turn it over?"

"Well, I'm looking at Roman Challis, Alfred Falsgraf, and Max Jennings. Maybe one of them, maybe all of them."

"Wasn't it Roman Challis who didn't get back to Nicki Pitts about his Russian girlfriend, Alina? Didn't Nicki tell Challis that Alina knew who was turning over records, and Challis did nothing? That sounds pretty damn incriminating to me, Miles."

"I have an idea about that. We're going to set a trap for Roman Challis and the others and see who falls into it. Then we've got our man."

"Or woman."

"Another interesting development I just found out about from Lakin," I said. "It seems the DOJ is sending out feelers to the Heinlein firm to take over Gray. What do you know about that?"

Frank shrugged. He pulled out a visitors' chair and sat down, removing his North Face fleece winter hat. He unbuttoned his overcoat and pulled off his leather gloves. "First, I've heard about Heinlein, but how does it affect what we're doing?"

"It will dissolve the law firm I just rejoined from outside-in. I can't see that happen. Too many people there I respect and want to protect. Why, what's your take?"

"It worries me. First, the DOJ could very well file bar complaints against Gray's Environmental team and get law licenses yanked for the negligent document handling. Client property protection is huge. Second, the DOJ might file a negligence lawsuit against Gray. Public uproar might make this necessary once the spy games become public. Americans don't like losing. Especially to the Russians."

"Lakin gave me a video we should watch. It's Tommy Gray and Gerry Heinlein discussing a takeover. Let's watch it together."

"Fire away."

I swung my screen around where we could both see it. I first registered the thumb drive with the computer system so it wouldn't set off the alarm system, shut everything down, and then inserted the USB into the laptop. Then we started watching.

"December twenty-seventh," I read on the video. "10:11 p.m. That's Gerry Heinlein on the right side of the desk and Tommy Gray on the left side by the two-drawer lateral filing cabinet. That's Tommy's office."

"Yep," Frank agreed. "You know that Tommy and Inga—"

I paused the video and held up my hand. "Don't go there. I don't want to know what happened on Tommy's desk unless it is this case."

Frank chuckled and nodded his head. "Sure, we won't go there."

"Let's just watch." I pressed play.

Heinlein was the first to speak. "Tommy, Heinlein law has been asked by the DOJ to enfold Gray into Heinlein. We would take over your firm and running the environmental show for the DOJ from here on."

Tommy replied, "That's preposterous. It's an unconstitutional seizure of partnership equity and private property. You would destroy our firm. Tell your connection at DOJ it just ain't gonna happen."

"I'm authorized to offer all shareholders one-hundred-twenty per share. That's a great price, Tommy."

"Ridiculous when you consider the shares have an appreciated book value of seven hundred and seventy-five dollars per share. What, you think the DOJ has authorized you to steal our law firm?"

Heinlein shifted his feet, then crossed his legs as he pushed on the arms of the chair. Now he was sitting very straight, emanating power. "The DOJ is ready to pull all its files out of Gray and transfer them to my firm. Should that happen, your share values will drop below fifty dollars. That means bankruptcy for every partner in here. We'd much prefer your cooperation so we can transfer Gray's key attorneys into the same files."

"After you've defrauded them out of shares worth seven-fifty for one-twenty? I don't think our lawyers will work for Heinlein on that basis. I would encourage them to look elsewhere or look for state work."

Heinlein sighed and shook his head. "Ok, Tommy, I didn't want to have to bring this up, but you're forcing me. As the chairman, the DOJ believes you have so misguided the law firm that you have criminal responsibility in allowing DOJ's documents to fall into the wrong hands. They think they can prove you're working as a Russian sympathizer. A Russian agent."

Gray stood and shouted, "Get the hell out of here, Gerry! That's a damned lie, and you know it is! I served my country in the Korean war inside a tin can on treads. We pushed the North Koreans back to China before they called MacArthur back. I'm a loyal veteran and have the medals to prove it. What do you have, Gerry? Anything? I thought not. You get back to your losers at Justice and tell them Tommy Gray says hell no! Now get the hell outta here!"

Heinlein stood and pulled a sealed letter out of his coat pocket. "This is our official takeover offer, Tommy. I suggest you read it with your attorney present. Then call me when you've come to your senses. Good night, Tommy."

"Get the hell out!"

The computer screen went black, leaving Hemet and me staring at each other.

"Jesus," I muttered as I tried to decide whether to fight or flee. "Tommy's found dead eight hours later, give or take. A self-inflicted shotgun wound. This is all just crazy."

"Is it?" said Hemet. "Or did someone set it up to make it look self-inflicted? Right now, I don't trust Heinlein one damn inch. I believe his people did Tommy in. Probably some hitman out of L.A."

"What are the police saying?" I asked. "Or have they circled the wagons?"

"Not a peep. I'm on Detective Douglas every day for his group's progress report. So far, he won't even return my calls. I'm about to go all FBI on him."

"What could he possibly know, anyway? They have Heinlein with a motive to kill Tommy off. We've got someone named Alina saying she knows a traitor's name inside Gray. Hell, maybe Tommy did himself in. Things were caving, and he'd had enough, you know?"

Chapter Sixteen

MILES STANDISH

I rode the elevator down to the basement and climbed into my Mercedes—which I had refused to let the FBI talk me out of that day. It was quite dark, but my team had assigned spots, and my number was 1. I was wedged in between a wall and a Chevy Tahoe. Three cars over sat the ever-present FBI follow-on, a Ford SUV that went everywhere I went. Agents armed with automatic weapons rode inside. I tried my best to ignore them as my driver got us out of the basement parking.

I dialed Inga's cell phone. She was home and hopeful, so I gave my driver her address.

Inga lived two blocks from the Potomac in Georgetown on Prospect Street, NW. I recognized her colonial townhouse, pulled up in front, and set my brake. I had been there many times for parties, get-togethers, and even a Super Bowl viewing party with a football game most people ignored in favor of drinking too much. Deonna wouldn't go, but I had thought it was rude of us if we stayed away.

I waited for five minutes to determine whether anyone

had followed me. During that time, no cars came from either direction except a city truck pulling a Japanese front-end loader and a plumber with three ladders stretching from cab to tailgate. The FBI follow-on was wisely staying out of my view. Several young mothers with babies in strollers passed by, so I soon felt safe enough to climb out and go up and knock. It wasn't about my personal safety so much as my caution in not wanting to blow this opportunity to get back to work.

The door flew open, and there stood Inga, a cigarette in her right hand and a whistle in her left.

"It's a deterrent," she said of the whistle. "Never had to use it. Come in, Miles Standish!"

"Thanks, Inga. I was wondering if we might talk for a few minutes."

"Oh, I already know what it is. Lakin briefed me over lunch in the most desolate burger bar I've ever sat my tush down at. Greasy burgers, I'm still taking Tums. Follow me to the kitchen. I've got two bottles of thirty-dollar champagne. Not the king's drink, but not the drink of amateurs, either. You do still like champagne, Miles?"

"I have to admit I do. Quite so."

The front door hallway led to a kitchen on the left and an open family room on the right.

"You scoot on in there," she said and motioned toward the family room. "Let me see if I remember how to open one of these jiggers and get to pouring."

"I'm quite handy around a corkscrew if need be."

She abruptly turned and smiled at me alluringly. "I've always heard you were excellent around screws, Miles. Do I have that right?"

But I ignored her poor attempt at humor and went into the family room, choosing a chair closest to the kitchen.

As she moved around the kitchen, I called to her, "So what is it, Inga? Are you in?"

"How's that?"

"Are you going to join my little crew?"

"Do you even have to ask? You're one of my idols, Miles, one of my special boys at Gray. I'd follow you into a burning building if you said. Of course, I'm with you. It sounds very hush-hush, which I find enormously attractive. Who do I have to shoot?"

"We'll go easy on the shooting."

"Is this all Lakin's idea?"

"It seems so. Our mandate is to find Tommy Gray's killer."

"I also mentioned illegal documents to Lakin. Are we on that as well?"

"We think they're related."

"So that's a yes?"

"Yes."

Inga joined me and handed me a flute of her special champagne. "Don't gulp it, Miles. It's to be savored."

"Thank you for telling me. Here I am about to make a fool out of myself with my gulping."

Inga chuckled. "Miles, please humor Inga. Let's move on to the couch. I need to see your eyes while I'm deciding for the last time."

"Good idea. You do that."

She reached and took my hand and led me to the couch, sat down, and patted the cushion beside hers. I sat as shown, keeping my knees together, so our legs didn't touch.

She was wearing a very loose-fitting pair of blue jeans and a yellow silk shirt with the top three buttons unbuttoned and the bottom two likewise. The violet eyes above the yellow silk melted me down. I shook my head and sat back. "Lord," I muttered.

"You're staring at my shirt, dear man. Have you never seen silk at work? Oh, that's right, your Deonna wore silk. How dumb of me. Do you miss her terribly?"

"Yes, terribly."

"Poor man. Max should be skinned alive for whisking her away. She was vulnerable, you know, Miles, change of life and all that."

"I guess I never realized that. Interesting theory. I just thought she slept around on me because she was bored with dear Miles."

"Slept around on you? I've only heard of two lovers. Were there more?"

"Oh, yes. I think so, but I didn't catch her."

"Don't give her another thought then, Miles. You're still relatively young and can do much better. Are you even looking?"

I set my champagne down on the coffee table before us. "Not a bit. I'd take Deonna back in a second."

"Then you've got it bad, Miles. All right now, give me my marching orders. This is so exciting!"

"I'd like you to approach five lawyers and ask if they have any thoughts about who the killer might be. Then record their comments on your iPhone and bring it to me for copying. The five are Roman Challis, Max Jennings, Renz Aldrich, Alfred Falsgraf, and Arnie Truckee. I've already got my suspicions, but we're just getting underway. I won't leap to conclusions."

"Miles, aren't you missing one?"

"Who might that be?"

"Me. I had daily access to Tommy. How can you just give me a pass?"

"I've known you since 1980. I know you, Inga. Why would you include yourself?"

"I lied to Frank Hemet. I told him Tommy was alive at five in the morning, and we had make-up sex. That wasn't it at all."

"What else was there?"

"When I entered Tommy's office, he was already dead, and I lost it. I saw the shotgun and wanted desperately to get it away from Tommy like I was protecting him. So I picked it up to move it, but immediately realized I was violating a crime scene and dropped it on the floor. Then I picked it back up and wiped it clean with the hem of my blouse. At least I hope I got it clean."

"This isn't good. Now you're a suspect."

She seemed not to understand or even to hear what I'd just said. Instead, she sat back and pulled a throw pillow to her chest. Her eyes had a faraway look. "Miles, do you remember how happy we were in the Eighties? What happened, Miles?"

"I didn't know you in the Eighties."

"I'm talking about how our generation was. What sad thing happened to all of us?"

"We grew up. It was inevitable. We became who we were always going to be."

"That's deep, Miles. I would've said we got greedy, wanted too much love and cars and houses and kids. Then we didn't get it, and we became depressed and drank too much. Then relationships went to hell. No offense, Miles, but your relationship with a cheating spouse is exactly what I saw coming years before for both men and women."

"Thanks for the warning."

She reached and touched my shoulder. "No, I don't

mean I saw you and Deonna specifically. I'm talking generalities now. Forgive me for not being clearer."

She didn't remove her hand. I felt the weight of her fingers as twenty pounds, and I wanted it gone and I wanted it to stay. Oh, for fuck's sake, I thought, tell her to move her hand and you'll always only be friends.

I squirmed an inch, but she hung in there, touching me and moving her fingers back and forth on my shoulder. Two things held me there: one, how rude it would be to reach and remove her hand; two, I didn't want her to leave the team or refuse to join. Oops, there was also a third: I liked her touch. But then I stood and took the champagne glass into the kitchen and put it into the sink. Then I returned to Inga, but this time remained standing.

"Come sit." She patted the couch again. "I need more details about my role."

I hitched up my pants and rocked back on my heels. I shook my head and said, "I would, but I have another meeting. Any chance you could come by the new office at noon tomorrow? I'll get some food ordered, and we can talk about you and the crime scene. You're going to need a top-notch criminal lawyer."

"What about you, Miles? Will you defend me?"

"I can't. Conflicts. But please come by so we can talk."

"Oh, I'm sorry, Miles, I have other plans."

That she had been outright rejected was etched on her face. I was set back since the look was very unattractive, and I'd never seen Inga in that space before. It unnerved me, but I couldn't think of how to fix it. I decided on the truth.

"Inga," I began, "you're a terrific woman and very attractive, but I'm carrying this terrible torch for Deonna. I just need to say that."

"Shush, think nothing of it. I'm just an old weepy

widow with too much time on her hands and nothing to show for it. I have the house and a paid-for car, but not much else because Kopovsky and I had no children. Miles, I'm just terribly lonely, and I know you are, too. I was hoping we had something to offer each other."

"Inga, you have something to offer. I'm the one who has nothing to offer because I'm still convinced Deonna will walk through my door at any minute. At night, I still listen for her despite my dying of the lonelies."

"Call me up at night when you're doing that, Miles. I can talk you down."

"All right. I have your number. I'll do just that."

"You'd best go now, Miles. I might need to have a little cry at my embarrassment."

"Please, don't."

"It was just another stretch for a man too far away. I need to take up gardening instead."

"Gardening is what I'm spending my time with."

"Really? Maybe sometime I could come to see your garden. That would be a thrill for me."

"Maybe sometime, sure."

"Call me when you're accepting visitors, Miles."

I cleared my throat and was about to walk away when I remembered I wanted to ask her an hour's worth of questions. "What day this week could you come to my office, Inga? We really must get you a lawyer."

"I'll call you, Miles. I'll call you when I'm free."

"No hard feelings?"

She smiled and pushed air. "Not to worry, dear man. I'm going to get your recordings. I'll have them by Friday and drop by with my phone."

"I'll be in the office all day waiting. And thank you, Inga."

"You're welcome. Call me about the garden now. Ta."

"Thank you for the wonderful champagne."

"Oh, stay and help me kill it."

"I'm sorry. Some other time."

"I'm sure, Miles. Some other time. Those words make me sad. I'm going to make coffee and get back to ironing my blouses. So long, Miles."

"Don't be sad. It's all good."

"I hate that expression."

"So do I."

"Bye."

Chapter Seventeen

NADIA

He'd stopped by his office after leaving the Russian woman's house. Nadia Karamov picked up her target at the intersection of 5th Street NW with Indiana Avenue. Now she paced him at forty MPH.

She was a dark-skinned FSB agent from Vicily, thirty kilometers north of St. Petersburg in Russia. Moscow had wanted the best FSB spy on Miles Standish. The order had come down after the DC FSB team watched Standish and FBI SAIC Marshall Lakin meeting at the house in the woods in Maryland. That had clinched it for Moscow. They knew Miles Standish was far from down and out, though he had been cast out at Gray. The Bureau had swept in and whisked him away, and it was now up to Nadia Karamov to confirm Standish was working hand in glove with the FBI. Or not. If Standish were still active, Nadia's orders from Moscow Center were to terminate him because he posed a threat to the Gray-to-Western Energy Reserve clandestine transfer of secrets. He had to go.

Standish drove eastbound from the courthouse at 333

Constitution Avenue NW. He was alone in his car, and it appeared there were but two FBI sedans tracking him, one three cars back, one a block north and running parallel. Pulling a secure phone from the gray bag lying in the van's passenger seat, Nadia called Kopovsky. He answered on the second beep.

"K," he said. "Go."

"I have made contact. He is alone and is moving from the courthouse toward his home. I have scouted the location. My best target will be his greenhouse—if the glass does not distort, I have a field of fire from the alley. Egress is two blocks away on the freeway. I can recommend taking this shot at seventy-five percent."

Kopovsky chewed his cheek. He immediately decided he wanted more confirmation that Miles Standish was indeed working with the FBI. Being seen in their company, without more, wasn't any kind of confirmation other than he was keeping company. It would create a major international incident to take his life, so Kopovsky had to make the right call. He had his decision.

"Negative that. Center requests audio or video that leaves no doubt. We must know that they are engaged in our cases. If they are engaged, and it doesn't involve our oil and gas, we won't take that shot, either. So go back to square one and get me a video of a conference. A video putting them squarely in the lawsuits at Western Energy Reserves. Do you understand me, N?"

"Can do, sir. Out."

She ended the call on her secure phone and turned her full attention back to following Standish. His vehicle began a northeast line of travel. She stayed two cars back, one or two cars behind the trailing FBI vehicle. It was a difficult job because it involved her following for a block or two and then switching over a street south and following for a block before hurrying back to Standish's street and falling back behind once again. She watched the two agents in the car ahead of her. Their swivel wasn't on, telling her they were not watching their six as closely as they should have been. The only monitor they had going was the rearview mirror. It was a plus in her favor. She took advantage of it by switching between streets less often and staying more on the same roadway as Standish. She even took to passing his vehicle and rushing to the upcoming light, where she made a legal U-turn and again fell in behind.

Finally, 5th Street turned into 395, and they approached New York Avenue NW. There was a delay gaining access onto New York, and while they waited, the FBI agent riding shotgun turned around and looked directly at her. She immediately flipped her visor down and covered her mouth with her hand as if she were applying lipstick. When he turned back around, she flipped her visor back up and cursed at the man in Russian. Traffic surged ahead.

At the intersection of 9th Street NE, they headed north and continued up to BrentStandish Road, where they made a right and then went back north two blocks into a very upscale neighborhood. Standish turned into a driveway and the garage door articulated upward on the far left. He pulled in; the door closed behind him, and the FBI sedan drove on past. Nadia held back before turning onto the remaining 100 feet of Standish's street. She stopped and put it in park and determined to wait there. Her van said Flowers and Ferns in a fancy script and a metro phone number that was just an answering device.

She put the seat back in the van and slipped a large pair of sunglasses over her eyes. A straw sun hat fit nicely over her forehead. Now she would wait.

It was time to see about catching him in the greenhouse. She had never missed a target in Europe, the UK, China, or the US, and she would not start now.

A sudden idea came to her, and she dialed her phone. Three researchers at the DC Russian Embassy immediately flew into action. Their quarry: the name of the glass manufacturer used to build the Standish greenhouse. She would need the thickness, distortion values, tints, and bullet deflection capabilities. It was a pro forma search; the embassy team would answer all inquiries.

She reached behind the front seats and pulled a large Igloo cooler toward her. She unlatched it and reached inside. She found a pork sandwich with mustard and a diet Dr. Pepper. The cooler contained provisions enough for a week.

She would wait until the house cleaners came. She needed only their name and address.

Only then would she leave.

Chapter Eighteen

BOARD MEETING

Roman Challis started off the board meeting. "My source at Justice tells me Miles Standish is going to be appointed as the Special Assistant US Attorney in charge of investigating and prosecuting whoever killed Tommy Gray. That means we have problems, ladies and gentlemen."

Several attorneys' files and yellow pads were plopped on the table as the meeting was just getting started. Coffee was poured even while Roman spoke.

Gathered inside that small deposition room at Gray were Challis himself, Max Jennings, Inga Kopovsky, Alfred Falsgraf, and Denny Walsh of Government Litigation. The five comprised the new board of directors of Gray. They were a close-mouthed group obsessed with making as much money as possible from all practices in which Gray was engaged.

"You said Miles as prosecutor means we have problems," said Walsh. "How so?"

"Think of it as human nature," said Roman. He looked around the table. "What else, people? Inga?"

Inga Kopovsky was silent because she was too close to the problem. As Tommy's lover, as someone who often fought with Tommy, she knew they could look at her as someone with motive every bit as much as Roman might have motive. So she was standing mute.

"Well, let's talk about the pink elephant in the room while we're laying our hearts bare," said Roman Challis. "I'm talking about the love-hate relationship between Tommy and Inga. We all remember times when they were fighting up and down the hallways, refusing to speak to each other at firm meetings, and even shouting so loud inside their offices the rest of us could hear them. It wasn't very comfortable, especially when we had clients with us and could hear the words through the walls. Yes, I'm still very upset about that. I think it is incumbent on Inga to undertake the same self-exposure that I'm taking and provide us with her bank accounts, financial statements, and communications with all Russians. Wouldn't everyone agree that this goes without saying?"

Roman surveyed the room. It was unanimous. Inga was going to have to disclose, too. Which relieved Roman since he needed the issue raised and had done it with great finesse and timing. Just like they had discussed before the meeting. Now it wasn't all eyes on Roman. It was all eyes on Roman and Inga.

And there was one more thing. Roman left that night for Zürich, Switzerland. He'd always preached cases were won or lost by whoever out-prepared the other.

The meeting ended thus, with Roman and Inga making full disclosure within ten days. The board would then resume its meeting.

As he lagged with Jennings in the hallway, Roman whispered to him, "My office. Fifteen minutes."

As soon as Jennings entered his office and closed the door behind him, Roman started right in. "You know, it's one thing to prove that I'm innocent by disclosing my bank and financial records and lack of communications with the Russians. But it's an entirely different thing to come up with a murder suspect as well. So that's exactly what we are going to do. You've been to St. Petersburg, and you have the bank account set up there, along with the opening deposit. Tonight I go to Zürich, and I transfer one-hundred thousand dollars from St. Petersburg to Zürich, all done in the name of Inga Kopovsky. Now we have a lady with a motive, and we have a lady with a large unexplained deposit from a bank in Russia to her secret account in Switzerland. We are just about to pull the plug on her at that point and turn our findings over to Miles Standish so that he can make an arrest."

"I believe things are about to wrap up nicely in your favor, Roman."

"It's only right," said Roman as he pushed back in his chair and placed his feet on his desk. "It's only right that she be prosecuted for Tommy's death. After all, she had motive, what with their knockdown drag-out fights. It won't surprise anyone if she gets indicted."

"Her files are bulging with sweet-talking emails and letters to Western Energy Reserves and other Russian companies. If one believes these communications, she is in bed with these people. I'd say we're good to go."

"Then off I go to Zürich. I'll be out all day tomorrow, so keep your finger on the pulse of the office. Also, I'd like you to set up a meeting between Miles Standish and us at his office to discuss our findings on Inga. Tell him this is newly discovered evidence that we need to present to him."

"Consider it done. Have a good flight."

"Of course, I will. I'll be taking our corporate jet and eating bonbons and wooing dancing girls before I set down."

The men laughed. Then the meeting broke up.

Was there a video of this exchange?

Never.

Chapter Nineteen

FRANK HEMET

I called Frank Hemet in. I needed clarity on Pitts going to Roman Challis with the stolen document. Did it really happen? I wanted Hemet to find out. I wanted Hemet to get into Roman Challis's visitors' diary and see whether Pitts had visited on the day he claimed. Hemet said it would be difficult, and he might get caught.

Sixty minutes later, he reported back to me. This is what happened.

Frank rode the public elevator up to the second floor of Gray and got off. He flashed his black works security ID and went inside the server room.

There were two rows of servers, right and left, in a relatively small room, extending about 20 feet to the back wall. Hemet guessed there were maybe thirty servers, plus a flashing array of other electronics he could not identify. He knew there would be an operator or two in the room, so he set off to his right to find them. Sure enough, ten feet away was a young man with a beard and thick eyeglasses hovering above his computer keyboard and watching sine waves on his screen. Hemet approached the young man and waited until he looked up. Then Hemet said, "I'm wondering if you can locate a file for me. It's the diary of entrances and exits for the office of Roman Challis on January 20 of this year. I need the entire day and a printout of the whole day, too."

Without answering, the young man turned back to his keyboard and stabbed in a row of words. The computer screen filled with dates, times, and names as Hemet watched within seconds.

"That's exactly what I'm looking for," said Hemet when the young man turned his computer screen to him. "Can you print that out for me?"

"No problem," said the young computer operator. "You can find the printer four aisles over."

Frank walked around the end of the servers and over to the far wall, found the printer, and collected the document he had ordered.

He then exited the server room, exited the computer processing offices, and returned to his own office, where he sat down in his chair and digested what the printout had to say. Halfway down the page, he found an entry for Nicki Pitts visiting Roman Challis for all of six minutes. Satisfied, Hemet then left for Standish's offices.

He had no sooner left his office and stepped into the hallway when Renz Aldrich accosted him. Aldrich's face lit up in a whimsical smile. "Roman Challis would like to see you immediately. If you want, you can follow me there."

"Unnecessary," said Frank. "I know my way there very well, thank you."

Chapter Twenty

FRANK HEMET

Never mind that Frank said he could find his way to Challis's office on his own, Aldrich took it upon himself to lead him there, anyway. They rode the elevator up to the seventh floor, where they got off, took a right, walked to the end of the hall to the corner office, and went inside. Challis's secretary waved Frank on through but held her hand at Aldrich and reminded him he was not invited to the meeting. He sat down in a visitor's chair with a flounce, disappointment on his face.

Frank went inside to find the conference table in Challis's office taken up with Roman Challis at the head, flanked by Max Jennings, Inga Kopovsky, and Alfred Falsgraf, head of Gray's mergers and acquisitions.

The farthest chair away from Roman Challis was available, so Frank chose that one.

"Welcome, Hemet," growled Challis. "Let me begin by saying I don't know how stupid you think we are here, but we have information you have been palling around with

Nicki Pitts. For your information, Pitts is no longer working for this firm, and we consider it seditious for you to meet with him. He not only is no longer a member of this firm, but we also have reason to believe Pitts is cooperating with opposing attorneys on several of our cases. We are frantically trying to understand what he knows about those cases and what he might turn over. Oh, I see that you're going to remain stony-faced and not acknowledge what I'm telling you." Challis then began shouting, "This is my God damn law firm, and I'll be damned if I'll have my black arts team meeting in secret with the likes of Nicki Pitts. Why are you not responding to me, sir?"

Frank spread his hands. "I'm not sure exactly what you're getting at. But I met with Pitts for the same reason, to understand if a disgruntled employee was the one disbursing company secrets to opposing attorneys. In that regard, I was doing nothing more than representing my law firm in doing my job. If you find fault in that, then we have very different ideas about my job description. Other than that, I have no other reason to respond except in a calm, sane manner. So I'm not sure what you're expecting by my facial affect."

Max Jennings loudly spoke up, "And just who the hell authorized you to begin this investigation in placing our secret documents into the opposition's hands?"

"Somebody needs to authorize me?" said Frank. "I would be a damn poor employee if I failed to jump on the biggest problem facing the firm. I wasn't aware that I needed authorization to do my job as the director of black arts. Part of my job is to remain anonymous and undercover when I'm working. If you find fault with that, please let me know, and I'm more than happy to discuss it with you. Otherwise, I sure as hell don't need these attacks as I will do my job the best way I see possible. If you remain dissatisfied with that, all of you, then perhaps you have the wrong man in black arts."

In just two exchanges, it had been made clear Frank was his own man, and titles or raised voices would not cow him. Challis shot a look at Jennings, who looked away because he did not know what to say next.

Challis continued. "Keep in mind that Nicki Pitts defected from my section when I oversaw DOJ lawsuits. I don't know what he took when he left, but I do not trust that man! He's a criminal, and I've made a report on him to the FBI. As I understand it, the FBI is looking into him and his activities as we speak. Please keep this in mind as you go about your duties. Also, please remember that I'm so angry with you for meeting with him without prior consent from me that I could almost throw the book at you. I don't know how you feel about going to prison, but that remains a possibility in the event it turns out you are up to no good. We don't know you that well, Hemet, and we don't know what you mean when you're meeting with the likes of Nicki Pitts. From here on out, you check with Mr. Jennings or me here before you run off half-cocked on your investigations."

Frank rocked his head. "There was nothing half-cocked about my investigation. It was all in due course, and it was all done to help this law firm. If that's not good enough for you, then fire me right now, and I will find another job. But I will not sit here and be abused by you, Mr. Challis, or anyone else. Now you have it, loud and clear. Make your choice, sir."

"I'm not at the point of wanting to fire you or any such thing. I just wanted you to explain yourself before the board here so we are all on the same page. Please carry on with your work. If anything odd comes up, please run it past me and keep me in the loop. You are dismissed."

Frank stood and, without a word, turned and walked out of the office. When he shut the door behind him, it was not gentle, nor was it meant to be.

Chapter Twenty-One

NADIA

Nadia Karamov got the name and address of Standish's house cleaners when they came on Friday. She had been awaiting them for three days. Night and day, she had remained near his house, rotating between three vehicles she had stashed for the job, so no one became curious about any one vehicle and investigated her.

They arrived Friday at eight. Miles Standish had already left for work at seven that morning. The FBI checked IDs, and the crew of three disappeared inside. Nadia slowly approached their van. *White Glove Cleaning* said the vehicle signage. It also provided an address in Maryland. She jotted it down and immediately left for Maryland.

She found the house cleaning business in a rundown section of Tuxedo, Maryland, an industrial sprawl within the unincorporated township. Nadia parked and went inside the walkup, taking the creaking wooden stairs to the second floor. They received her and listened to her request for a job application. Then came the interview. She needed work desperately, she told them. And she would prefer working in the northeast part of DC to save on transportation costs, as she was unmarried with four children and had to scrape and save every penny to make ends meet.

They reviewed her ID, American passport, DC driver's license, and New York birth certificate. All phony, of course, but who cared? It wasn't NASA hiring, just house cleaning. No need to check references or documents or licenses or certificates.

It was post-pandemic, everyone in America was hiring, and she left that day with her uniform blouse and instructions to be back at six in the morning.

Which she did, arriving at 5:35 in her uniform with a travel cup of Twining Tea from London, a favorite among Russians living in America.

She sidled up to the manager's office and said good morning. It was a Friday, and she wondered if she might see her assignments for the day. With fingers crossed, she read down the list of six homes her crew would clean that day.

Miles Standish was number four on the list.

Chapter Twenty-Two

MILES STANDISH

The following day, Detective Alvin M. Douglas met with me. Douglas had made the appointment himself, calling to tell me we needed to speak about an upcoming grand jury. I called Marshall Lakin to attend because I knew the FBI needed to know what I was about to learn.

We met at my office at seven a.m. The day was windy and cold, with a late-rising sun that hadn't broken through the cloud cover. The cherry trees around the Capitol were rimed with ice on the thinnest branches, threatening to snap them off with the slightest breeze.

Douglas wasted no time. "I wanted to meet with you today because I have just been briefed by Mr. Lakin here on the role you will play in the parallel investigation. As I understand it, Mr. Standish, you will look for Tommy Gray's killer at the same time the DC Police Department is also looking for Tommy Gray's killer. Your mandate is to find the traitor giving Western Energy Reserves hundreds of confidential documents of the Department of Justice."

"Yes, that is my mandate. And I'm happy that the DC

Police Department has been advised and will work with me."

"I want to give you a heads-up that my Assistant Attorney General, Devon Bradley, has called a grand jury to meet over Tommy Gray's death. Devon will call Challis and Jennings to testify, among many others. Our commitment to the Standish investigation is to provide you with all grand jury testimony after DOJ vets it to ensure no national secrets are divulged. After that, it's all yours. I only hope you will reciprocate by sending file memos as you go about your investigation. Can we confirm we have this agreement?"

"Yes, we have such an agreement. As of now, I have minimal turnover as we're just getting established in the office. Soon, we'll begin talking to some people. But I will update you through the US attorney's office, which will help keep things in order and keep a record of what's come over the transom and what hasn't."

"Going through the DOJ is fine. Devon Bradley will call Mr. Challis and Mr. Jennings in the next few days. It would help if you sat down with your people and came up with questions for them both. I'm sure our goals will be the same in this, and you will help us as well. Is this possible?"

"Absolutely possible, and I'll make sure it happens. This is a free shot at these two, and I'm happy to take it. Will the grand jury be limited to Tommy's death, or will it also be going into leaky documents?"

"The grand jury will go into all violations of law. There will be an emphasis on Tommy Gray's death, of course. Still, the grand jury will also look for lawyers on the Challis team who might leak documents to Western Energy Reserves. That much I can promise you. Whatever else will be gone into, we'll have to wait and see."

"So it's more or less a fishing expedition," I said. "That's just fine. We'll have plenty of questions ready for Assistant US Attorney Bradley before the questioning begins. As soon as you leave here today, I'll begin on that with a few members of my team. But right now, I'm pretty well tuned in myself to things that should be asked, and I will revise more of that right away so that Bradley has my questions before even the first witness is called."

"I would expect no less, Mr. Standish."

"By the way, are your people aware that Challis and even Jennings himself are possible killers and are possible leakers? Just so we are on the same page."

"Challis has always been a strong suspect. He has the most to gain by the death of Tommy Gray because he rose to lead the firm when Gray died. Likewise, Max Jennings had much to gain. He was promised the Environmental law group. That is a lofty and much better paying position than the staff attorney position he previously held. So these two are strong suspects."

"I think you're making good judgments. Challis and Jennings had much to be gained with the death of Tommy Gray. Others in the firm, not so much."

"Maybe yes, maybe no on the others. I'm keeping an open mind there."

"Fair enough. And there's one other possibility we need to keep very much in mind. The Russians at Western Energy Reserves might very well have wanted to do away with Tommy Gray. We all know about the letter that Heinlein delivered to Tommy Gray. We know that Heinlein's law firm was threatening Gray with a takeover. Keep in mind that Tommy Gray's son left Gray to go out on his own just months ago. Bobby Gray took a large list of Gray clients who went with him out of loyalty. So, Gray was already hurting when Gerry Heinlein paid his visit to Tommy just before he was murdered. That being the case, Gerry Heinlein should be called to testify before the grand jury. I would get hold of him and shake him like a rag doll. Especially ask him what other attorneys work for him or just above him. Their testimony should be taken down in hopes there's a chink in the armor, and we might find out something about their plans for Tommy."

"This is great," said Douglas. "We hadn't been considering a Russian angle through Heinlein, but it certainly is food for thought and more. I'll bring this up with Assistant Attorney General Devon Bradley immediately, and we can get a subpoena out to Gerry Heinlein without fail. Thanks so much for this, Standish."

Chapter Twenty-Three

MILES STANDISH

I took a call two hours later from Devon Bradley at DOJ. He wanted to see me immediately. Could he come right over? Of course, I said.

When he arrived, I saw Bradley was relatively young, maybe late twenties. He wore very thick, black-framed glasses and had blond hair, which he had combed over to the side. His nose was broad, and his lips were small, giving him the look of a pugilist wearing black eyeglasses. I had done some nosing around and had learned that Devon Bradley was a graduate of Yale law five years earlier. He had served on the editorial board of the Law Journal, a lofty enough position for any lawyer and an indicator of an up and coming government career. While he might have resembled a pugilist, he was, in fact, a star law student.

I indicated Bradley should sit right down and get started.

Bradley wasted no time. "I'm here because I want to talk to you about the upcoming grand jury in the Tommy Gray case. You know the players and the law firm members in the case in much greater depth than I could ever hope to. You know their accomplishments, their quirks, and their strengths. This information would put the Department of Justice in a good position in questioning these witnesses at the grand jury. So, I am here to ask you to join me as a special assistant US attorney and take over the questioning of the law firm witnesses. I'm wondering, would that be possible or something you're amenable to?"

I drummed my fingers softly on the desk before I replied. "You know, I had never thought about that. In one way, it makes sense, and in another way, it tips my hand to the Gray firm I am involved in investigating Tommy's death. It makes sense for the reasons you stated and because I have a strong desire to find out what the hell is going on. I'm reluctant to let the Gray firm know I'm now investigating. Of course, they were going to find this out eventually, so I'm just wondering right now whether sooner is any worse. Please give me your thoughts, Devon."

"Like you, the same thing has occurred to me because I know you are involved in a down-low investigation that we would never want to cause to become public. One thing is very compelling about this, however, and that is that Washington DC is a tiny town at our level. Your involvement will be known almost immediately after you make your first phone call to your first possible witness. So, I wouldn't let that stand in the way of your jumping in with me. I'm hoping we're on the same wavelength."

I nodded. "Pretty much. No doubt word will get out quite fast once we question lesser lights at the Gray firm. I had planned to build a strong foundation for my investigation by first talking to the staff attorneys at Gray, by whom I mean the attorneys who form the backbone and do the drudge work every day. Within one or two meetings with those people, Jennings would certainly find out, and then he would tell Challis, and the cat is out of the bag. All things considered, it makes sense to me that I would join with you in examining the Gray firm witnesses. So, count me in. Who is the first witness, and when?"

"The first witness will be Max Jennings tomorrow morning at nine at Justice. I'll call you around eight-thirty and give you the suite number."

"Sounds good. I'll be there, ready to go with my questions. I would also ask that you have your questions written out that you wish me to ask Max Jennings."

"I certainly will."

Devon Bradley then stood, and we shook hands. I watched Bradley as he left. Now I had a title. Special Assistant US Attorney.

It had a nice sound to it.

Chapter Twenty-Four

NADIA

Nadia Karamov was assigned windows. She was to clean inside and outside. There were floor-to-ceiling windows in the dining and family rooms, and she saw she'd need a ladder. She was told she would find a stepladder in the garage.

The sky looked like rain, she told Marie, the woman running her team. It only made sense to begin outside. Marie, hungover and a little out of sorts with the world, brushed her off, telling her it was up to Nadia where she started and finished. Just don't bother her with too many questions and interruptions. Nadia promised that wouldn't be the case, that she was a self-starter. Marie seemed relieved.

There was a connection from the laundry room into the greenhouse. Nadia went there with her bucket filled with glass solvent and long-handled squeegee.

The greenhouse was perhaps twenty-five feet long and twenty feet wide, constructed entirely of glass panes eighteen by twenty-four inches. The walls arose from a concrete pad up to waist height and then climbed another ten feet at a canted angle that joined at a steel lodgepole at the apex, running the full length of the elegant glass structure.

Nadia drew near the glass wall facing the alley. The glass was heavily mattered with water spots and stains that ran down the glass wall. Nadia looked up and decided the staining was corrosion of the lodgepole. It would require elbow grease and lots of it.

She set about squeegeeing the entire alley-side wall, starting at the pinnacle and chasing the water down the wall, top to bottom. But it was working. Within an hour, the entire glass surface shone on the alley side of the greenhouse.

Then it was time to take her stepladder outside and repeat her efforts.

A clear view of her target was imperative. It began with the ability to visualize her target clearly through the glass. While she prepared, she studied sun angles and shade problems with the oak and cherry trees long-established in Standish's backyard. She even became so bold as to locate a handsaw in the garage and return to the backyard, where she openly cut down a cluster of oak branches that might cast shadows on her target.

When that portion was all said and done, she went back inside the greenhouse and worked at the other wall and ceiling until Marie called to her to cease and join them for the ride to the next job. Nadia carefully stowed her tools and left the greenhouse looking untouched.

Unless one looked up from one's plants and stole a look outside, the distinction between indoors and out had all but disappeared, clear as the glass walls were.

Miles Standish didn't even notice. But he had become a

prime target, clearly visible from his alleyway, and he hadn't a clue.

The shot was almost too easy for an expert sniper such as Nadia.

Now she only needed Moscow Center's order to proceed. She bundled up all monitored email conversations from Standish's computers. A Russian FSB tech group had hacked the files for her. She sent them by satellite uplink to Moscow. Maybe now they would confirm the connection between Miles Standish and the FBI as joint operators. When the order to take the shot came late Monday next, she was elated.

Now it was her turn to shine. They left the job site at 11:04 a.m.

Chapter Twenty-Five

BENJI

Three hours after my Bradley meeting, I was home and working in the greenhouse when I received a text from Benji. "Come get me. Home."

My Big Brother child. My heart jumped as he lived in a terrible neighborhood with a mother who wasn't always around.

I dropped what I was doing—cultivating the plants with a 3-tine—and went inside, where I washed my hands in the kitchen sink. Then I threw on an all-weather Carhartt and headed for the garage. My driver slid behind the wheel and asked for an address. Thirty minutes later, I was entering the lobby of Carver Terrace and ignoring the young dudes gathered on the stoop, smoking and making snide remarks as whitey went past. I took the stairs, avoiding the elevator and whomsoever might ride just then.

At his door, I tapped with my car keys. Three times, easy, very polite. I didn't want any trouble with Immanuel Rayito and his knife. The door opened just a crack on my third knock, with the interior security chain drawn tight. It was Benji. He was red-eyed and rheumy, and he looked very thin, even frail.

"Benji?" I said, "What's going on?"

"I want to come with you."

"Sure. Is your mother here? Shouldn't we ask her?"

"She hasn't been home in a week. Immanuel's here. He won't share his food with me. I'm hungry, Mr. Standish!"

"Bastard! Come on out, and let's get you something to eat. Then we can talk about your mom. Will you come to my house with me, Benji?"

"That's what I wanted."

"Then come on out. Don't bother bringing anything. We'll replace what you need."

The chain went slack, and the door opened, casting a right triangle of yellow light on the asphalt tile floor. He closed it behind him, and we hurried toward the stairway. Then the entrance door swung shut behind us, and we were double-timing down the stairs before Immanuel became aware Benji was gone. Not that it mattered all that much: Immanuel was neither Benji's parent nor guardian. He had no right with the boy at all, except what he could conjure up with his anger at Benji and the world around them.

Then we were on the sidewalk. The toughs on the stoop insulted Benji with names only insiders would recognize as hurtful—but I read his face now, like his family member. Benji heard it all and pulled his hoodie up over his head. He jammed his fists into his blue jeans and picked up the pace until we were climbing into my car. I knew Benji wanted nothing more than to speed away, so I had the driver floor the Mercedes, and we laid down rubber a respectable distance.

When we arrived at my house and went inside, a sudden

silence arose between us. We had nothing to say from out of our usual bag of topics. So I plunged ahead.

"Where's your mom, Benji? Do you even know?"

"She has several men she hangs with down around 12th Street and Massachusetts Avenue."

"Homeless neighborhood."

"Skid Row."

A look of desperation crossed over his angular face. His eyes turned away, and I studied his strong chin, perfect teeth, and braided hair. He was only ten, but, as my stepfather always told me about me, he would break some hearts.

"Okay, has she done this before? Just taken off and been gone for several days?"

"She goes on a bender when we get our check."

"Every month then?"

"Yes. Then she's gone until the check is all gone. It takes about a week. That's how long she's gone for."

"And how do you eat? Who takes care of you?"

"I steal food from the supermarkets. They're my bitch."

"How do you get to school?"

"Bus. City bus. The driver don't charge me for school rides."

"Why haven't you told me all this before? We've known each other for years?"

"It makes me ashamed. No one taking care of me. It's like I'm invisible out there."

I got up and went to the kitchen. I returned with two Fiji water bottles and passed one to Benji.

"Thank you."

"So we need a plan. How would you feel about living with me?"

"That works great, but the man won't allow it."

"What man won't allow it?"

"CFSA."

"Children and Family Services won't allow you to live with me? I'll call them and become a foster parent and give you a good place to grow up."

"You'd do that for me?"

"Yes, I would."

"Shiiit."

'I'm calling them right now. You go out back while I talk to them. Decide where you want our basketball court."

"What?"

"We're gonna ball. I'm no good, but I'm your competition until you get bigger than me."

"I'm on it, dog."

"And no more dog and dude. Call me Miles."

"Sure enough."

"Now go."

I called the child agency. The upshot of it was that they would need to come right out and inspect and check the boy. Then they'd decide about temporary placement while I went through foster parent qualifying. It seemed to help that I'd been his Big Brother for going on five years now. That's when the lady began talking about temporary placement. They would be out this evening. We hung up, and I started reading the DC Code on child custody. I found I qualified for temporary custody and, at ten years of age, some judges might allow the minor to tell the court their preference for placement. Both helped us.

First the house. I used a weekly cleaning service and seldom disturbed anything, so the house was pretty much immaculate.

Then I checked the refrigerator. There had to be food for the child. Mine was all but empty because I ate out three or four evenings a week and was never home for lunch. So, I went grocery shopping on Instacart. A roast, a ham, fried chicken, fresh vegetables, peanut butter, Sprite, and on and on. I called Benji in, and he listed his likes and dislikes—most of it starch and candy. He even wanted cigarettes, or at least an e-cig. He got neither, of course. But I knew my kid: he was only testing me to see just how safe he really was, how good the parenting was going to be. He must have been relieved when he saw we would eat healthily.

We had no decent food while waiting for Instacart, so we made peanut butter and jelly sandwiches. I started to pour milk but sniffed it first. Sour, so I poured it out.

Once the food was taken care of, we browsed over to Amazon.com and began shopping for Benji's clothes. Of course, he needed everything, so this ate up the better part of an hour. He wanted gangsta; I wanted prep schoolboy. We settled on pieces of each, but we agreed he had to wear 50-50 every day to school. There might be a hoodie and sunglasses (outside only), but there would also be khaki pants and loafers. Poor kid, but I was struggling, I admit. This was my first time being in charge of a ten-year-old boy or ten-year-old anything. I was going to have to learn as I went along. It would take me a month or two before I realized that 50-50 would get the kid attacked by both groups. Slowly, we slipped into gangsta.

Next, we picked out a room for Benji. He chose the violet guest room because it had a trundle bed, and he envisioned friends staying over. I was good with that. Then we went to Posters.com and picked out posters.

Just then, the doorbell rang, and I went to answer. I saw two women wearing slacks, shirts, and open sports coats through the glass. They carried clipboards and had their phones to record and photograph. They looked all business and impatient, waiting for the door to open.

I opened up, they stepped inside, and off we went, details, details, details. They even asked Benji about his placement preference. "Here with my dad," he said.

He now owned my heart.

The temporary placement was made that night with me, and a temporary hearing was set for two weeks off. Notice of the proceedings and the whereabouts of Benji would be left at Philomena's apartment at Carver Terrace. That would be his mother.

Later, we made popcorn and watched *The Outlaw Josey Wales* when they were gone. My favorite western.

When Clint Eastwood meets the Indian chief, Benji turned to me on the couch, his eyes wide.

"Was I wrong to say you were my dad?"

"I'm your dad. Now let's watch the movie."

He sat back, a huge smile plastered on his face, and raced me to the bottom of the popcorn bowl.

Chapter Twenty-Six

MILES STANDISH

The following morning, I met with Frank Hemet, and he updated me on what he had learned about the visitors' records at Gray proving Nicki had been to see Roman Challis with the compromised expert report.

"Here we have a printout of the January twenty visit confirming that Nicki Pitts visited with Roman Challis. As you can see, the visit lasted all of six minutes, but it occurred just as Nicki has told us."

"So what happened, according to Nicki, that Challis had ignored the purloined document, is very believable. Of course, there's nothing in this written record to prove there was a document, but why else would Nicki have visited?"

"What I plan to do now is pay a visit to Nicki and collect up that document. We will need it at trial at some point, whether we are helping prosecute Tommy's killer or bringing our lawsuit against Western Energy Reserves. The record will be key to either at some point."

"Good idea. Once you have the document, please bring it here and enter it into our local database. I'm trying to set up our little law firm here, complete with our own document retrieval system. It would be a very nice beginning to all that."

"Of course, I will. So I'll see you again later today."

"Thank you for stopping by."

Chapter Twenty-Seven

MILES STANDISH

When the clock struck nine the following morning, I sat in the US District Court grand jury room where Bradley had directed me. Alvin M. Douglas of the DC Police was also present, as was a court reporter, a closed-circuit video system, two bailiffs, and two security officers. Security was tighter than usual because top secret DOJ documents might come into play, and bags and briefcases would be searched as witnesses exited the grand jury room. All grand jurors would also be searched after breaks and again at the end of the day.

The witness, Maxwell Jennings, had just been admitted into the grand jury room and was getting settled in his chair.

Jennings was 50 years old with black hair and bushy black eyebrows, and he wore eyeglasses that were always a light tint of gray, thus disguising his eyes to some extent. He was rather heavyset yet looked athletically fit as if he might work out on a regular schedule. I honestly couldn't understand what Deonna saw in the man. She was gorgeous, a goddess. And Jennings--well, he wasn't even all that attractive, but there was a certain air about him, perhaps in the way he held himself, confidence that must have appealed to my poor Deonna. But I would bet it was all a façade, and he had sucked Deonna in with his conniving ways instead.

When he took his seat, he crossed one leg over the other, opened a notepad, and withdrew a Mont Blanc pen from his shirt pocket. He jotted a quick entry at the top of the page of his yellow pad and then looked up. He nodded at the grand jurors and offered a small smile, then turned his gaze to me and narrowed his eyes as if he were going to pursue me instead of the other way around.

I was ready. I met his gaze and did not break away when I asked my first question. "Mr. Jennings, you have been called here today to testify regarding the death of Tommy Gray. Have the rules of testimony been laid down for you by your attorney?"

"I'm not sure. I've never been under grand jury scrutiny before."

"Fair enough," I said with a nod. "So let me ask you this, Mr. Jennings. Are you comfortable with the rules of the road and the grand jury room? Or do you need me to explain any part of what's happening here today to you?"

"I am comfortable enough that I am ready to answer if you will only get to it, Mr. Standish."

The great intimidator. I'd heard tales about Max from other lawyers who talked about his pushiness and exaggerations to frighten lawyers off. Welcome to the real world, Max. We've only just begun.

"In the twelve hours before Tommy Gray was found dead in his law office, please tell the jury where you were and what you were doing. I am talking about the hours between seven o'clock the night before and approximately eight o'clock the next morning when Tommy Gray was found dead."

"Well, let's see. At seven o'clock the night before, I was having dinner with my girlfriend."

"And what is your girlfriend's name?" I knew. Everyone knew. And I hated to hear it, but this was a grand jury.

"Deonna Standish."

I cleared my throat softly before continuing, trying not to let any emotion betray me. "And what time was supper concluded?"

"When we were finished, it was eight-thirty, and I went into my office, spread out some papers from my briefcase, and worked until about eleven o'clock when I turned in. Deonna was reading the new Stephen King book on her Kindle when I went to bed, so I put my mask on to block out the light, turned over, and was asleep almost immediately. The next thing I knew, it was six-thirty in the morning. After my morning prayers, I jumped in the shower and prepared myself for work. Does this answer your question, Mr. Standish?"

"At what point did you learn that Tommy Gray was dead by a gunshot wound?"

"I would say around eight a.m. since my condo is only a fifteen-minute walk from my office. So, I was there by about seven-forty-five a.m. I was then called out of my office by Inga Kopovsky, who had sounded the alarm. She told me that Tommy Gray was not answering his door and was not answering his phone messages. That was extremely unusual and alerted me because Tommy was always at his desk and working by seven a.m. She said to meet me at Tommy's door, and so I exited my office and walked two doors down to his corner office, where a small crowd had already gathered. Someone produced a key to Tommy's office and opened the door. We squeezed inside."

"I would like you to tell me exactly what you saw upon entering Tommy Gray's office."

"I was probably the second person through the door and the first or second into Tommy's inside office. I was jolted to see him flung back in his chair with part of his head missing. Obviously, he was dead, as the missing part of his head was scattered across the wall behind him. Entering with me was Arnie Truckee, who went to move the shotgun lying on the floor. He was abruptly stopped by Frank Hemet, the criminal lawyer in the Gray firm. Frank gave a quick order to Arnie not to move the shotgun because we were standing in the middle of what might've been a crime scene. Frank talked to us a bit more, and we ended up backing out of the office and retreating to our firm's large conference room, where we all took a seat. I believe it was Inga who dialed 911 and asked for police officers to come."

"Now, you told us that the night before, you had worked in your office from about nine o'clock to eleven o'clock. And you have also told us it was approximately a fifteen-minute walk from your home to the offices of Gray. You also told us that Deonna, your girlfriend, was reading her Stephen King novel when you went upstairs to bed. Tell the jurors how long your live-in girlfriend had been upstairs reading."

"I didn't say she was my live-in girlfriend."

That stopped me up. The bastard had caught me, but I wouldn't let him get me again.

"What do you call her?"

"My fiancée."

"Your married fiancée?"

"Not for long, Mr. Standish."

"Please answer the question: How long had Deonna Standish been upstairs reading?"

"I have no idea."

"Tell the jurors how many times you saw her between nine o'clock and eleven p.m."

"I didn't see her even once."

"So there were two hours of the night before he was found dead where you have no witnesses as to your whereabouts, isn't that correct?"

"Well, she might have seen me, and I didn't know it."

"Have you discussed this case with her?"

"I have."

"And having discussed this case with your girlfriend, did you ever ask her whether she observed you in your home office in the hours between nine and eleven?"

"We have never discussed that, no. There was no reason for us to discuss that."

"So you don't know if she observed you?"

"That is correct. Her habit is to disappear upstairs with a cup of decaf, climb into bed, and read while I go into my office to work for a couple of hours. It's just a way of having time to ourselves and being comfortable with it, not like we're abandoning each other in those intimate hours before sleep. At least that's how I see it."

"Well, your girlfriend—excuse me, your married fiancée—is waiting outside to testify next. Can we count on you not to discuss this matter with her before she testifies?"

"I didn't know there would be an opportunity for me to discuss this matter with her before she testifies. I know we're being kept in separate offices before we come here to testify, so I don't even know where she is."

"Mr. Jennings, what proof do you have that you didn't

go to Tommy's office between nine o'clock and eleven and shoot him yourself?"

"I suppose the only proof I have is my testimony. And let me say that I've never had my testimony refuted in any court or deposition. I have never been convicted of lying in court or of perjury, and I have never been convicted of any other crime. Let me also say that I'm a law-abiding, God-fearing citizen who would never in your wildest dreams shoot somebody. My life is full. I am a happy and fulfilled man, and Tommy Gray was one of my closest friends. I hope this answers your question."

"Rather nicely done. But I've learned that the Gray video surveillance system went blank that night and was off for the rest of the night. Have you since learned how this happened?"

"I have. What I have been told by the company that installed and monitored our video system was that a server went down in their offices. The system quit recording at about nine-fifteen. I have been offered no other explanation."

"Is it possible for the office-wide video to be shut down from the offices of Gray?"

"It is possible. I checked that out with our video company, and they have said an alternative reason for the video failure could be the fact that someone in our offices turned off the video."

"How does your video company know the difference between a server failure at their office and a person turning off the video at the offices of Gray?"

"I have been told they have no way of knowing the difference. I don't believe that, and I'm having an expert look at the why."

"Still, it leaves the possibility that you turned off the video yourself at nine-fifteen, isn't that correct?"

"I did not turn off the video."

"I did not ask whether you did. Instead, I asked whether it was possible. I'll ask again. Is it possible?"

"I suppose anything is possible," said Jennings. He sat back with a loud sigh and pursed his lips as he studied me. At least I had his attention.

"Mr. Jennings, do you own any guns?"

"I do. I own two Glock pistols. A model 26 and a model 17. Both are holstered in the type of holsters I could wear concealed when I was out and about when my children were younger. It's long been my habit of doing so because I don't want to be a target or have my family be a target for that person who comes into the movie theater and randomly starts shooting people. Many people would agree that this caution I take is supported by the never-ending random shootings our country experiences. And let me head off your next question, which is no, I do not own and have never owned a shotgun."

"We have already subpoenaed your credit card, bank card, and bank account transactions for the last six months. We are looking for transactions where a shotgun was purchased. We have not finished our examination of those items, so let me ask, are those transactions going to show the purchase of a firearm?"

"Yes, they are going to show the purchase of my Glock 26 from guns-dot-com. But it will also show there are no purchases of a shotgun. The Glock 26, like I stated earlier, is carried concealed as a defensive weapon."

"Mr. Jennings, I'm going to continue your grand jury testimony at this point because I need to call your married fiancée so that she can get back to her counseling practice for a scheduled appointment at noon. Please remember that you are still sworn under oath and must follow the rules of grand jury testimony and discuss what is said here today with no one. Do you understand these rules?"

"Of course, and I shall follow them to a T."

At that point, we took a break in the testimony. Restrooms and fresh coffee came next. Break time was a slow process. What the jurors took to the bathrooms had to be searched by the officers outside. For myself, I refilled my travel mug with coffee and then returned to the counsel table to review my notes for the testimony of Deonna Standish. The bailiffs had a list of those I had subpoenaed to testify that morning, and Deonna was being retrieved from the office where she was comfortably held, waiting to give her testimony.

Chapter Twenty-Eight

MILES STANDISH

After the grand jurors had their break, the bailiff brought my wife, Deonna Standish, into the grand jury room. She looked as beautiful as always in a flattering pantsuit, heels, and her hair short and combed to the side. With her bright lipstick and glasses, she looked so young. My heart lurched even though I was finished with her. She gracefully took the witness stand and flipped her head to remove a curl of hair below her eyebrow line blocking her vision. She then looked up and smiled at the room and seemed ready and willing to participate in whatever was to follow.

I moved to the lectern and laid my notes before me and then looked up and smiled at her. "Let's get this out of the way first. Your name is Deonna Standish, and you are a psychiatric counselor at a private practice in Washington, DC, correct?

"Yes, I am Deonna Standish, and I'm a clinical psychologist. Just recently, I opened my private practice in the Watergate complex."

"Your boyfriend, Max Jennings, just testified about

certain things that happened on the night before Tommy Gray was found dead in his office. Do you remember that night?"

"I've been over this with Max's attorney. I've had to tell him I don't remember that night because it was like so many other nights since we've been together. I can tell you what I think happened, from habit, but not what actually happened. So I'm afraid I will not be much help to you in your investigation, Mr. Standish."

Was her use of my name a go at me? Or was she angry I had brought her there? I continued. "Please tell me what you think happened that night."

"After a long dinner of conversation and good food, Max and I go our separate ways. I get my coffee and go upstairs to my bedroom, change into my T-shirt, and start reading my latest book. Max is in his office during that time, working on office stuff. We seldom see each other during these two hours because I never come downstairs. By nine o'clock, I am done with downstairs. After I am upstairs, Max will lock the downstairs doors and check the windows before moving into his office and doing his thing. I know he has a cup of coffee during this time, but I don't know whether he did that night."

"Given what you have just said, would it have been possible for Max to leave the house, walk to the Gray firm, and shoot Tommy Gray without you knowing about it?"

"Max could have done just about anything, and I wouldn't have known about it. I am not keeping track of Max while I am upstairs reading. I have my headphones on, and I listen to brain-dot-com as I read. Sorry, I can't help more. But there is one thing, and that is this. Max would never shoot anyone. He's not that kind of person. He always works things out by having a sit-down talk. We express our *feelings*. Ever since we've been together, I haven't known him to be violent or aggressive. He's a mature man, kind and generous."

That was a go at me. But I'd take it standing up. "All right, Ms. Standish. That is all I have. You are excused now."

Chapter Twenty-Nine

MILES STANDISH

Max Jennings was then recalled to the witness stand.

I asked him, "Mr. Jennings, your married fiancée, Deonna, has just testified. She stated she did not see you between nine and eleven p.m. on the night Tommy Gray died. That being the case, have you thought about anyone else who might have known your whereabouts during that time?"

"I have checked my cell phone records. My cell phone never left home that night. It is my habit to take my cell phone when I leave the house. Had I left the house that night, I would've taken it with me, and my cell phone location records would show me at the offices of Gray that night. But those records show no such thing. So I did not leave the house that night."

"Or if you did, you did not take the cell phone with you, correct?"

"That would be correct, except I always take it with me no matter how you might phrase the question. I did not leave the house that night, and you can't prove that I did."

"Mr. Jennings, I'm going to change the line of questioning now. I want to go into the hierarchy of Gray's senior management when Tommy died. Are you familiar with that hierarchy?"

"Definitely. I was and am part of it."

"At the time Tommy Gray died, he was the chairman and managing partner of the law firm, correct?"

"That is correct. Tommy ran the whole firm from top to bottom daily. His word was final, and no one ever crossed him because he was so well respected. You could say that Tommy was beloved by his employees."

"And who was second-in-command?"

"That would be Inga Kopovsky. She was number two behind Tommy and now is number two behind Roman Challis. I know you're going to ask me next who is number three, so I'll tell you right now that I am number three. However, I have no designs on being number one and pray that will never come to pass. I have never wanted to be the head of the Gray firm and don't want to now."

"Tell the jury why that is."

"Because the job takes so much out of your day. Please remember that partners in our firm are paid based on their earnings and the earnings of their associates. The chairman is also paid an extra one-hundred-thousand a year for managing the firm, but that falls far short of the time he actually loses in managing the firm. It's a losing proposition to be the chairman."

"Fair enough, Mr. Jennings. Tell us how the employees of Gray look at Roman Challis."

"Well, Mr. Challis is still new to the position. Even though Roman has been with Gray for almost as long as Tommy was there, I think most of the lawyers are taking a wait-and-see attitude. So far, the reports coming back are good; people are feeling better about him every day and are letting go of Tommy Gray."

"What about you, Mr. Jennings? How do you feel about Roman Challis?"

Max shuffled his feet in the witness chair and looked uncomfortable for the first time. He stared at the ceiling as if deep in thought but then finally looked back at me and then at the jury. "We have a problem in Gray. I don't know if you've gone into this yet with the grand jury, but allow me to tell them that our law firm is losing top-secret documents to the lawyers representing Russian oil and gas companies in litigation we have filed against them. We've been trying to discover just who's leaking documents for some time now. We are not taking anybody for granted, and we do not give anybody a pass. The five board members believe Tommy Gray was innocent. As for Roman Challis, the jury is still out on him and still out on everyone else in the firm."

"So the jury is still out on you, as well?"

"I guess you could say that. No one gets a free pass. What's been going on is too much of a problem for it not to be taken seriously. Everyone is a suspect."

"Isn't it true that the FBI is now investigating Gray?"

"I hadn't heard that. But it wouldn't surprise me. That you are here today, helping the government, puts me on alert. You are just the kind of man the Department of Justice would hire as special counsel to investigate the leaking documents. How I would love to ask you whether that's what your job is, Mr. Standish."

"I'm going to tell you right up front that yes, that is my job. I am looking for the killer of Tommy Gray, and I am also looking for the person or persons leaking top-secret documents to the Russians."

"I'll keep that in mind."

"Please do. And please do not tell this information to anyone else in the law firm or anyone else anywhere. It is confidential, covered by the federal grand jury rules, and you could be in grave trouble for telling anyone what happened here today. Do you understand this?"

"I understand that. I am a lawyer, and I understand my obligation."

"All right, then. I am finished with you, Mr. Jennings, but please don't be surprised if you are recalled to this room later. I have the right to do that, and you must come as a person still under oath. Thank you for being here today."

After I had finished with Max Jennings, I called for a lunch break and excused the jury for 90 minutes.

One thing ran through my mind again and again: we needed motive.

A jury always wanted to see a defendant's motive, but the law didn't require proof of motive at all.

But I wanted to own this jury, and they would be given an inescapable motive.

It had only just begun.

Chapter Thirty

MILES STANDISH

After lunch, the FBI driver reversed course and returned me to the grand jury room at the Justice Department. This afternoon would begin the testimony of Roman Challis. And I was so ready for him.

My thinking of Roman Challis went like this. For openers, he was now the chairman at Gray. He had arrived at that lofty level by being alive when Tommy Gray died. The title meant that Challis had the second most longevity at Gray.

Roman Challis had joined Gray when he was 24 years old after having clerked in the First Circuit Court of Appeals for one year after graduation from law school. He was a hot catch, and Gray had landed him.

Challis was known for being a hard-nosed litigator but a lousy people person. He seldom attended Bar Association conferences and shied away from social interaction with other members of Gray. His interests were traveling to medieval locations in Europe and taking photographs of long-forgotten battlefields. He had a wife who traveled with him, a ditzy little woman who graduated Phi Beta Kappa from Alabama and was the secretary of her Pi Beta Phi sorority. Her name was Betsy, and she raised English sheepdogs and showed them every year at Westminster. Roman and Betsy went everywhere together and sometimes could be seen sitting in the front row of the U.S. Open tennis finals. They were an odd couple that no one could figure out. I would break down fifty percent of that couple this afternoon, meaning the Roman half.

We took up again at 1:30 when the grand jury was seated and settled in, and I had the bailiff bring in Roman Challis.

Challis arrived wearing a conservative Brooks Brothers suit with a traditional straight collar and a conservative club tie. There were cufflinks, a tie bar, and perfectly combed JFK hair. His nails were manicured and shiny, I noticed, as he sat at the witness table, took out a pad of paper, and rolled back the first page. He produced a $2 Bic pen and sat there poised, awaiting my first question.

I said, "You are Roman Challis, age forty-five, and the chairman at Gray, correct?"

"That is correct."

"How did you become the chairman at Gray?"

'I did it by outliving the previous chairman. There is no skill required for that, just plodding longevity, which most people would find very boring. It was my norm."

"How well did you know Tommy Gray?"

"Like a brother. Tommy and I had been at Gray almost an equal amount of time, and I doubt there was anything about him of any importance that I didn't know."

"That being the case, who killed Tommy? Was it Tommy himself, or was it someone else?"

"I thought that's why we were here today. I thought you

were going to pull that rabbit out of the hat for us, Mr. Standish."

"I am, but the rabbit is taking it quite slow, Mr. Challis. He seems to want your help. So again, let me ask you to give us your best estimate of who killed Tommy Gray."

"This much I know. It was not suicide. Tommy was a Catholic, and suicide is a mortal sin to a Catholic. Tommy was a better Catholic than that. Plus, Tommy was neither depressed nor going through a terrible family problem. I had lunch with him the day before, and we talked about how things were for us. He was thrilled, had a trip coming up to Europe, and had just traded in his seven-thousand-dollar Canon camera for the newest iPhone and its triple camera. He thought that was a hoot."

Challis provided great detail about this, so much so that I grew drowsy. Then I snapped fully awake, angry at his digression. "Frankly, I don't give a damn about iPhones or any smartphones."

"Sir?" he asked me, his brows raised to his hairline.

"So, let me come back to it for what is hopefully the last time. Who, in your mind, killed Tommy Gray?"

"The Russians. They sent in a killer, and they took out a man who they knew loathed them. However, it was a fatal mistake because they put me in his place, and I'm a man who loathes them even more than Tommy did. I hate the Romanovs. I hate Lenin. I hate Stalin. I hate Khrushchev. I hate *glasnost*. And I hate Vladimir Putin. They could not have promoted a bigger hater of all things Russian than me. Incidentally, is my testimony confidential? I don't want it loose on the streets what I just said, and so I am counting on the confidentiality of this grand jury testimony."

"Absolutely," I exclaimed, "what you say here stays here. Now, let me ask this, having told us that a Russian killed

Tommy, could you help us by narrowing that down more? Do you have any names or known persons who had an ax to grind against Tommy?"

"I have no names. I did not work in environmental law, so I wasn't interacting daily with Western Energy Reserves or the other Russian-oligarch-owned companies. I am an antitrust lawyer, and the two don't mix."

"You have seen the video between Gerry Heinlein and Tommy Gray where Gerry tells Tommy that the Justice Department wishes Heinlein law to enfold Gray into Heinlein. As he said, that would mean Heinlein would take over Gray and run the environmental show for the Department of Justice. You have seen this video, correct?"

Challis shuffled his feet, and a brief look of discomfort crossed his face. It was the first time he had allowed even the slightest emotion loose in the grand jury room. Everyone picked up on it. They waited for what came next.

"Yes, of course, I've seen the video; everyone has. It is a horrible suggestion for the DOJ to take over Gray's Environmental practice and give the work to Heinlein. That would be instant death for our firm and mean bankruptcy for about forty attorneys within the month. I'm concerned that we are here today because the Justice Department seeks more information before it takes over my law firm. Please tell me that's not the truth, and I can relax tonight and get some sleep."

"I'm not included in those discussions, if there are any such discussions, at the Justice Department. I have no idea if what Gerry Heinlein was telling Tommy Gray had any truth to it or not. But one thing I want you to comment on is that, at the end of that video, Tommy Gray throws Gerry Heinlein out of his office. Gray is tremendously upset with

Heinlein. That being the case, do you feel Heinlein had anything to do with the death of Tommy Gray?"

"Oh, I'm afraid that's so tenuous that I have no comments."

"Tenuous?"

"Preposterous. I've never even heard that until right now. From you, Mr. Standish."

"Now, Mr. Challis, I want to get down to the meat and potatoes of your testimony. We—meaning the Justice Department—have information that a Gray employee named Nicki Pitts brought to you a document that the Justice Department had given Tommy Gray. It was intended for Gray's use in an EPA lawsuit in Colorado. However, it immediately wound up in Russian hands and was used against the Department of Justice and won a critical case. Nicki Pitts says that he brought this document to you and asked you to act on it. He said that you all but refused to discuss it with him and that you walked him right out of your office offering no help, and to this day, you haven't gotten back to him with any offers of help. You recall Nicki Pitts's visit to you?"

"I remember Nicki Pitts coming, yes. The document that he produced differed from the one you described here today. The document he brought into my office had to do with the list of attendees for our monthly noon luncheon at the firm. It had absolutely nothing to do with anything else. It was ridiculous."

"Nicki Pitts has told us that the document was, in fact, the report of an expert witness. The Department of Justice had hired the witness to investigate Colorado fracking. The witness said that the Colorado groundwater problems were most likely the cause of upstream farming, ranching, and mining. Are you sure you didn't see that document at the time Nicki Pitts came to you?"

"I'm sure I've seen no such document. If Nicki Pitts had brought such a thing to me, fire alarms would have gone off, and I would've taken every step possible to circle the wagons and find out how the report had gotten out of our office and into the hands of the Russians. It would've taken up the next week of my focus at the law firm. It would've been huge. Is there any other way I could say this?" He gave a slight dramatic pause. "It would have turned our office upside down."

"Well, that's what I would've expected. But that's not what happened. So either you're telling the truth about what the document was or wasn't, or Nicki Pitts is telling the truth about what the document was or wasn't. The only thing is, Pitts has produced for us the key document, and it is clearly marked 'received' by the Western Energy Reserves attorneys. How would you explain the WER attorneys having that document at all?"

"I have no explanation. Nor do I agree it came from our law offices. It could've come from anywhere, ranging from the expert witness's own office to the Department of Justice or wherever else it might have been sent, which could be anywhere in America. I cannot vouch for the etiology of that record."

"Mr. Challis, I am next going to take Russian grand jury testimony, and then I am going to bring you back. Please do not leave the U.S. over the next few weeks."

"What? We have a Slavic tour planned to begin the first of the month."

"Please remember you are under subpoena here until I dismiss you."

"So I stay."
"That is true."

Chapter Thirty-One

MILES STANDISH

I didn't know who I wanted from Western Energy Reserves to testify before my grand jury, so I sent a general subpoena, which said I wanted them to produce the person most knowledgeable about WER's litigation with Gray. Sure, it was a fishing expedition, but a bunch of law is a fishing expedition, so I didn't mind at all. Besides, this was my grand jury. I could go after five or ten other Russian witnesses if I needed to. Whatever it took was what I would do.

They sent a man by the name of Anatoly Mikael Studov. I had never heard the name before and did not know who Mr. Studov was, but he was scheduled to testify the morning after Roman Challis. He was a white-skinned Russian with his hair parted down the middle and a wave on either side in front. His eyes were very sharp and darting, and it suddenly occurred to me I had not asked for an interpreter. I had assumed he would be English-speaking. We might all be wasting our time right now.

After he was settled and had shot a pinched grin at the grand jury, I walked up to the lectern and smiled at him.

"Mr. Studov, my name is Miles Standish, and I represent the United States in this prosecution for the death of Tommy Gray of Gray law. As you may or may not know, Tommy was found with a head wound from a shotgun blast, dead in his office. He was the law firm leader that is suing you in the case of *United States of America versus Western Energy Reserves, Colorado*. While he was not actively involved in that case, he was the man who would make the key decisions about strategy, settlement, and trial. He was a kind man, brilliant, and had a family that loved him. We all miss him, and we will get to the bottom of whoever killed him and bring them to justice. So let me begin by asking, sir, do you speak and understand English?"

"Oh yes, I am a graduate of the University of Moscow and have a Ph.D. in engineering from Oxford University. I have done more of my higher education in English than in my native tongue. And of course, now, living in the United States as I do, I am even regionalized in my English. I speak pretty good Okie."

I looked over at the jury. I didn't know if they would be insulted by the man's use of "Okie" or if they would find it humorous. There were some smiles; evidently, he had not wholly lost his audience.

"When I subpoenaed Western Energy Reserves, I asked for that officer or director who had the most knowledge about the lawsuit Gray had brought against Western Energy Reserves in Colorado. You were picked regarding my request. Please tell us why it was you who was picked."

"I was picked because I am currently running five different lawsuits that have been lodged against Western

Energy Reserves. As I told you, I have a Ph.D. in petroleum engineering, but I also have a law degree from New York University. Rather than spending my days buying and selling petroleum products, I studied law, and today I practice law in a corporate setting. With a degree in petroleum engineering and a law degree, it was quite simple to join Western. My knowledge of the cases is vast, and while I do not pretend I could be a trial lawyer if someone got sick, I probably could step right in. So yes, I am ready to discuss your lawsuit with you. However, the death of Tommy Gray is something I know nothing about. But I'll try to do what I can to help you."

I liked the guy. His educational background was impeccable. I got the feeling he wasn't the kind of man who would jeopardize all of his work, his diplomas, and his law licenses to defend Western Energy Reserves by lying in a grand jury inquiry. I could feel the energy in the room and knew that the jury felt about Studov the same as I did. My decision not to go after him was quick. I would drain what knowledge I could out of him and then let it go. I would see if I could turn up a witness with more knowledge of Tommy Gray and Western's dealings with him.

"Mr. Studov, is there anyone in your company who dealt with Tommy Gray in the litigation that alleges environmental negligence?"

"Yes, one of them would be Kenneth Kravitz. Mr. Kravitz is an American hired by Western as the lead attorney on several of the lawsuits. I'm sure you've seen his name on some pleadings. Mr. Kravitz would often come to Washington DC and appear before various bodies and inquiries regarding this or that oilfield or fracking or gas pipelines. I know he met with Tommy Gray in person more than once. But would Mr. Kravitz know something about Tommy Gray's death? Highly unlikely."

"Mr. Studov, getting right to the point, do you know anything about the death of Tommy Gray?"

"I know nothing. If I knew something, I would tell you."

"Mr. Studov, what is the role of the Russian FSB in Russian overseas oil and gas projects?"

"I'm sure I don't know."

"Well, in case you have forgotten, the FSB is the Federal Security Service of the Russians that replaced the KGB. The FSB roams the world far and wide and has infiltrated every modern civilization outside Russian borders. Please tell us the role of the FSB where it touches upon the commercial exploits of Western Energy Reserves."

"I am told there is no FSB in America."

"Oh, come now! Who in the world told you such a lie?"

"It's common knowledge where I work that there is no FSB. If there is, I have never seen them, and I have never been in touch with them, anyway. So I'm sorry, but I cannot help you there, either."

"Would it be unusual for the FSB to murder lawyers who were suing a Russian company if it looked like Russian interests might be damaged?"

"I know nothing about any of this."

"You read the papers, sir?"

"Sometimes. I mostly watch YouTube and Netflix. We don't have those in Russia."

"No news?"

"No news. I'm sorry."

"I'm sorry, too. It looked for a while there, like you and I were going to have a mutually respectful relationship, one where we could believe each other. Now I see no such thing because we both know the FSB is very active in America. The FSB is very active in Russian commerce in America. It wouldn't be beyond the FSB to murder an adversary lawyer if he created too many problems for a Russian company. But you deny this, is that right?"

"I deny that. I know nothing about the FSB. Had we known you wanted to ask questions about the FSB, we would have referred you to the Russian Embassy. The rest of us will know nothing."

Our time together was just about spent. He would not tell me one word about the FSB because he knew, and I knew, it was likely the FSB had killed Tommy Gray at the behest of some officer or director of Western Energy Reserves. It was that fast that I had shifted from Max Jennings to the Russians. Sometimes, it only took one word, and my instinct kicked in. I had relied on it much of my career as a trial lawyer, and rarely had it failed me. The Russians were tickling up my spine, and this was going to be much more difficult than I had known going in when I thought it would be impossible to implicate the FSB through the grand jury. The likelihood of our ever getting a step on the FSB was probably 10,000 to 1. I saw no need to continue harassing the man and ended the testimony with my thanks to him. He collected up his few things and left the room.

Next up for testimony was Inga Kopovsky. It would have to be delicately handled with her for obvious reasons, and I needed time to work out just exactly how I was going to do that. I also needed to sandpaper her so that professional matters did not cross over into personal. Thus, I set the grand jury free for the rest of the day and told them I would need them at nine in the morning.

It had been snowing and icing, I found as my FBI driver steered away from the DOJ. I was looking out of my window for a place to have my lunch alone, where I could review witness interrogations. Our windshield wipers soon brushed ice aside that threatened to cover the windshield and make driving very hazardous.

Finally, we found a pub at the edge of downtown.

Over the noon hour, I caught a look at the TV screen in Houlihan's Pub, where I had a bowl of stew and a Pepsi. The TV news predicted an ice storm that would blanket DC by four o'clock and make travel home extremely hazardous.

I quickly jotted down my Inga questions and noted the ones I would need to go over with her that night.

Then I returned to my stew.

Chapter Thirty-Two

MILES STANDISH

That afternoon, after court, it was still snowing. Undaunted, I headed into my bedroom and changed into my jogging suit. Inga was coming over for the night but wasn't home yet, and I remembered she had said something about a late-running deposition, and she would be over around seven, which was just fine with me. Benji wasn't home from school. I had a slot to jog, and I hurried out.

Benji's bus pulled up just as I closed the front door behind me. He climbed down and came jogging up to me.

"Running?"

"Something like that. Go put on your sneakers and sweats. We might as well get you going too."

"Roger that."

He scrambled inside and reappeared five minutes later. White running shoes, wine red sweatpants, a white sweatshirt, his school jacket, and a watch cap. "Fucking cold," he said.

"No, no fucking cold. Just cold. We don't talk like that."

"Roger."

We headed out for my unwell jog, the one that was more of a lurch than a glide, and tonight my right side was aching more than usual, most likely from standing in front of the grand jury for two days in a row. Our escorts—two agents in the lead, two behind—went with us but stayed out of our sight. Down through the park and alongside the Potomac, Benji easily stayed up and often ran ahead to inspect something interesting to a 10-year-old boy. When we got home, my heart jumped because Inga's car was in the second slot of our four-car garage. Inside the house I went, filling with dread with each step. "Go into your room and stay until I come to get you."

"All right."

I found her in the bedroom and told her we needed to talk. She looked up and said, "That sounds ominous. What are we talking about?"

"I'm just wondering if it would be good if we stayed apart tonight, so there will be no chance of anyone saying or asking if we live together tomorrow."

"Uh-oh," she said. "Methinks Brother Standish is having second thoughts about our bump and grind relationship. Not to worry. I'm throwing my stuff in my overnight bag right now and heading home. We can sort all this later. For now, I am long gone. Enjoy your supper."

"I'll see you tomorrow at the District Court's grand jury room, where we'll take your testimony."

"Yes, we will. Please don't spring any surprises on me. Be kind, Miles."

"You can count on it. I will call you in about an hour and go over my questions for you. Goodbye."

"I need that. Thanks." Then she left.

I went into the kitchen, feeling every inch a liar and a cheat. I dumped a can of soup into a pan on the stove. I stood there, thinking and rethinking the Inga relationship while slowly stirring and warming my clam chowder.

I hollered for Benji, and he was beside me in a flash, studying what I was cooking.

"Soup?" he asked.

"Campbell's clam chowder. One of my faves. Do you like it?"

"Never had it. Can I fix grilled cheese sandwiches with it?"

"You know how?"

"Does a bear—"

"Whoops!"

"Is the Pope Catholic?"

"Cheese and bread are in the refrigerator?"

"Long story."

I sat down at the kitchen island with my bowl and began noisily slurping at the spoon. The warm meal was doing its work, and my spirits were lifting when suddenly in walked Deonna. She slammed her purse on the island, walked right up to me, and stood at my side. "Miles, when in the hell were you going to tell me?" She didn't bother to acknowledge Benji.

"And what is it we're talking about, exactly?"

"Marshall Lakin called me this afternoon. He wants us to go into judicial hiding while you're doing your thing with the Russian mob or whoever you're entangled with this week. Were you going to mention this to me, or did you force Marshall to do it? No matter, I will tell you the same thing I told him, and that is that you can both go to hell. I'm not leaving my house because you have concocted a ploy to get me to leave. Do I really look that stupid? Do I?"

"Hey, this is the real deal. The Russians are after me,

which means the Russians are after you." I set my spoon down on the table and dabbed at my mouth with a napkin.

"Neither Max nor I am giving up this house. The court will soon give it to me."

"That's doubtful. You were just leaving?"

"I saw your girlfriend out at her car with the trunk open, putting her bag inside. Love on the rocks? And about my plants. Would you please stay the hell out of my greenhouse and leave my goddamn plants alone? With both of us watering them every day, they're going to die. They are not your plants, you didn't plant them, and I did. So please, leave them alone."

"I guess the possibility of you going into judicial protection is zero then?"

"No one's after me. I haven't poked the bear."

"Good luck, then."

"It'll be good if you're gone. I can move right in without a fight."

"Don't try me."

"And leave my goddam plants alone!"

Chapter Thirty-Three

BENJI

The Children and Family court proceeding went without a hitch, and I was made Benji's foster parent while he was declared dependent and his custody placed with me. The judge was a woman in her early forties with early-onset gray hair that she didn't bother to color. She wore a turquoise necklace that went perfectly with her hair. She had listened intently to the social worker's testimony. She had listened intently to the deputy sheriff who laid in wait, trying to serve Philomena with court papers. He had finally given up and slid them beneath the mother's door. Whatever, she hadn't shown up at court.

Benji and I celebrated our win by going to a boat salesroom and marina. We carefully looked over the 30-foot cabin cruisers, deciding what features were a must and what was a want. We got a brochure and made notes, putting our heads together as we considered. Benji wanted a jet boat with a wave rider; I wanted a triple Evinrude with a cabin where we could spend the night.

The salesman said he had exactly what we wanted and

showed us a 30-foot boat, the Sea Ray 320, brand new, that had a stern drive propulsion system, the ability to get up and make a wake the wake riders loved, and a lounge where Benji could sleep and a cabin for me. $322,000 and out the door. I placed a call to Bobby Doyle at my bank, and my check was good. Benji and I selected a covered slip, then went for a ride. The salesman tagged along as we had our shakedown cruise. It was freezing on the Potomac, but neither Benji nor I noticed. We had our names on a boat! And we were free!

I would let my lawyer hammer out the details with Deonna's lawyer. But it was my separate debt so that she couldn't squawk too much.

Benji and I filled our phones with pictures and headed home.

"What's her name—dad?"

"You choose the name, Benj."

"I think I like *In Recess*."

"That's clever, Benji. Very. Where'd you get that?"

"The judge said it when we were done.' The court stands in Recess.'"

"*In Recess* it is. Nicely played."

Chapter Thirty-Four

MILES STANDISH

It was the question I most hated to ask Inga, so I got it out of the way upfront. There could be no secret at any point about the romance between Tommy and Inga, which meant that if I didn't bring it up, it would look like I was trying to hide something. Still, the look of dismay on her face made me feel terrible and made me wish I could do something right then to support her. She reeled backward in the witness chair, looking vulnerable and cornered. I knew she was collecting herself and preparing her response, but, most of all, I knew she was a lawyer with over three decades of experience so that she would be okay in the end.

"I had a romance going with Tommy Gray at the time he died. Does that make me an expert about the cause or manner of his death? I know no more about why he died or how he died than any of you. I have an opinion but no facts. I'm sorry, but I don't have any great insights for you today."

"Well, instead of looking for great new insights, let's

review what we know. For openers, when did you last see Tommy Gray alive?"

"That would have been about five o'clock in the morning on the day he was found dead."

"That would have been about three hours before the body was found, correct?"

"Correct."

"And you next saw him when?"

"I was one of the first ones in his office at eight o'clock. The security officer produced a key, and we went in."

"Tell the grand jury what you saw when you went inside that office."

"It was a tragic sight. Tommy was slumped back in his chair behind his desk. There was a shotgun on the floor beside him on his right. His eyes were half-open, and much of the side of his head was spattered on the wall behind him. I immediately went to his desk and looked for a note of some sort. But there was nothing. He had left Mona with no sign of what he was doing."

"And who is Mona?"

"Mona is Tommy's wife."

"How did you feel about Mona since you had been cheating with her husband?"

"How the hell do you think I felt? I felt awful. I felt like a cheater and a bad person, and I still do. If I could take it all back, I would. It was the biggest mistake I ever made in my life."

I bent to my notes, giving her a chance to collect herself. Of course, I was not in an adversary position with Inga, and I did not want to give off that impression. I jotted down a few questions I wanted to ask her to humanize her and cast her in a more favorable light.

"Inga, the other side of that coin is that you had much respect for Tommy Gray, isn't that correct?"

"That is correct. Tommy is an honorable man, no matter what the circumstances. His wife is very sick and is confined to her bed with a massive stroke. She is incapable of engaging in any physical relationship with her husband. She has difficulty speaking, and she must be hand-fed. He changes her diapers. Tommy had fallen into a time of tremendous loneliness, and I was right there with him. Bottom line, we were two lonely people, Tommy and I, who found each other and held on for dear life."

"Your relationship with Tommy was a rather tender one, isn't that correct?"

"That is correct. Sure, we had our difficulties, and we even had our fights, which were quite nasty but short-lived, maybe an insensitive email or two, and that would be it."

"Let's talk about Tommy's death. Suicide or murder?"

"Murder. Tommy was the last person in the law firm I would expect to commit suicide. He had become happy. We were planning a vacation together, and he was sticking by his wife as long as she lived, which made him very proud and was something he would never abandon by suicide. She needed him in her way, and he was always there for her. On the professional side of the street, Tommy was very successful both as a lawyer and as the manager of Gray. His salary and bonus were over one million a year, so he had no financial problems to speak of. But there is one thing I want the jury to know. Tommy was in a lot of pain and shame that someone in his law firm was turning over top-secret documents to the Russians. We talked about that, and we discussed various traps he might lay to catch that person. However, we were amateurs and needed something more than what we could do, so

Tommy called the Department of Justice and requested help."

"Did you and Tommy ever discuss the takeover offer from Heinlein law?"

"We did. And Tommy, rather than succumb to Heinlein's threats, went straight to the Department of Justice for help. He was determined that Gray would escape any such takeover and remain sovereign. "

"Tell us what you discussed about the takeover letter."

"Tommy decided the takeover could be overcome by demanding and receiving help from the Department of Justice. Remember, the DOJ had hired Gray, and thus there was a contract between DOJ and Gray. DOJ couldn't just pull the rug out from under our firm and turn the work over to Heinlein law. That would have been a breach of its contract with Gray right out of the gate. So, Tommy never believed the part of the takeover letter that said the Justice Department supported Heinlein."

"Help me understand the timing here. Gerry Heinlein delivers the takeover letter the day before Tommy Gray is found dead. Had takeover threats occurred before that time?"

"Oh, my God, yes. This had been going on for something like six months. But there had never been a formal demand in writing before. That was the ultimate threat and the ultimate insult. That last time I saw Tommy, he was in a rage at Gerry Heinlein and was ready to turn the dogs loose."

"What do you mean by 'turn the dogs loose?' What might Tommy have done?"

"He had talked of suing the Heinlein firm for interference with contract. That meant he would sue Heinlein for going to the Department of Justice and persuading it to give the work to Heinlein law. I expect he would have done that, too, had he lived."

"Is that threat still in play today? If so, what steps might Roman Challis be taking to protect the firm?"

"We just met about that. A lawsuit is being prepared against Heinlein law. Gray is damn serious about protecting itself from any so-called takeover. It just will not happen."

"I want to go into one last area with you before we end this testimony today. Please tell the grand jury what you know about documents being leaked to Western Energy Reserves? And tell them who you think is guilty."

Inga shifted in the witness chair, but I couldn't tell if it was just discomfort from what was happening in terms of her testimony or if she was tired of sitting on her tailbone and needed to move around. I decided it was the latter, so I didn't help her.

She replied, "My best judgment about who is turning our documents over to the Russians is a junior lawyer out of the two-hundred Environmental litigators in our firm. Someone is going to have to do a standard-of-living analysis of those lawyers. By that, I mean, someone is going to have to compare their lifestyle to their income. Do they have a new boat? Have they traded up in houses? Has there been a long tour of Europe or Asia? Are bank accounts filled to the brim with disposable income? These are the kinds of things that could show one of our attorneys is receiving payoffs from Western in return for top-secret documents."

She knew, or at least had a strong suspicion, that my people had already undertaken such a standard of living inventory as to each of the 200 attorneys practicing environmental law at Gray. Where we needed bank documents or IRS documents, the FBI was right there to get those for us. We were building an extensive database, and we were going to begin several mathematical analyses of lifestyle, earnings, and bank accounts. Maybe Inga knew about these things, and maybe she didn't, but her testimony was right on point. Which jolted me to a stop, and I realized her answer might mean she had insider information about my firm and what we were doing. God forbid.

"Inga, do you have any specific names for us we might like to bring in for testimony for a deeper look into their lifestyle and assets?"

"I don't have any names. But I can tell you that Roman Challis tasked Max Jennings of Gray to do the lifestyle inventory I've been talking about these past few minutes."

I knew I had to have access to Max Jennings's work product. He would have much more background on the employees than I could ever get. And so I did the next indicated thing. I asked Inga whether she had access to Max's workup.

"Inga, regarding the study that Maxwell Jennings is doing. Do you have access to that study and its records?"

"I do. I am one of three members on his team, and I have full access."

"Would you be willing to share with me the documents and studies that Maxwell Jennings generates?"

"I could not do that voluntarily, as it would jeopardize the duty I owe to the firm. You're going to have to subpoena me back before the grand jury and make me give you those things, and of course, I will be happy to do it."

"Fair enough. This grand jury will continue for a few weeks yet, and that will be plenty of time for Max to complete his study and for you to bring his documents and reports and share any conclusions before this grand jury. Is there anything else I've missed or failed to ask you about?"

"You haven't asked me who I think shot Tommy Gray. I don't know if you omitted that on purpose or what."

"Who shot Tommy Gray?"

"That would be Max Jennings, who has the motive. Remember, Max is next in line to head up Gray if Roman Challis leaves or passes away. Plus, I believe Max is Russian-friendly. Last, I don't trust the man. What I just told you is confidential, as you and the grand jury know. And so, I feel free to discuss these things with you and give you my best insights. However, all of what I've just said is my opinion, and I have no facts to back up my opinion. So take it for what it's worth."

"All right, and thank you for coming today."

Inga sat back in her chair and visibly relaxed. "You're welcome."

Chapter Thirty-Five

NADIA

Nadia pulled into the alley behind Standish's house and crept along his backyard fence. She got out of her van and stole a look at the greenhouse from the alleyway. Sure enough, the greenhouse was frosted in ice, like so much of DC. There was nothing to be done now except await the melt.

Moscow Center was contacting her every day now. What was the problem? When did she expect to take the shot? Was she still up to the assignment?

She slid back inside her van, angry at the uncontrollable turn of events dropped in her lap by Mother Nature. There wasn't anything she could do about it, and she knew it. The iced-over glass was impenetrable by her Leupold VX-5 HD scope on her Henry 45-70 rifle. By now, she had her perfect angle and field of fire and was beyond ready to make a headshot. But the icy glass made the shot just like shooting into a cloud. She did not know where her bullet might go.

Still, she checked the setup every day without fail. Soon,

the ice would yield its grip, slide down into the grass, and disappear.

The same end she planned for Miles Standish.

Chapter Thirty-Six

MILES STANDISH

Gray law held a Tommy Gray One Year Memorial one year following Tommy's death. I attended because, although there had been hard feelings between Tommy and me, I still felt an allegiance to the law firm and wanted to show my support. The memorial was open to law firm members, families, and anyone who shared a kinship with Tommy.

The day of the memorial was dark and foreboding, and by 7:30, blowing snow filled the air in Washington, DC. The local TV channels carried stories of driving delays and film clips of fender benders across the city. I listened half-interestedly while the TV droned on in my bedroom. I chose a black suit and white shirt and an off-red necktie. Tommy's memorial was not a festive occasion, and we attorneys would all be dressed the same.

The memorial was scheduled to begin at 10 a.m., so I stopped for breakfast at a nearby IHOP pancake house, my favorite place when I'm looking for comfort food. I ordered the farmers' breakfast. The food came after about five minutes, and I dug right in. The coffee was awful and was probably made in a coffee maker at least ten years old in dire need of a good cleaning.

After paying my bill, I stepped into the snow and saw that my Mercedes windshield was covered in a good inch of the white stuff. My driver scraped and brushed, then held the door while I climbed inside. All around us, traffic was coming and going. I thought I recognized two more FBI vehicles back behind us. Those guys were very good at what they did, and I had gotten to the point where I no longer cared about the stalking. They were there, and they were looking out for me, given that there was still a killer loose, and my initial repugnance at having a tail had turned into gratitude.

We pulled out of the IHOP lot and headed for the Georgetown University conference hall memorial in the grand ballroom on Reservoir Road in downtown DC. The venue accommodated approximately 700 people, fifty less than the full strength of lawyers alone at Gray. Nowhere near 750 people from Gray would attend. Maybe a third of that, I thought as we approached the venue. Construction was underway on the campus, but when wasn't there? So it was tricky finding parking at the hotel after entering from Canal Road. We found a space on level P3, parked, and headed for the elevators. It was 9:40 a.m. when I walked inside the meeting room and waited to sign the guest book.

I had moved into the group to mingle and search out the people I knew as friends when Nicki Pitts approached me. Nicki's face was contorted, and his eyes glassy as if there were chemicals in his system. He came up and began spewing sentences. He was speeding.

"Hold on, Nicki," I said. "Slow the hell down. What did you take this morning?"

At that point, Nicki pulled open his suit jacket and displayed a gun that he carried inside his waistband.

"Miles, I do not wish to alarm you, and I consider you a friend. But Alina needs help now. So my offer is this—your life for her immunity. Plus, she's not a citizen, so she wants asylum. You have the connections to make it happen, and I am watching you from here on out. If she isn't granted asylum by the end of this month, I will come looking for you. So far, everyone's ignoring me, and I'm fed up."

"Nicki, I am one of those who have not been ignoring you. I plan to get asylum for Alina. She deserves it, and I'm going to deliver. However, it might not be done by the end of this month, and I'll tell you why."

"Yes, tell me why."

"The process that I have undertaken, which you know about, is going to take time. But there will be an exact moment that will come when the government needs Alina's testimony. That is when the iron will be hot, and that is when I will cut a deal that guarantees her asylum and a path to citizenship. Please bear with me as I do this. I know what I'm doing. Unfortunately, you are not in the circle of people I work with every day who know what I'm doing. You're just going to have to trust me."

Two agents had come up behind Nicki and were ready to jump him. I raised my hand to hold them back. A man with a loaded gun was angry at me, and they were prepared to haul him off. But I didn't want that. I needed Alina, and I needed him to testify regarding Roman Challis's inaction when Nicki took him the stolen report.

So, I tried to defuse. "What do you say we get some coffee? I'm ready for my first cup of the day, and I'll bet they have finger food. Join me?"

"Well, okay then."

We proceeded to the refreshment bar and got our drinks. Then I turned to him and said, "Okay, I'm going to mingle now. You should move along and do likewise. Remember, you want to be friendly to any government officials or agents you encounter. It also wouldn't hurt for you to put a sentence or two in their ear about Alina. Every little bit helps, and I am only one of the players you need in her corner. You have me, so move on along. And please don't expose that gun in here. I'm under guard every minute, and I don't want to see you get taken down."

He shot a look in both directions. "Of course, you have protection. Never thought of that. Well, look, I'm going to take this gun outside—no, I'm going to get out of here and leave. I won't be back. But I'll be trusting you, Miles."

"Now you're talking. You're smart to trust me. I always deliver, Nicki."

He pivoted and headed for the exit. The two agents split up, one of them following as far as the exit, one staying near me.

I was curious about who was there, and I was especially open to hearing from Gray attorneys and staff who might have something to share with me about the law firm under the guidance of Roman Challis. I moved back into the crowd.

I didn't get far until Frank Hemet caught up to me. We shook hands and said the usual howdy do's at such functions. He asked me how the investigation was going, and I shared it with him. We shared a few more goings-on and then moved apart. Just as we did, there came Roman Challis himself, making a beeline at me. Max Jennings was close behind with his nose up Challis's ass, where I can only guess his nose spent most of its working days.

Challis pressed right up into my space and got his face within a foot of mine. He began with a smirk, saying, "Well, well, if it isn't Miles Standish, the snoop. How am I doing, Miles? Have you been going through my underwear drawers while I'm away? Have you been hacking into my bank accounts to make sure I'm not the one getting payoffs from the Russians? Come on, Miles, make a clean breast of it with old Roman."

"So... you've been drinking, and you still can't hold your liquor. But luckily, you're in good company here, a group that's friendly to you that already knows you're out of control after one drink. Congratulations, you've just given me another reason to hate you. Run along now, Roman, and make someone else uncomfortable. I'm not here to listen to you."

I moved away when suddenly Roman reached out and shoved me so hard I went down to my butt on the floor. Suddenly, a circle widened away from us, with several dozen people watching. The FBI immediately surrounded me, and I climbed to my feet and turned away yet again when Challis rushed and broke through the agents. He swung at me and connected with my jaw. It all went black. This time, I hit the floor hard with my knees. Then the side of my face, and I was stunned. The FBI agents had Challis by the coat-tails and pulled the chairman off of me. Things were fuzzy as I tried to stop the world from going round and round. All around me, I heard voices and knew the FBI was there and watching and had grabbed Challis and was moving him away.

Then I felt hands pulling me up from the floor and turning me over into a sitting position. I looked at the man helping me and saw he was wearing an FBI badge beneath his coat. Good, they had done their job before I got hurt much worse. Roman Challis was a large man, and I was not. So I was grateful the cavalry had arrived.

Just then, Detective Alvin M. Douglas broke into the circle of men helping me and asked me to file assault and battery charges against Challis. I told him, "No, no, no. He's not worth it. I'm not hurt, and I don't want to waste time in the lower courts of Washington DC, watching the moron get a hundred-dollar fine and thirty days probation. But thanks for offering."

"I get it," said Douglas. "Still, maybe an order of protection?"

"Let's just forget about the whole thing," I said to Detective Douglas. "Roman Challis is not worth the effort. Besides, I have my methods. This mugging will be evened up, and more, in time."

Chapter Thirty-Seven

MILES STANDISH

Max Jennings sauntered over after the FBI had hauled Challis away, with Detective Douglas following. "Miles, that was uncalled for. Sorry on behalf of Roman, who probably has exceeded his bourbon limit."

"Roman made an enemy out of me. I don't know why. I have never tried to usurp him, and I have never operated behind his back. There are suspicions regarding the next in line to Tommy Gray, but those are the typical suspicions any observer of human nature would have."

"So what do you do with my two missing hours the night Tommy died? Am I a prime suspect?"

I was shocked; even I hadn't known Max was this nervy, even after running off with my wife. But I kept my cool and responded professionally.

"Come on, Max, you know I can't discuss grand jury matters with you."

"Hey, let's talk off the record for a minute. There are nights I can't sleep. I'm so worried about being caught up in this. I want you to know that I would have no reason to murder Tommy Gray. Tommy and I always had a great relationship, almost father and son. Did the fact that I told the grand jury I was number three behind Roman Challis in succession hurt me? Is that going to play heavily against me?"

"I have given little thought to anybody's grand jury testimony yet, Max. And even if I had, it's the same answer as before. I wouldn't discuss it with you. I'm sorry, but I know you wouldn't want me discussing Roman Challis's testimony with him had he testified."

"Did he testify?"

"You know I can't tell you anything else about the grand jury, Max. Let's change the subject. Let's talk about Tommy Gray, who we're here about today. There's a guy who beat me out as chairman and then booted me out the door. But truth be told, there was a real silver lining there. I've had my freedom from the practice of law. I've been away from the everyday fights and arguments between colleagues. I haven't had lawsuits taking up all my thoughts. And I'm enjoying myself with my greenhouse and alone time. So I hold Tommy Gray as one of those who made my present life possible, and I really wouldn't trade it for anything."

"But you have, haven't you? You've taken over as a Special Assistant Attorney General, and now you must be busier than ever. I don't quite get why you would do that."

He had me there. It made little sense to go charging back into a law practice setting, but I had. I think, deep down, some of it had to do with impressing Deonna by having her see me in a role superior to Max Jennings. I knew that sounded crazy and off-the-wall, but I had never been one who acted sane in matters of romance. Husband-and-wife issues could be written off as mostly losses for me.

I didn't win the arguments a couple would have, and most of the time, I overanalyzed and disappointed my better half. They wanted to be heard when they spoke, and I wanted to run right out and fix whatever was bothering them. I understood that wasn't my role, and I knew that's not what the woman wanted, but my legal training was all about problem-solving, so I was stuck.

"Sometimes, I wonder myself why anyone would do that, Max. It just seemed to be a community service, and I needed a pick-me-up after being forced out of Gray."

Max took a sip of his coffee, which I was certain was spiked with alcohol because I could smell alcohol on his breath. I didn't want another one-on-one like with Roman Challis, so I started trying to break free of Max and get to a group where I might feel comfortable.

"There's just one last thing I want to tell you, Miles," Max said. He moved a step closer to me, and I took one back.

"Please, I don't want to talk anymore about the grand jury or my investigation. Now, if you have some topic that isn't about Tommy Gray's death, I'm all ears."

"It's the goddamn video that has me so worried. When I arrived at the office, the video goes on the blink. You have got to believe me, and I swear it on my mother's grave. I had absolutely nothing to do with the video going out. We've had a maintenance team looking into it ever since. So far, they have no answers, so we have no answers. It's just a damn snafu like I'm back working in the Army again. You knew I served honorably in the Army, right, Miles? I know you did, with your drawerful of medals. What was the big one? The Silver Star? They aren't exactly giving those away to just anyone."

The last thing I wanted to think about that day. Or any other. And it embarrassed me.

"I think we're done here, Max. I'm going to move on and mingle with some others before the memorial begins. But it's good talking to you, and I hope this whole thing isn't taking too much of a toll on you. I understand your side of it completely."

I found a place to sit near the front since the service started in five minutes. I just had enough time to take a second drink of my coffee when I suddenly found Inga settling in beside me.

"My goodness, aren't you the brave one sitting up here where you might be asked to say a few words? You're amazing, Miles."

"I don't think amazing is a good word for it. I've had Roman Challis take me down to the floor, and I've had Max Jennings buttonhole me about his grand jury testimony. I've had Nicki Pitts approach me and show me a gun in his waistband that he plans to use if I don't get asylum and citizenship for Alina. Son of a bitch, I have never felt more put upon or more personally in danger since the time in the sandbox."

"What?"

"Afghanistan."

I sighed. "Now to sit back and hear a few words about somebody dying from a gunshot wound. That rounds out my morning. And so, how are you doing?"

"Holy shit. You've had quite a morning. As for Nicki Pitts, I wouldn't pay him any mind at all. I'm sure he was under the influence of something when he approached you."

"He was on meth and out of control. Not to worry. I

can handle the amateurs without breaking a sweat. Now I need to relax."

"So, if I wanted to talk to you about my grand jury testimony, this probably wouldn't be the time or place?"

Chapter Thirty-Eight

MILES STANDISH

It felt good sitting beside Inga. She was an oasis of sanity smack dab in the middle of the Gray family. I already had a great insight that morning, which was this: I was never taking on the role of special counsel for the prosecution of any crime again—ever. I hadn't realized how everybody and his brother would walk right up to you and start talking about their role in a case.

I was talking about lawyers here, the people who were supposed to know that grand jury testimony was holy and that word of it or any news out of the grand jury room was a crime. But I couldn't escape the fact that my whole reason for being there was that, deep down, I knew I had spent years in the company of Tommy Gray, litigating cases together and managing the law firm together. I loved the man, even though he double-crossed me and forced me out of Gray.

I remembered a case we had against Dow Chemical for dumping and polluting. I remembered a case against Billings Lumber Company for clear-cutting 2500 square miles of timber before anyone found out about it. What they had done was create an illusion that the forest was still there by leaving a swath of full-grown trees, maybe 100 feet deep, alongside the public roads. Then, on the other side, they had clear-cut across a mountain range, down the other side to a river, and beyond that to a public highway, again leaving in between another hundred-foot swath of full-grown trees. By the time we arrived on the scene with our team of attorneys, the damage was already done.

Over those same years, Tommy and I saw our Gray law Environmental Division grow from five attorneys to 200. The department had started with oil and natural gas fracking and when the Department of Justice was frantically trying to staff enough lawyers to sue all lawbreakers. DOJ had had to hire outside counsel to assist in work arising from that fracking. Gray became enormously expert in those cases and had established all the right contacts with all the right witnesses to bring expertise into our courtrooms to shut down companies seeking to profit from their purchase of subsurface rights.

Suddenly, Inga nudged me with her elbow, and I realized the service had begun and that I was snoring softly. I came awake from my thoughts abruptly, sat up in my chair, and made myself listen to the homilies about Tommy Gray.

Forty-five minutes later, the calendared speakers had finished, and those who wanted to step up and say a few words had done so. The service was closed with a brief prayer from an Episcopal minister. We were then dismissed.

Chapter Thirty-Nine

MILES STANDISH

Inga and I left the conference room and had just stepped into the hallway when Gerry Heinlein seized my upper arm and spun me around. Inga saw me turn away, and she turned around, too. An FBI agent sidled alongside to protect me. I don't think Heinlein realized. Another from behind reached between us and removed Heinlein's beefy hand from my arm. Heinlein looked startled, but the agent had a good six inches on him, so he turned back around to me.

Heinlein was red-faced and had a murderous look in his eye. He was shorter than me by a couple of inches but had the rounded belly of a drinker. He was balding, a gray crown of hair sitting just above his ears and around the back. Here was the man who had met with Tommy Gray the day before Tommy died. Several of us had watched the video of their meeting, and some thought that Heinlein's threat was enough to push Tommy over the edge to take his own life. Others thought the threat had been a warning and that, true to his word, Heinlein began the takeover by murdering Tommy Gray. I had no opinion one way or the other for the record, except the whole thing sounded pretty empty to me.

Heinlein stood there glaring at me but then suddenly spoke. "I know Tommy was leaking documents to the Russians. And I believe you were leaking documents to the Russians before him. This is part of what enrages me about Gray and why I keep going to the Department of Justice and turning you bastards in."

It came across to me as almost comical after what I had already been through that morning. I replied, "I'm one of those bastards, so you can go right ahead and turn me in. For what good it's going to do you. For the record, Heinlein law will never take over Gray and tear the heart out of the firm by hanging onto the Environmental section of two-hundred lawyers while telling the other five-hundred-and-fifty lawyers they're on their own. It's just not going to happen, and so you might start looking elsewhere for someone to rip off. Just seeing your ugly face makes me want to take you in front of my grand jury and drill your ass into the dirt. But a prosecutor can't have those feelings, so I will not do that. Still, you've been warned. Now take your goddamn ugly face away and stand aside."

He did anything but. Instead, he moved his body close to me and shoved me into the crowd of people streaming out of the meeting room. The FBI agents reacted instantly and blocked him away. My nearest agent saw me rocked back and steadied me from falling. Now, Heinlein found himself surrounded by my entourage of FBI agents, who quickly cordoned him off and moved him away from me. It was over that fast.

"Come on, Miles," said Inga. "Let's get you the hell out

of here and back to your office. Hang onto my arm. I'm running interference."

Grateful, I followed as she elbowed her way through the crowd. We had just come into level P3 of the parking garage and were stepping out of the elevator when Inga nudged me and cried out, "Look!"

She pointed at three police cars, lights flashing, surrounding a black Volvo with a license plate that said, "Sue Em."

All the lawyers in DC knew that license plate belonged to none other than Roman Challis. We moved a little closer. They had the car's trunk open, all four doors open, and the floors vacuumed with a portable vacuum cleaner. A man in the trunk attempted to get the back seat loose. Once he did, he was handed the vacuum cleaner, and he began vacuuming the trunk. The funny thing was that all the guys going over the car wore black suits, white shirts, and black ties. These were not police; they were not detectives. Challis had the FBI up his ass, big time.

"Come on," I said to Inga, and we approached the police officers standing guard around the car. I showed them my Department of Justice badge and said, "Who are these guys?"

The nearest police officer was a sergeant with a dark red mustache and wavy, dark red hair. He didn't smile, but he said, "IRS. This is a CID team."

CID meant criminal investigation division. Which meant the IRS had sent out a team of investigators who knew the IRS criminal code forward and back, and they were now going through the car of Roman Challis with a fine-tooth comb. It made me feel happier than I had felt in months. There was justice.

Inga pulled close to me and whispered, "Mr. Challis has

been up to no good. IRS criminal investigators do not just turn up. He has been the subject of an audit, and the auditors have now called the criminal investigators. This gets better by the hour."

"Let's get in my car and get the hell out of here. I don't think I can stand many more happy endings today."

Just as we were climbing into the back seat of my car and were about to tell the FBI driver where we were headed, I heard a man's voice cry out, two cars over, "Hey, get the hell out of my car!"

I didn't even bother to look. Who wanted to see Roman Challis taking on the IRS criminal investigators? They had a search warrant and had pounced on his car--no need to stay for the fun.

I had other places to go.

We made it back to my office thirty minutes later and sat down at my desk.

"What a morning," I moaned. "There is a lot of emotional baggage riding on what happens with Gray. I think I can expect more, not fewer fireworks. And I also think Marshall Lakin was brilliant in surrounding me with FBI agents while I did my work. It would've turned out a lot differently this morning if they had not been there."

Chapter Forty

MILES STANDISH

I was reviewing lawyer communications between Gray and Western Energy Reserves when I got the call from Frank Hemet. Nicki Pitts had approached him. It seemed Alina wanted to talk. For the longest time, Pitts would not reveal Alina's location and, until that moment, we hadn't been able to get her to agree to a specific date to meet. Now she had—for whatever reason—changed her mind.

Good enough, I thought. If Alina's the real deal, she can give us a leaker out of Gray. It will come at a price—asylum in the US—but Justice had already told me the US is a big country with room for just about everyone. They were amenable to asylum if she had the goods. I would be the final judge of that. My word would decide her fate.

Alina wasn't willing to come to my office or meet us nearby at a coffee shop. She wanted it more complicated than that to lessen the chance of me leading the Russians to her. So, Hemet came by and picked me up, and we set off on a course that Alina dictated to him by phone as he drove.

First, we navigated through George Washington University, where the college students' footsteps were so many the late-spring snow had melted through to cement, and the square was barren of snow where students crisscrossed.

After following a series of seemingly random turns and twists, we were directed down along the Potomac River until we were close to leaving DC. She then directed us straight north then toward Maryland, where we finally came to the restaurant to meet her in Annapolis. Alina told us by phone she saw Frank's car just outside the restaurant window, so we had found the right place after nearly an hour of driving.

"This lady's serious," said Frank.

We climbed out of Frank's car and went inside Norma's Restaurant and Bakery. Behind the cash register, the first thing that drew my attention was the entire wall of fresh pies and cakes for sale. I loved lemon meringue pie and promised myself I would take home a slice—or maybe two slices. We passed on by the pie display, and Frank led us to an alcove containing four tables and two booths. Nicki Pitts was seated at one booth with a woman who had to be Alina. He waved us over, and we joined them, sitting opposite.

"Alina, this man wearing the Italian threads is Miles Standish. Miles was once the chairman at Gray but got pushed out by Tommy Gray. This other gentleman, Frank Hemet, is a recent hire at Gray, specializing in criminal defense plus behind-the-scenes duties. Gentlemen, meet Alina. Alina was born in Russia but raised in Los Angeles and, after a series of educational and employment moves, she found work as a paralegal at Western Energy Reserves. From there, she got a job at Gray. So, you see, she is the most valuable person to you right now. No one is more valuable. She can give you a plethora of information—you representing the United States. But she must have a guarantee of asylum and full citizenship in America. If you can work with her on this basis, there is much to discuss. But if you cannot, or will not, then we will buy your coffee and leave you to drink it in peace."

I didn't hesitate. "My initial response is to say that the Department of Justice has assured me there is always room for one more American citizen. It only depends on two things: her knowledge of Russian oil mining and oil strategies and her knowledge of the documents passing from Gray into Russian hands. If she has these two capabilities, we have much room to talk. I would suggest that we begin by allowing me to ask her a few questions and gauge her responses. If it sounds promising, then I would want her to be lodged in a place of safety and accessibility by me so that we could then go into a deep transfer of knowledge. If this meets with what you have in mind, I'm ready to begin right now. Even without coffee."

Alina looked to Nicki as if wanting his advice. Frank and I made our coffee orders, and the waitress soon returned with a hot pot and poured coffee for our group. Nicki seemed ready to answer and further engage as he sat, nodding his head slowly and making eye contact with me.

"Miles, please proceed with your first three or four questions, and let's see how that goes."

"Alina, as Nicki has told you, my name is Miles Standish, and the Department of Justice has appointed me to do two things. One, I am to locate the person who murdered Tommy Gray. And the second thing is to locate the person responsible for top-secret documents going to the Russians. Are you able to speak to either or both tasks that lie before me?"

"I am," said Alina in a stronger voice than her affect suggested. While she was thin and fine-boned, and her facial features classical, her voice was the contralto of a practiced trial lawyer speaking in court. It pleased me because the voice alone was 50% of whether a jury liked or disliked a witness. With that alone, she was already successful, which was vital for me.

"Regarding the identity of Tommy Gray's killer. Do you have a name for us? And how did you get that name? I'm not asking you to divulge the name."

"I have a name for you, but I can't go into too much of that right now. But regarding the person's identity leaking documents, she was inside Gray, and I dealt with her face to face when I was at Western. She was professional and was grateful for the money I paid her. It was a rock-solid relationship with the American spy. But it all fell apart when I refused to give up my source to the FSB. From that point on, I've been on the run."

"The next question I have is this. Did you possess a stolen document leaked to the Russians?"

She stirred her coffee and glanced outside. I noticed her eyes were constantly moving, sizing up the crowd coming in and who was going. I knew that life was horrible for her, given her anchor-less existence. "Did I possess a stolen document? I possess many stolen documents. Which one did you have in mind?"

"I have in mind the document that you gave Nicki Pitts that he gave Roman Challis."

"I had that document. And I have many more just like it. You're going to be stunned when you see the mass of information the mole has transferred from Gray to Western Energy Reserves. It will boggle your mind, I promise you. If it gets out, this is front-page news. Not one news cycle, not two news cycles, maybe six months or a year. Heads will roll. The DOJ will make their estimates of the damage done. The matter will become political and suffer irreparable damage because the problem has been institutionalized as a conservative versus liberal rallying cry. So, the United States loses because nothing gets done. But there is one solution, and that solution is for you to take the information from me and act on it yourselves before it becomes institutionalized."

"And how do you see us acting upon it ourselves?"

"The custom would be for the United States to eject Russian spies, and the ejection would this time include Russian lawyers and staff. But that still doesn't muzzle the American spy. That's a whole different matter. As far as the spy is concerned, I have a name, and the United States can then take whatever action it needs to take against an operating spy that is killing it. Were that spy to disappear, I would have no questions, only gratitude that my new country has taken steps to defend herself in a time of war."

I couldn't help myself. "That is an amazing answer. I think we are going to work very well together. Your ability to move from the micro to the macro is highly sophisticated and will serve my team well. I can say that I am ready to set up a series of future meetings between you and me. Nicki, what say you? Do you have any idea where we could meet?"

Said Nicki, "All she is asking is immunity and asylum. Who profits most in the arrangement will be hugely weighted in favor of the United States. Asylum plus a new identity and witness protection. That's not too much for her to ask. You will be one hundred percent on board with it tomorrow at the end of your first meeting with her, where she will go into detail. For now, I'm going to leave with her. She will go first. I will wait five minutes and then follow. Alina? Please tell these gentlemen you'll see them tomorrow, and let's be on our way."

"I will see you tomorrow, Mr. Standish," said Alina. "Bring a windbreaker. The air temperature will be quite cold out on the water."

With that, she disappeared outside like a nymph once here, then gone. Hemet and I purposely did not turn to watch. We drank coffee in silence while Nicki Pitts counted down five minutes, then he was gone, too.

Chapter Forty-One

MILES STANDISH

We met the following day at noon at a Potomac boat rental. Nicki chose a brand-new Bentley Pontoon, ruby red, with room for Alina and me to sit across from each other at a small table and do our Q&A. I supplied the recorder and the credit card, which required a $200 advance payment for boat cleanup at the end. I thought that was high but paid without a whimper.

"Thank you, and we're off now!" I had noticed the FBI sitting nearby in its own boat, waiting for us to cast off. They never quit.

We glided into the Potomac, which was a very slow-moving river that day. In the winter, it can be quick. We headed for the far shore, then turned and began drifting downstream. Alina and I commandeered the small table in the bow and sat on the upholstered cushions surrounding it so we were face-to-face. Nicki Pitts took over the captain's chair and appeared entirely happy to motor us along. At one point, he called out to tell us that the boat had a fish finder and how he wished he had brought along some fishing gear. We ignored him and got into our talk.

"Alina, I'm placing this recorder between us on the table. It is turned on, and I will first ask you to acknowledge that you know I'm making this recording and that I am doing it with your permission."

"I know you are making the recording, and, yes, you are doing it with my permission. I just wonder how long it will take because I feel very exposed out here on this river. Everyone can see us."

"That may be, but this is where Nicki chose, so here we are. And I can assure you no one is watching who knows anything about our work. Let me begin by asking, how old are you and where were you born?"

"Let's just say that I'm in my early twenties, and I plan to stay there for the next twenty years," she said with a light laugh. "Seriously, I was born in 1999 in Novosibirsk, Russia, to Lili and Karpov Grunsky. We moved to the States when I was little and lived close to the University of California, Los Angeles. I roamed the university with my science-minded friends, passing many afternoons in the science buildings, sneaking into the laboratories, and studying the fetuses in their jars and the wild animals stuffed and attached to their branches. The rest of the time, it seemed like we spent an excessive amount of our lives in a Russian Orthodox Church across the street from where I lived. I'm not kidding about this. My mother had me in church every day from as far back as I can remember. Her goal was that I would be relieved of my sins. I wasn't familiar enough with sin to know even what my sins were, so my mother took it upon herself to detail all the sins I was carrying. It scared the living hell out of me, and I began thinking that I belonged in church every day, as she said."

"You still attend any church, or have you fallen away?"

"Oh no, I still attend weekly. Well, I did until I went into hiding. My mother makes me come home and attend with her Sunday mornings. It's turned into more of a happy thing for me because I love seeing my mother and father. But I will share this. My mother's imaginary sins no longer burden me. I've committed enough sins now to have my own things to talk to God about. You know, the kinds of things women in their mid-twenties don't want anyone to know about.

"When I was in my late teens, I was too far advanced for the boys my age, and a group of women I was running with was spending more and more time around the docks at Long Beach. There's huge money there, some great clubs, and they had fantastic bands to dance to. I've always loved to dance. Do you like to dance, Mr. Standish?"

"I do like to dance. My wife and I took dancing lessons and became quite proficient at ballroom dancing at one time."

"Oh, you still do that?"

"Not right now. Other things have interfered that take precedence. That's all I'm going to share about that. Now tell me, when did you get your first job?"

"I began working as a bookkeeper for a small company on the waterfront. It provided transportation services for ships' crews as they came ashore. I'm sorry to say I began hanging out with some of those men, and they were way older than me. During those few months, I learned all I would ever need to know about men. Then I met the captain of a tugboat at Long Beach. We moved in together, and he did the strangest thing. He told me he loved me and wanted me to stay but that I couldn't stay as long as I was drinking and partying around with my girlfriends. For once,

I heard the voice of reason, and I did as he said. I gave up my drinking and drugs and started staying home at night with him. He next encouraged me to get an education. I found a program at UCLA that I got into on a scholarship, learning how to be a paralegal. Following graduation, I bounced around with the Russian firms—we speak Russian at my parents' home—and the American firms. Then I landed my job at Gray. I had also worked at Western Energy Reserves, and I know I learned valuable information that might get me citizenship."

"Information like what?"

"Like the name of an American spy.

I wanted to jump right in it, to have her give me a name and immediately rush back to shore and subpoena that name for grand jury testimony. Instead, I settled back in my boat seat and made myself put two feet flat on the deck of the boat. I told myself to steady down; there was much territory to be covered first.

"Take your time, but please tell me how you came to know who killed Tommy Gray."

"Working at Gray, I was working for Ginger Cobblestone, who's a divorce lawyer in Gray's family law department. Ginger had been copied on an email from Max Jennings to Roman Challis. Her practice was so busy that I read all her emails and gave her summaries at noon and night. She would then dictate back to me and tell me which ones to answer and what to say.

"Anyway, the email sent by Jennings to Challis contained two words: 'Thanatopsis tonight.' To make a long story short, Ginger had represented Max Jennings in his divorce and was often copied on his emails even though the divorce was long past. That seemed to be the case with this one. I had to look up the meaning of the word 'thanatopsis' and then came to understand that it meant death, the consideration of death. So here was Max, telling Roman that tonight was the consideration of death or some such. I thought little about it at all until I arrived at work the next day and found out that Tommy Gray had been murdered. I instantly knew who had done it, and I knew that the email was a smoking gun, no pun unintended. The other side of it was this knowledge put me in immediate jeopardy because Max would eventually realize his mistake and realize that he had copied that smoking gun email to Ginger, which included me. These are brilliant people, and I knew that eventually, my name would come up as someone who might have seen the email if I stayed around the firm long enough. What I did instead: I went home in the middle of the morning, packed my things, and left. I had been staying with Nicki Pitts as he was another great employee, and we had hit it off."

I noticed she lifted her eyes then and looked back at Nicki in the captain's chair and made a judgment about what he could and couldn't hear us saying. She must have decided he was out of earshot because she then added, "I wasn't in love with Nicki; it was just a situation. I would leave him soon anyway, so I didn't think twice about disappearing from his life. He eventually tracked me down through my girlfriends, and he's been helping me ever since. Now, I am developing feelings for him, so it's getting bizarre between us. But I've stuck around, and we'll see where it goes this time, so there's your update as far as my romantic status."

She then continued. "There's one more thing you need to know. As a floater, I accessed the attorneys' files and records on their private servers in the computer room. Each attorney was assigned their own server. It's done for security.

Floaters like me required all kinds of access to all kinds of information. We had all been vetted, and we had passed background security checks and had been given Level I access to those files. Only the floaters and the board of directors had that access as Level I security workers. To make a long story short, on my last morning there, I logged into Max Jennings's server and scanned through the files as fast as I could. I didn't know what I was looking for, but I was hoping I might find something that convinced me Max had nothing to do with Tommy's death. I liked Max immensely and knew he was the best litigator in the Gray firm."

What the hell did Max Jennings have that women liked so much? I didn't get it.

She continued. "I wanted Max's email to Challis to come up innocent. But then I stumbled onto his bank statements from East Coast Savings and Loan. I scanned month after month, looking for anything that interested me, and then I found it—an innocent-looking purchase from Wilson's Hunting and Fishing Supply in Fairfax. I opened the invoice, and my heart blew up because there it was, the purchase of a Browning shotgun, 12-gauge, two weeks earlier. I cried because I knew what it meant, and I knew I needed to print a copy of that bank statement and invoice, which I did and which I still have hidden away in a bank vault."

"This is astonishing. You have found who killed Tommy. When we are again onshore, I suggest you let me immediately enroll you in the witness protection program. Your testimony is crucial, and we cannot guarantee your safety except inside the program. What do you think?"

"It scares me. I know I'm dealing with important and powerful people, and I am not. But I think Max should be made to pay for his crime because Tommy Gray—there was no one better. He was a huge loss, and I still cry about it sometimes."

"So you'll go into witness protection?"

"I don't think I have any choice, do I?"

"I think not. If you were my daughter, I would insist on it."

"Then that's good enough for me. I'm just going to allow you to do with me what needs to be done to protect me. Does Nicki come with me?"

"I think he does. Nicki has more of the story himself and will also be a witness in the trial I'm putting together in my head the more we talk."

"Oh, I'm so glad to hear that. We make a good team, Nicki and me."

We had been drifting for about thirty minutes, and it seemed the water was picking up speed, so I asked Nicki if he could turn around and head back upstream for the next hour. We immediately came about and headed northbound.

Alina got into her bag and produced a thermos of coffee and two plastic cups. "You?" she asked.

I told her that would be very welcome, but only if there was enough for Nicki as well. She reached back inside her bag and pulled out a third cup, a red plastic cup just like ours. She poured three cups, doctored one, took it to Nicki, and returned. We both did cream and sugar, and she put the condiments away. I took a sip and was quite relieved to find that it was a bold Colombian and hit the spot just fine. Then I got back down to business.

"Let's go into what is probably the most troubling part of this entire case, Alina. You know the part I'm talking about?"

"You're talking about the missing documents."

"Exactly. Let me preface this by saying the United States has not suffered this much damage within its borders by a foreign power since September 11, 2001, and the World Trade Center. Russian fracking has drained Oklahoma and turned it into an earthquake zone. The same is underway in Colorado and North Dakota. Huge damage has been done, which is what my job's about. My job's preventing as much damage as possible from here on out."

"I'm thankful you're doing it."

"Please help me understand how the law firms representing the Russians are getting American documents, enabling them to kick ass against the Department of Justice. Can you give me an overview?"

"I can do better than overview. I can name names. But there is one caveat about that even. You will catch the mole and eradicate her, but soon the Russians will put another in her place because they have money to burn and human nature to assist them. Greed is greed, whether it's done in English or Slavic. So I can help you plug this leak; plugging future leaks is up to you."

"Please give me the name of the person inside of Gray who is currently providing secret documents to Western Energy Reserves and its lawyers."

Just then, the boat throttled down, and the water rushed up behind and rocked us deeply in a trough. "Hey, boss," Nicki called to me. "There's a van stalking us along the shoreline. It has a radar dish on the roof. But maybe it's not a radar dish; maybe it's picking up what you're saying."

"When did you realize it was there?" I shouted at Nicki.

"Maybe ten minutes ago. I wasn't sure, so I watched it out of the corner of my eye as we came upstream. But yeah, this van is stalking us, and I think it's picked up every word you and Alina have said."

"Take us in, Nicki. We're going to continue this in my office." With that, I reached inside my jacket, pulled out my sat phone, and made a call to Lakin. It only took a minute to explain to him that Alina would accept the benefits of the witness protection program and that Lakin should have an agent at the boat rental waiting to take her away. I also told him we were being eavesdropped upon, and I could hear him groan over the phone.

"Stay in your freaking office, Miles, stay off the goddam water," he all but shouted at me. "The entire world is one cesspool of eavesdropping and videoing. They will find you even out on the Potomac River, and they will listen to every word you say. So return to shore, and I'll have Agent James waiting there to whisk Alina away."

"Nicki Pitts is part of the bundle. He goes, too."

"And Nicki Pitts. Why take one when you can get two-for-one, eh?"

Then we were ashore, and two burly FBI agents helped Nicki and Alina off the boat and into a waiting Lincoln SUV that then disappeared, leaving me to explain to the boat rental operator why we hadn't stayed out for a minimum of three hours. I got that sorted, including paying for the entire three hours and then left.

My time on the water was done.

Chapter Forty-Two

MILES STANDISH

FBI agents assigned to my watch transported me from the Potomac boat rental to my office on M Street NW. We stopped to jump out and grab a hot dog and a Pepsi from a sidewalk vendor, then swept away.

A pink message waited on my desk. The caller was Roman Challis, and he wanted to meet. He asked me to be at his office at three o'clock that day, so I had my secretary call; she confirmed that I'd be there. I did this because I had no desire to have Challis on my home turf. I sent my phone to our transcription team to untangle Alina's recorded interview and get it all down in a Q&A format. The recording was then uploaded to our servers and saved under lock and key.

A receptionist showed me into Challis's office at three o'clock. We sized each other up and shook hands. Then he launched right into what he had to tell me.

"Miles, we have assembled a vast set of documents, and we have acquired video, all of which proves your killer and leaker here at Gray is Inga Kopovsky."

"You must be joking," I said, thoroughly thrown off by his accusation. "Inga's as steady and devoted as anyone here."

"Please. Before you defend your friend, allow me to show you what we have."

"Be my guest. This should be good," I said with all the sarcasm in my voice I could muster. "But you're only going to embarrass yourself, Roman."

At that point, he passed me a thumb drive, saying, "Take this and read everything on it, Miles. These are the documents Inga has printed from her computer, which we can only assume she took out of our offices. Considering the video I'm about to show you, it only makes sense that she then turned these documents over to Western Energy Reserves. So have a look there, first, please. I'm going to swing my screen around and show you a video. You can see her face several times; she's the female in the video who's in the nude. Here we go.

"As you can see, the timestamp on the video is just over two weeks ago. My investigator videoed it in Oklahoma City, where we followed Inga over the weekend. She met with Dimitry Kopovsky, the lead attorney for all Western Energy Reserves litigation. He is also her ex-husband."

I leaned over the desk and watched the video play. It opened with a head-to-toe view of Inga—I could see her face now—lying on a made bed with a man sitting beside her. He was also nude. She had her face in his lap, and it was apparent what she was doing. This went on for 4 minutes—I timed it—and then the parties shifted position and began making love missionary style. This went on for another five or six minutes. We saw the man's face twice, and we knew who he was. At that point, Roman commented he would show me the man's still photo in just a moment so that I could make a connection and put a name to the face. The scene then devolved into serious sex play, intercourse, and many minutes filled with more fellatio. The video ended with both parties lying side-by-side on the bed, her face on his chest, his left arm beneath her neck and head, and it was clear they were talking and smiling. There was no audio.

"Now, Miles, I'm going to show you the man's corporate photograph taken from Western Energy's website. Here we go. As you can see, this is the same man as the one in the video. Just look at the short bio next to his photograph. Notice it says he is the senior attorney for Western Energy Reserves litigation and that he has been with the firm for almost twenty years. He was once married to our own Inga Kopovsky. During that time, she gained US citizenship, and at first, we thought the marriage was one of convenience so that he could apron-string onto her citizenship and gain citizenship for himself. But that didn't turn out to be the case. He had citizenship eighteen months before she did. She was tying herself to his citizenship to gain her own. Incidentally, her employment here at Gray was ended last night at five p.m. Her desk has been cleaned out, her credit cards returned, her ID badge canceled, and she is long gone."

I was staggered to see the video and what it meant. I'd never even had a glimmer she had someone else. Inga had told me her husband had died in an accident, and here he was, alive and well, and a potent sexual partner. And as recently as two weeks ago! That was when we were together, when she disappeared for a weekend, ostensibly to visit relatives in Philadelphia. I was surprised and could only tell Roman that we would carefully look at all documentation before deciding on any action.

"So, Miles, how on earth did the Department of Justice

uproot you from your greenhouse and con you into taking on your role? I thought you were way too smart to be dragged into the mess called Gray again. What is your play, Miles? I am all ears."

I sat back and drew a deep breath. Challis, of course, had to personalize my visit there and exercise the winner's role over the loser. I plunged ahead, remembering why I hated Roman Challis even as I began speaking. "You may not realize this, Roman, but I still have many friends at Gray. Those friendships primarily drove my decision to become a Special Assistant US Attorney. At the Justice Department, a law firm couldn't be trusted to investigate its own nest honestly. Wake up, Roman; the Department of Justice does not trust you. And so they went outside and asked me, and I couldn't say no. But my question back to you is, when can we set your testimony before the grand jury based on this new evidence to be looked into?"

A pained expression crossed his face, and I knew it had not occurred to him I might want to take him back before the grand jury based on his so-called Inga findings. But I was going to let him squirm and listen to what he came up with.

Then he spoke, choosing his words carefully. "I am unwilling to cooperate with the grand jury at this moment. Maybe later, I will be willing, but for right now, my attorney has told me to stay away."

"You are still under subpoena. There is no staying away."

"And for that reason, I am asking you as one attorney to another to honor my needs instead of forcing me to return for more questions and answers."

"But now you're going to pressure me to prosecute Inga Kopovsky without giving me a chance first to hear the testimony of the key witness against her, which is you, Roman. How fair is that to her? No, I'm going to have to insist on your attendance at the grand jury. I'll send your attorneys a letter with the date, time, and room number at DOJ. We will proceed, and if you're not present, I will have the court issue a bench warrant for your arrest. Is there anything else?"

"Still the same old bastard, Miles. Except maybe worse. Please show yourself out; we are finished here."

"Yes, and thanks to you, too, Roman, for inviting me today. It has been informative. I'll see you in about a week or less."

I then left his office and rode the elevator back down to the ground level. I burst through the rotating door onto the sidewalk where I could, at last, inhale a mighty breath of fresh air. Only then did I realize how clammy I felt being inside Gray, and especially around Roman Challis.

It was distasteful, and it was disgusting, and I knew I had just been in the presence of an accomplished criminal mind.

Chapter Forty-Three

MILES STANDISH

After the Challis meeting, my staff sent a letter to Challis's lawyers demanding that he return for his continued testimony in five days. That was certainly going to light up his Christmas tree. Then I sat down at my desk and thought about how sad it was that a great law firm like Gray was now in the hands of a cheat and a liar named Roman Challis. I decided that whatever else became of my work for the Justice Department, I would drive Challis out of Gray and hopefully see him go to prison. Even worse was his treatment of Inga.

In my mind, her coupling with her ex-husband amounted to only a simple coupling with one's ex and had no more criminality than that. I would look at the documents that Inga had printed off, and I would confront her about them in the privacy of my office. It would be a disservice for me to drag her back in front of the grand jury and attempt to question her on the record. I knew that she would have some innocent reason for the printouts. In the end, she would tell me something to the effect that the printouts were all about one key lawsuit she was working on or several related lawsuits she was working on, and she was getting her trial notebook ready. At any rate, I was convinced it was innocent, and I was equally convinced that Roman Challis had pounced on the random printouts and tried to infer guilt against her because he was worried for himself.

Well, I held the cards, and it would not go any further. I would expose his scheme to divert my attention away from him and onto Inga. The exposure would certainly be enough to motivate the Gray Board of Directors to unseat Challis and install another chairman instead. He would be ruined, and he would have to quit the practice of law. Further, I would still look for ways to hang his ass and destroy him.

I had to pause and ask myself whether my intent to destroy Roman Challis was because he now sat in the seat as chairman that was rightly my own. Or was he double-dealing and maybe had murdered Tommy Gray? Maybe he was running the scheme to turn over documents to the Russians. None of this was anything I had evidence of so far. But I told myself I had only just begun. He had thrown down the glove when he had conjured up an imaginary prosecution against Inga and had terminated her.

My secretary told me that a call had come in from Roman's attorney, and he was furious. I told her to tell him I was no longer in the office, but I had left a message that if he called and tried to squirm out of next week's grand jury testimony, I would cause a bench warrant to be issued and have Roman arrested. She understood and returned to her telephone.

Alina and Nicki arrived for their working lunch with me at 12:30. Against FBI advice to keep all our meetings at my office, we met at Sandy's Sandwiches. My attention went immediately to what Alina had to tell me about the person she believed was leaking documents to Western Energy Reserves.

She was very confident. "Previously, I have said the mole is a paralegal. I did this to ensure I didn't give away my secret and get nothing in return. So now I am going to tell you the truth. The person making the leaks is Inga Kopovsky, and I know that for a couple of reasons."

"This better be good. Before you proceed, let me remind you I am conducting a federal investigation, and it's a serious crime to lie to me. Now proceed."

"First, my friends at Western Energy told me that Inga and Dimitry, who were once husband-wife, are still having an affair. Second, I have previously told you that the Board of Directors has Level 1 access to all documents on the Gray servers. It would be a simple matter for her to randomly select what appears to be unrelated documents and print those out. She would then deliver them to Dimitry. It would always depend on his latest need, and they would make sure the printouts were rare and unrelated to other printouts."

"I see. But I'm still unconvinced. I need to see a smoking gun. What else could you possibly give me?"

Alina smiled broadly at my question. "I knew you were going to ask that, and so I am ready." She pulled out her phone and turned to me. "These are the documents that Inga Kopovsky delivered to Dimitry Kopovsky on September eleventh last year. I have acquired these from a friend at Western Energy, and if you look closely, you will see that this is the document that cost the Department of

Justice the state of Oklahoma. Here's the smoking gun where the expert witness for the DOJ states the downstream pollution was caused not by Western Energy but by upstream farming and ranching."

"But how do we know these are specifically from Inga?"

"Because my friend was there when they were delivered to Dimitry. Now, look up here at the top. See where it's stamped *received WER* by the Russians? Here's proof it's from them."

"I see, and this is all very interesting and tells me I will have to bring you before the grand jury and let the jury hear you. The grand jury is waiting for something like this."

Nicki spoke up. "Miles, can you give us an approximate date when this will all be wrapping up? Alina and I have decided to marry, but we first want this stuff behind us."

"In a hurry, are we?"

"Alina's pregnant. This has to end soon for the baby's sake."

"Congratulations," I said and meant it. But as to the accusation against Inga? I found that very weak.

I was disappointed, and I was elated it wasn't my friend.

At least, it wasn't yet.

Chapter Forty-Four

MILES STANDISH

Monday morning in Washington, DC, and I could feel spring coming on as I stepped into the garage for my Mercedes. The air was probably ten degrees warmer, and the sun was shining outside, clearing the snow and ice from the streets.

The FBI driver came through the open garage door. We backed out of my driveway and headed for M Street NW.

It was 7:30 a.m. when I arrived at the office. Several people were working while Alina and Nicki waited in the reception area. As I walked through, I saw she was reading a *People* magazine, and he was reading *Sports Afield* magazine. Mutual interests, sure.

I said hello over my shoulder and entered my office. I shut the door. It was the first day of the *United States of America versus*—versus who? The indictment I had filed had the name of Max Jennings on it as the person who had murdered Tommy Gray. But it was a funny thing. I did not feel entirely comfortable with that indictment. But again, it was not my indictment; it was the indictment that was the work of the grand jury. So I had had very little to do with it other than produce witnesses in a grand jury room and then let the jury decide who had killed Tommy.

After the indictment had come down, I spoke with several grand jury members about the case against Max Jennings. *How did you decide on Max?* I wanted to know. Was there ever anyone else who you felt might be involved?

The grand jurors who responded told me that the 15-minute walk from Jennings's home to the Gray firm capped it off. He had no way of proving where he was between 9 and 11 o'clock that night Tommy Gray died. And they thought that Max Jennings had a compelling motive: he wanted to be the chairman and knew he needed to get Tommy Gray out of the way first.

They found it compelling that the Gray firm video system had gone dark at 9:15 p.m. They couldn't accept this. And it blinked off just when Max would be at the office with no one else around except Tommy. The grand jurors next said they had been very impressed with Deonna Standish, Max's girlfriend, and they became suspicious after she testified she had not seen him between the hours of nine and eleven.

It just seemed too convenient that Max had left his cell phone at home, so there was no way of checking his location for a couple of hours. "Too much of it was just too many little things that kept us from knowing where he was and what he was doing," said the grand jury foreperson.

But the worst part of it? Max was just very unlikable. He was pushy, unaware of how he came across to other people. As a witness, the jury had not liked him, which went a long way.

They eventually left the grand jury room, and I was left alone to decide how to make the case against Max in front of a trial court jury. My head was spinning. I decided I would go home since the Max Jennings trial would have to wait until tomorrow for me to think about it. But one thing was for sure, and that was the grand jury had given me an indictment that was my official duty to prosecute.

And prosecute it, I would. Tomorrow I would make an opening statement after jury selection, and I'd call my first witness Alina, and I'd bury Max Jennings.

After all, that was my job. It didn't hurt that he was also the man screwing my wife.

Chapter Forty-Five

NADIA

Like all of DC, Nadia celebrated when the last remnants of ice and snow slipped away one warm spring night. She was up the following day to find her windshield—she parked overnight on the street—devoid of all moisture.

Now she could proceed with the shot.

Driving across town, she felt her pulse jump when she was sure she wasn't being followed and could proceed to Standish's alley. Fifteen minutes later, she arrived there and pulled to a stop behind his fence. Ever so carefully, she hazarded a peek over his fence at the greenhouse.

The greenhouse glass tiles were clear, just as she had left it in December. Now there was nothing between her and taking down Miles Standish. Moscow Center would be delighted, and she would receive a new assignment overseas as the hunt for the assassin raged in North America. The Embassy's Tupolev jet was on standby, waiting to wing her away.

She stood at the fence, the Leupold scope in one hand, alternately sighting the greenhouse with her eyes and then with the rifle scope. She failed to notice a black Ford Bronco nose into the alley and head toward her as she was preoccupied. Inside were two men dressed in dark suits, white shirts, and black ties. Their hands were on their guns as they approached.

As soon as she saw them, she slipped the rifle scope down the sleeve of her windbreaker and prayed it would stay there. Here they came, opening doors, hands on guns, approaching her from two sides.

"Morning, Miss. What are you doing out here?"

For a moment, she considered playing like she had no English but immediately thought better.

"I'm a realtor. I'm always in this neighborhood looking for houses to sell. I approach the owners and see if they're interested in listing with me."

"Realtor? Got a card?" said the looming Hispanic man.

"Not with me. I left my case back at my office."

"Who's your broker?" asked the other man, with a stature like an NFL running back. He was light on his feet as he moved, and she knew that at some other time, under some other circumstances, she would never outrun him, fast as she was.

"My broker is me. I work out of my kitchen."

Fast, she thought. Now, if only they don't ask for ID and run her through DC licensing, searching down her broker's license.

"Hand me your ID, please," said the huge man. He held out a saucer-sized hand and waited.

"Nothing on me. Turning in here was a spur-of-the-moment thing as I set out for donuts."

"What's your address where you work out of?"

Her mind flashed ahead, and she saw the DC police

searching her rat nest of an apartment with a search warrant. She decided she had no address.

"I'm just visiting today. I flew in from San Francisco to visit my sick sister. But the neighborhood looked prime for gentrification, so here I am, snooping. I'm sorry if I've done something wrong."

The halfback peered inside the driver's window of her van.

"Is that a long rifle case behind your seat?"

"Definitely. I compete in the cowboy shooting competition at Durham Ferry. My sporting rifle is a Henry 45-70."

"Christ," exclaimed Mr. Huge, "that gun can kill anything on the North American continent. Sexton, that's the rifle the big game guides carry in Alaska. Miss, you are seriously loaded for overkill. Doesn't it bruise your shoulder?"

"I keep a thick pad on the butt. I'm not stupid."

"It's also a brush gun," said Mr. Halfback. "It's the perfect gun to shoot through that greenhouse back there."

Mr. Huge and Mr. Halfback stared at her, waiting.

"I don't know about that. I brought it along to show my brother-in-law. He owns the Marlin all-weather 45-70. The Marlin's the better gun, but Marlin went bankrupt, and now we're hoping Ruger brings them back. The stores are full of backorders."

"You know your guns," said Mr. Halfback, clearly impressed. "I might even believe you, Miss. If only you had some ID."

"We're going to follow you back to your sister's," said Mr. Huge. "We'll just have a look at that ID this morning."

Nadia's heart flipped in her chest. She knew she could lose them if it were just the one Bronco following. But if there were other cars giving chase, they would probably drive her to the ground and catch her.

"Pull on by us," said Mr. Huge, climbing behind the wheel of the Bronco. "We'll follow you."

She thought she saw him then key a microphone on a cord and start talking. The roof was quickly caving down on her.

But if the FSB/KGB had one key piece of training for the new spies, it was extremely serious about the art of losing a tail. So, she drove out of the alley and took a left, headed for the secondary roads leading to the freeway.

She headed for Union Station on Massachusetts Avenue. A dash through the stores and a hidden seat on an outbound train awaited.

Twenty minutes of nervous driving followed. The men all but tailgated her. She was had.

When she had pulled into the Union Station parking area, she made her way to the Massachusetts Avenue entrance. She suddenly leaped from her car, abandoning her gun, her scope, her supplies—everything—while she made her escape, running at the speed that had made her first in her FSB class. Arms pumping and legs driving, she quickly left the men behind.

She disappeared from the men when she merged into a mass of commuters hurrying for their connections. At the Street Level - Westside Shopping Concourse, she flew into the Neuhaus Chocolatier, pulled her windbreaker off, turned it inside out, and pulled it back over her upper body, changing her profile from light brown to forest green. She pulled a watch cap from the pocket and pulled it down over her ears. Sunglasses followed, then she was seated with her back to the door and making her order. While the waitress prepared her order, Nadia slipped out and slipped into The

Body Shop next door. Then it was into Hudson News and stealing outside to the Amtrak waiting area. Tickets could be purchased when the train was underway. Within five minutes, she was seated on a Maryland Rail Service train, pulling slowly down the tunnel, headed for daylight, and then rolling free of the station and heading northeast.

She shut her eyes and drew a deep breath.

They had won—this time.

She had already moved on, for there was a second way, an even surer thing, though her chances of getting away were very low, probably impossible.

So be it. Moscow Center was frustrated and angry--as was Nadia.

It was time to deliver, even though it might mean her death.

Chapter Forty-Six

MILES STANDISH

Alina and her testimony led off my case against Max Jennings when Jennings's murder trial began in the U.S. District Court. She took the stand, wore a brave face while being sworn in, and jumped right into the heart of her testimony when I asked her who murdered Tommy.

She replied, "Working at Gray, I was a pool paralegal. I would circulate among the lawyers and their full-time paralegals and do odd jobs and rush jobs and emergency jobs, just depending on where they needed me from day-to-day." She then explained the email she received that said "Thanatopsis tonight" and how that meant that Max, who emailed Roman Challis, was the killer.

When Alina was finished and had left the courtroom, I knew I had just lost the trial, that Alina's testimony indeed amounted to reasonable doubt. It just wasn't there.

Chapter Forty-Seven

MILES STANDISH

The trial didn't care what I thought; it just continued on. Never mind that I had set it in motion when I coaxed the Max Jennings indictment out of a grand jury that didn't know any better. I'd let my rage at Max indict a man who I thought to be innocent. Time for some serious meditation.

These thoughts moved along when the bailiff stood and went for the next witness, Inga, who entered the courtroom and took the witness chair.

Little did I know she was about to set Max Jennings free once and for all. Another dagger in my heart. But I could handle it; I had to. Off I went with the usual line of questions.

"Please tell us your name and employment details."

"Inga Kopovsky. I worked at Gray law until a week ago."

"What happened a week ago?"

"I was let go."

"Why was that? If you know."

"It was about the people I kept company with. Roman

Challis was distraught, and in a fit of anger, he tossed me out the door."

"Today, do you come here knowing who murdered Tommy Gray?"

I asked the question, knowing full well she did not know. I expected her to say as much, and we'd get on with the balance of what she knew—and didn't know.

"Frank Hemet killed Tommy Gray."

I was stunned--she had never said that anytime, anyplace, and especially not to me during our hours together.

"You said Frank Hemet killed Tommy Gray? How do you know that?"

"I know it because Tommy and I were lovers. And he admitted to me he had been sloppy with DOJ records several times, and they had wound up in Russian hands."

"And Hemet?"

"Tommy and I had a terrible, loud fight the night he died. But then we texted after we had parted for the night. By pre-dawn, I was ready to go to him and make up. I pulled my car into the Gray parking garage and saw Hemet in the garage. He was passing through the parked cars and seemed to stay in the shadows as he moved for the elevators. He was carrying a long package wrapped in newspapers. I took the elevator after him and went inside. Just as I rounded the corner to Tommy's hallway, I glimpsed Frank Hemet, letting himself into Tommy's office. I took a phone video of him putting a silver pick into Tommy's lock, followed by the second, then letting himself in. I scurried inside my office."

"This is the first time you've told this story?" I was in shock. This couldn't be happening in the middle of my case against Jennings. Plus, it was Hemet she was accusing? Hell, Hemet was undercover FBI. Impossible!

"So, what about the video you say you made? Do you still have it?"

"Of course."

"And do you have it with you today?"

"I do."

I asked the judge to play the video through the phone connection the courtroom maintained. There was no objection because, of course, Max's defense attorneys were delighted to have the blame placed elsewhere than on Max. So we took a few minutes and hooked up the phone video to the court system and then pressed play. The jury watched the video with totally rapt attention. As it moved through the frames, I knew it stopped short of convicting Frank. There was never a large object wrapped in newspapers, there was never the sound of a shotgun blast, there was only a picture of Hemet exiting Tommy's office in no apparent hurry. The video ended there.

Immediately upon the video's end, Max's attorneys made an oral motion for mistrial, claiming the video proved beyond a doubt it was Hemet who was last seen in Tommy's office early that morning. They needed more time to analyze the video and interrogate Inga. I argued vigorously at length, but the judge had been swayed. A mistrial was granted, and the trial broke off right there.

Court was then dismissed. There was nothing more to say.

Max and his attorneys left the courtroom jubilant. Max winked at me as they passed by. I nodded and looked away.

Later that day, Inga was waiting for me in my waiting room, and I took her right into my private office.

"Inga, I don't know what to say. I feel betrayed, and I

feel relieved all at once. Why in God's name did you mention none of this to me?"

"That's an easy one. I knew that Roman Challis and Max Jennings would eventually attempt to persuade you I was the killer because of my loud fights and my time with my ex-husband, a Russian working for WER. So I held the evidence in reserve to prove my innocence to you when it all went bad against me. As you can see, it served its purpose in a rather obtuse way. By that, I mean it wasn't I who was saved, but it was Max Jennings, which is all fine with me. The truth is out, and my testimony and my video will serve the truth. That's good enough for me."

"Still, I can't imagine why you didn't think you could have trusted me with it. I always thought we were good friends, Inga."

"We *are* good friends, Miles."

"But what about Max? It would've saved me from proceeding against an innocent party."

"That was your responsibility. My responsibility was to myself, and I had to wait for the ultimate moment to defend myself."

"I don't know what to say." I was honestly floored and did not know what direction to go with Inga. She'd been my friend for years and then my lover. She'd spent nights in my *home*. I was beyond angry. "I'm going to have to live with this for a few days and see. Until then, please take yourself out of my office and just let me sit alone and try to get a handle on what you've just done."

"I'm on my way. Please don't judge me too harshly."

"I'll be fair. But I'll do it away from you. Please leave now."

"As you wish."

With that, she left my office, gently shutting the door behind her.

Chapter Forty-Eight

PHILOMENA

The door wasn't shut three minutes before my paralegal Katelin came bursting into my office with a clutch of papers. "You ain't gonna like this, Boss."

I started reading. The poverty law clinic had taken on Benji's mother, Philomena, in her effort to set aside the court's order granting me temporary custody of Benji. A long affidavit was attached, signed by Philomena, that recounted her recent hospitalization with hepatitis A. She had stayed in bed for eleven days while the doctors got her disease and symptoms under control. Of course, she made clear she hadn't had notice of the court's session where I was granted temporary custody of Benji. She would never allow that to happen, she said. Also attached were hospital records and the report of her treating physician, which backed up her story.

By the time I finished reading, my hands were shaking. It felt like a knife in my guts, and I was dying from pain. My mind raced for the next ten minutes while I considered whose help I needed. When a name surfaced, I called him, Marshall Lakin. The FBI? On a child custody case? Really? No one does that.

"I need a huge favor," I said when he came on the line.

"Such as?"

"I need to know when a woman was home when her kid and when she was not home with him. My theory is that she abandoned him alone in the apartment for days, even weeks at a time. Her lawyers deny that."

"Custody case? Benji's mother?"

"Yes, and yes. I don't know how to do it. I only know if it can be done, the FBI can make it happen."

"We'll start with CCTV cameras around the building. He's still at

Carver Terrace?"

I sat there, speechless. It would never cease to stun me how much Special Agents knew. Almost frightening.

"Yes."

"How far back you want?"

"Beginning of this year."

"Some video might not go back that far."

"You'll do what you can," I said, confident in their efforts.

He paused. Then, "Is that it? Are we done? I know just who I want to assign this to. Hanging up now."

We disconnected, and I made a list of chores for me, including researching proper service of process by leaving documents slipped under the front door. After that came research on the degree of negligence required to sever parental ties. It was surprisingly easy to sever parental ties once you got over the initial degree of negligence required

Then we went to court. Benji's mother was the first

witness called by her lawyer. She painted a charming, if not eccentric, picture of herself. "There are a few times I've had to leave Benji alone because I was sick with hepatitis A and afraid of giving it to him. So I lent him money for food and clothes and checked in with him by phone."

I cross-examined her and, with the help of the FBI's data findings, proved to the court her absences were every other week and sometimes more. She then stepped down from the witness stand, and her lawyers called Benji to the stand without having first spoken with him, which was a mistake, because Benji told a story of years of neglect, of strange men coming and going in the house every few weeks, often when she wasn't even home. And he told about having no food and no money to get any. Toward the end, he even sneaked in his preference for me as his custodian. After Benji left them in ruins, he stepped down, and the mother's case ended.

The judge held up her hand. She said it was over. She'd heard enough, and she was going to allow the current custodial placement to remain with me, thus denying Philomena's motion to set aside my custody. Benji would remain with me.

Afterward, the caseworker got me aside in the hallway outside the courtroom.

"After a few months of placement with you, we'll be moving to sever parental rights and proceed with the adoption. It will go through without a hitch because mom cannot hold it together for that long to make herself look reformed. She'll go out again and maybe not come back home at all this time. I've seen thousands of cases just like this one. You can trust what I'm telling you, Mr. Standish."

I thanked her, and Benji thanked her with a hug, and we went our separate ways.

It was a warm enough day, so Benji and I headed for *In Recess* and took the boat miles and miles in both directions, learning the river. Then we got out the hibachi and made our dinner of sirloin steaks, fries, and root beer ice cold from the boat's kitchen refrigerator.

All was well, thank God.

Chapter Forty-Nine

MILES STANDISH

The FBI ID'd her, and Deonna let herself in my house through the front door just as I arrived home that night and came in through the garage. She was waiting in the kitchen when I went to get my first cup of good coffee. She was wearing a jumper with a white blouse with very delicate roses across the front, one of my favorite outfits, one we had picked up at Seaport Village in San Diego several years ago while on vacation. It had been a wonderful three days, and in the end, I was so exhausted from our lovemaking movement without pain was brutal. Her wearing it that night, my hackles went on alert. I knew she was lying in wait for me, that a big plan was about to develop right in front of my eyes.

"Miles, for God's sake, slow down. I want to talk to you for a few minutes. Is it a good time?"

Was this a good time? She was asking if it might not be good for me? When had that ever happened before? Jeopardy bonus answer: never. So I was taken aback, and I stirred my coffee longer than necessary. Then I answered, "Sure, I have time to talk. Is right now okay?"

"Yes, let's sit down at the dining room table."

So we sat at the massive oak table we had picked up one Saturday morning in Long Lake while we were antiquing outside Chicago. $1750, and that was a steal. I couldn't get it loaded in the back end of my Ford 150. But it was still with us. The truth was, our entire house was nothing but a mass of memories for me. While she had been off living with Max Jennings, I had had those memories pushed back and all but forgotten. But when she returned home that day, it was like the furniture came to life and spoke to me of things we'd done together in our great years. Here was our life, measured out in antiques and her one-of-a-kind clothing finds. It was more than I could deal with, and that's why I would retreat into my room, close the blinds, and read.

"All right," I said. "You spent your nickel; let's talk."

"Miles, Max, and I are calling it quits. It's a long story, and I don't need to go into ninety percent of it, but the important part, the ten percent part, is about you. I miss you and realize I still love you, and that will never stop, so I would like us to put the divorce on hold and see a counselor together to see if we can put this thing back together. Now, what do you think?"

I was stunned and immediately felt sorry for her. She thought all along—and rightly so—that I would take her back on a moment's notice and love her for eternity. But she was too late. I didn't have someone else; I just didn't want Deonna. At that point, it was only about survival for me. I couldn't do another abandonment by her, and I would never trust her again after this one.

Deonna, of course, couldn't have known any of this and

was acting in the dark when she came for me to whisk her away again.

"You asked what I think, and I want no part of it. My heart no longer cares, Deonna, I'm sorry to say. You are one of the most accomplished women I know. You are beyond beautiful and a wonderful conversationalist. You hold a world of knowledge about different countries and cultures and books and music right in your mind. And at one time, those things meant everything to me. But no more. I think the fire went out the first time I realized you'd be spending the night with Max in his bed. After that, the fire went out a little more with each passing night until, today, the fire has been extinguished. It won't come back either, I promise. So no, I do not want you back. I hope only the best for you, and my best wishes go out to you. I know you will have a wonderful life once you get beyond this. But I will not be part of it, and we will not see each other anymore once we're living apart. And that will happen soon."

Several minutes ticked by. I sipped my coffee and washed my face with a paper towel and sink water. It was clear I was finished. Her face was stone as she said, "I'll finalize the papers this week. I'll get them signed on Friday, and we'll be divorced by Friday night. Thanks for your honesty."

With that, she stood, then bent to me and kissed me on the top of my head.

Then she was gone.

Chapter Fifty

MILES STANDISH

One afternoon, I abruptly came awake on the leather couch in my office—an unexpected nap. I remembered the first night when Marshall Lakin first solicited me to take on my current role. Present at the mansion that night was Paul Worthington of the CIA.

I took a seat at my desk and turned on my computer. Then I looked up Paul Worthington in the government directory and called his office.

After battling through his staff hierarchy, I finally reached Mr. Worthington's secretary. Explaining to her who I was and how I was related to Paul Worthington in what I was doing, I made an appointment through her to see Paul at seven a.m. the next day. We hung up, and I knew I was doing the right thing.

The following morning at seven, I was making my way through obtaining a visitor's badge and being escorted by a man who refused to discuss even the weather with me as we made our way through the CIA's inner sanctum on the way to Paul Worthington's office. At last, I was delivered into his waiting room, but didn't have long to wait. At 7:10 a.m., I was shown into his office by his secretary. Worthington and I shook hands, and he indicated we would sit in the two wingback chairs set at his window. The view looked out on an enclosed area of grass and benches and tables for dining.

"Miles, would you care for some coffee?"

I refused, but thanked him. I needed steady nerves because I felt like I was on hallowed ground, and I was not just a little in awe of my surroundings.

"Is it all right if I just lay it all out before you, Mr. Worthington?"

He smiled, which surprised me because he had never smiled, not even once the night I saw him at the mansion. I would have to say that he had been grim that night.

"By all means, let 'er rip," I said.

"Why is it Western Energy keeps winning the DOJ lawsuits? Aren't you slipping a cog here?"

"Not at all, because we have just discovered the identity of the Gray mole who is passing stolen documents that are top-secret to the Russians."

"I suppose you won't share their name with me?"

"Certainly I will, because we're looking for the same man. The man I'm speaking of is Renz Aldrich, with whom you are very well acquainted. Renz went active approximately eighteen months ago, and his cooperation with the Russians has slowly blossomed into what is almost a full-time career based on the money they are paying him for the documents. He's the real deal, and he has over five-hundred thousand stashed away in the Dominican Republic."

"So, what are you going to do about Renz?"

"Yes, that is the problem because CIA hands are tied. So I'm going to give you the name of Renz Aldrich, and then I'm going to let you build your case against him and take him down. That is your mandate, and I will stand aside and let you do your job."

Right on the spot, I made up my lie to the CIA because I had already drawn this same conclusion after finding the "Dummy" books."

"To say I'm shocked would be an understatement," I said. "Renz Aldrich, of all people. I would not have thrown his hat in the ring of suspects in a million years. I just had lunch with him about a month ago, and he was all obsequious and bowing down and currying favor with me. I thought it was strange, but it never occurred to me he was ingratiating himself so that he would be on my good side in the event I returned to Gray. What would you suggest I do first to nail his ass?"

"If it were me, I would confront him directly. He has a weak personality and will not stand up to any close examination. So, were I you, I would ask him. Preface it by saying that government agents have followed him, and we know what he's been up to. That'll put the fear of God in him and light a fire under his ass to come clean and cut a deal. That's always the MO of people like Renz Aldrich. So good luck with that. Please keep me abreast of what's going on? We're finished here; it's time for my next appointment. Thanks for coming in, Miles. Let me buzz my secretary, and Jimmy will show you out again."

"Jimmy, you mean the gabby one?"

Paul Worthington chuckled. "Yes, the chatty one, indeed. Have a good one, Miles, and stay in touch."

And so ended my visit to the CIA, the most powerful spy

agency in the world, with zero power inside its own country's borders.

Whoever established the CIA knew what they were doing. No one wanted that monster loose on American streets.

No one.

Alone later that night, I made a strong coffee and sat in my favorite chair, my reading chair. Ever so slowly, I went back over the last time I had seen Renz Aldrich at our lunch date. First, he had accosted me in Gardiner's books when my back was turned to him. He had made a point of seeing what I was reading. And he had given me his book about home repair to pay for. He promised to repay me at lunch.

So what was there about that? What didn't quite fit?

I thought and thought, refilled my coffee, and then thought some more.

At last, the round nut revealed itself. Lawyers didn't keep home repair books. Lawyers couldn't repair jack shit. They always hired tradespeople to keep their lives running smoothly and their electrical and plumbing systems worked as intended. Which begged the question, what in the world was Renz Aldrich doing with a home repair book?

My mind continued going over the next day, and I remembered taking his book to lunch with me on the front seat of my car and then after we were finishing lunch, I remember telling him I had taken his book inside my house and I would drop it by his office. The funny thing was, I never delivered it. And the even more amusing thing? He had never contacted me to get his book. I swung around and looked at my bookcase. I still had the damn thing. My mind froze on the cheesiest trick of all. The hollow book trick. Surely a spy would have better than the hollow book trick.

But I had to go have a look, anyway.

I stood and walked to my bookcase and began looking through the shelf of my to-be-reads. Included among them would be my most recent purchases. My fingers did the walking, and there, eight books in from the end—I had been busy with even more purchases—stood Aldrich's book, *Home Repair for Dummies*. One of those.

I pulled the book out and looked inside the front cover. I turned a dozen pages. Nothing was unusual about it, nothing that should alert anyone to anything. I then grabbed the book with a finger at either end of the spine and shook it, fanning the pages to allow any free papers to fall out.

Nothing fell out, but I had found what I was looking for, anyway. For there was a cutaway inside the book just the size of an envelope. The fucking hollow book trick. *Does nobody innovate today?* I knew the rest of it. Aldrich had just received his payoff and handed me the book after he'd removed the money. It was a payoff to Aldrich for documents he had turned over to the Russians.

I shook my head and slid the book back into its slot on the shelf. Now I had all my cool together. I was on the trail. Spies used drop boxes and hiding places to pass back and forth to other spies. Aldrich's hiding place was the home repair books at Gardiner's books. The line of books would be the "Dummy" books because the title of his book was *Home Repairs for Dummies*. It was a resolution I would be embarrassed to ever tell anyone about.

Ten minutes later, my driver and I were heading for Gardiner's books in an FBI SUV.

I had to see for myself. It was a long shot, but I wouldn't sleep that night if I didn't take it.

Gardiner's it was.

An hour later, I returned home empty-handed and tired from the drive since the roads had turned icy. And I was exhausted from the long day. But there was one bright spot. Two FBI agents were now watching the Dummies section and would be until Renz Aldrich arrived to select the book beneath all the others, the one that held his cash.

I pulled my briefcase up off the floor beside my chair and balanced it on my lap. The files inside were filled with documents allegedly filched by Inga and turned over to the Russians. These were the files provided me by Roman Challis late that afternoon when he delivered his so-called "vast" collection of files, as he had called them at his office.

It was in this upcoming, protracted, long drawn-out, boring assay of Inga's printouts from the hundreds of pages I got to thinking about the lawyers at Gray to whom I was closest. "Closest" not in a good sense but "closest" in the sense that I kept them close because they had been my problem children when I ran the show. Inga's printouts were from lawsuits, all of which I had put my hand to. We had worked them together, many of us, Challis, Jennings, Aldrich, Inga, and many more. But the files were lightweight in terms of how heavily those people had once weighed down on me.

The procedural working parts of any trial were a trifle compared to how I always believed Challis and Jennings were in a never-ending conspiracy against me. Had I been paranoid? Not when they started shooting at you, the old saying went. After all, look at me now. They had been instrumental in me being forced out of Gray when the flow of documents from Gray to Western turned from a leak into a gully washer. And the opening salvo against me, made before the directors, was that I was the leak--that I was delivering documents to the enemy.

Of course, there had been no proof. Nor could there have been because I was guilty of nothing crooked.

The real truth lay somewhere between Tommy Gray and Renz Aldrich. But for now, the tail was pinned on Renz's donkey. And such a shame. He wouldn't make it much beyond year one when he came to understand he had to endure a lifetime of prison food. He was all about Italian and French cuisine. Fried bologna would be new, and it would be soul-killing to Renz. He would wither and waste away. Then he would know he was in prison.

Max Jennings, probably the best trial lawyer at Gray in the last twenty years, bitter and angry that Gray hadn't done more for him in return for his dozens and dozens of wins. What was he now, something like 105-3?

He had maintained that I was purposely losing cases because I had been paid off by whoever the enemy was at the moment. Proof of this? None, except for his intense anger Tommy Gray kept whipping into a frenzy even while he was yapping at my heels. He tried to get me to jump off the high wire without a net—to leave Gray with nowhere to go. When I didn't go peacefully, Jennings, Challis, and Gray had three board votes and forced me out with a 3-1 vote. Simple enough. Only Inga remained in my corner as I, the fifth vote, wasn't allowed to vote on my early retirement, according to the by-laws.

Besides my strict lordship over Gray, they hated me because I knew who they were and where they came from. Tommy Gray had avoided Vietnam by enrolling in med school, following law school, to maintain his student deferment. Then dropped his medical studies the day the American flag came down at the American Embassy in Saigon when the North Vietnamese Army overran the last city. He knew I knew. And me? I tried twice to enlist and was turned down both times—excess of albumin in my urine. Kidney troubles, they said. My best friend became a Marine and went to Ia Drang Valley, where he died in a brave hail of Vietcong mortar fire. I would've been right alongside him had I had my way. But not Tommy.

And Roman Challis, his truth? His father ran a small loan company in Orbit, Illinois, where he loaned money at 26% and foreclosed on widows and hail-stormed farmers. His father spent more time in court suing his customers than he did back at his office, calculating interest. From that gutter stumbled forth Roman Challis, Harvard bound and never looking back at EZ Loans. Later in life, he would claim his parents were dead, and his father had been a banker. Neither one was true. That was Roman, and he knew I knew. I had their personnel records; I had to know.

And Max Jennings.

Max spent most of his teen years in juvenile court and juvenile facilities for three sexual assaults at beer parties. Of course, that was all tossed out when Max became an adult. He hadn't publicly sinned since his teens--but he knew I knew. Again, I had his records.

Tommy Gray hadn't been born; there were no reliable records, only a church baptismal record and a letter from an aunt who swore to a birth date that might or might not have been accurate. Why no birth certificate? "We were living south of the border while my father bred cattle on Mexican grasslands, then crossed them back into the US to take advantage of US prices for beef on the hoof. I was born on either side, wouldn't you think?" Laughter from that birthday party where he told us his story. "Birth dates weren't written, and anniversaries of birth dates weren't celebrated. I grew up a cowboy in West Texas until I was twelve and possessed few official documents about myself. The Dean of Admissions at the University of Texas stepped up for me, took pity, and began pulling official documents out of his ass. I still do not know where my birth certificate came from. But I would need it to gain admission to the University of Texas law school four years later. As an undergraduate, they made me into a petroleum engineer. Today, I belong where I belong, here in the greatest environmental litigation firm in America."

Hadn't some of us heard that? A true blue-blood he was not, though now he spent more time at his country club than Eisenhower with his golf Thursdays and Sundays.

Now there was Renz Aldrich to contend with. A quiet Iowan who came to us by way of University of Michigan law school with a heavy concentration in UCC, creditors' rights, banking, and business torts. Prime rib for the banking section. He had wanted litigation when he came on board, but he scurried home from court with his tail between his legs and a withered look set upon his uncomely face, and we had demanded he move into office practice. There, he had thrived. Not in the sense of making it to the seventh floor, but on the second floor, he was a god—to the typists and copy machine operators, the court runners, and the shipping clerks.

The FBI detail I left in place at Gardiner's to photograph an unknown Russian and Renz when they next made their drops and pickups would flesh out my case against Renz. The Russian who regularly brought the payoff and stuck it in the *Dummies* book would testify against Renz on a deal I'd cut for him, then I'd boot his ass out of the country. He'd be welcomed back to Russia as a hero and get a rundown, dreary studio apartment without windows in the state housing in Moscow as his reward. He would know what his neighbors on four sides were having for dinner, and he could choose to listen to any of four TV programs coming at him through the uninsulated walls. So long to the wide-open spaces of Oklahoma and the Cherokee gal in Stillwater.

And as for Renz? I was going to deal with him myself.

Or, as we said in the sandbox, I was going to make him my bitch. It was a term I hated, but it described exactly what I meant for Renz Aldrich.

Chapter Fifty-One

MILES STANDISH

The following day, I placed a call to Renz. I wanted to set up a lunch with him and confront him personally about his massive crime against the United States. My phone recorder would be on, secretly, to memorialize whatever he might say. I was going to get some wine in him first and then bully him. Renz Aldrich was very susceptible to bullying, which is why he crumbled before federal judges, and those bastards always launched themselves after the weak. So I placed the call on my office phone and waited. His secretary soon had him on the line.

"Miles! How good of you to call me! I hope this is very important because I have been feeling left out of all the clandestine meetings and agreements being made under the table about Tommy's death. I hope I can help improve that. I'm standing in wait, Miles. I'm all yours."

"Renz, I need to set up a lunch meeting with you next week. What day can you give me?"

"Oh, next week is not good. I'm going on *Jeopardy*."

"Come again?"

"*Jeopardy*, the game show. It has come to town, and I auditioned for getting on the show, and guess what? They selected me! And I know some amazing models are going to be on the show. Who knows, Miles, I might come away with a trophy wife on my arm yet. So much depends upon me brushing up on world facts and American history. I'll be secluded next week, Monday through Wednesday, and then Thursday, I'll be on the show. Friday is recuperating. Can we try the next week?"

"I wanted to work you in before Tommy's murder trial began. That's next Monday, one week from today. You're going to have to give me a statement between now and then, or I am going to have to subpoena you, and you will miss *Jeopardy*."

"Oh, Miles, you absolutely cannot do that to me! What if I come to your office and give my statement?"

"No, it has to be lunchtime when we meet. I'm going to suggest we get together tomorrow and quit playing dodgeball. If you're unable or unwilling, then I'm going to subpoena you, and you will miss your TV show. Now, what time?"

"Lunch tomorrow? I'll have to make that happen. Where should we go this time?"

"Let's meet at the same place at 11:30. We can be done by 12:30, and you can return to your office and get back to your studies. Does that work for you?"

"I'll have to make it work. My American history tutor is an American history professor at George Washington University. He is scheduled to come in tomorrow for a tutoring session with me that will last until noon. I'll have to cut it short. *C'est la vie*."

"That makes sense. I will see you at 11:30."

"And Miles, please bring my book. You still haven't delivered it to me despite my many calls."

"Will do. I'll bring the book along."

Renz canceled on me 30 minutes later. His message said I should subpoena him because he didn't want to short-change his American history tutor. He said that too much was riding on him winning *Jeopardy*, and he could not pass up his opportunity for a starring role.

I crumpled his pink message slip but then unwrapped it and left a note to file in Aldrich's file. Even though it was the weekend, I also asked my assistant to set up lunch with Renz Aldrich the next day. Saturday at noon, no excuses.

Just as I was about to order my lunch at my office, I received a call from Inga. She wanted to know if I'd like to take her to lunch, and I immediately grabbed the chance. I was over being stunned and enraged by her withholding the killer's identity testimony until trial. I'm like that—I don't do long grudges. Resentment has killed more PTSD vets than any gun anywhere. Let it go, which I'd done.

Then I remembered my tight schedule. "I wonder if we can't meet here at my office. My schedule is jam-packed, and I don't need to be fighting in noon-hour traffic in Washington, DC. Traffic is impossible between eleven and one. So please let's meet here. Possible?"

"Miles, with you, anything is possible. You should know that about me by now."

Every time she spoke, the nude scenes came to mind. I thought it was a little sick and resolved to quit thinking about her that way. She was practically still a married woman with her Russian ex, and I did not like to think of married women that way. It was just a longtime practice of mine. It helped keep me out of trouble.

"All right," I said, "I'll see you, and we'll order something wonderful with a bottle of wine."

"I'm going to shower and change, and then I'm on my way. Don't eat without me, Miles."

"I can fight off the hunger pangs to see you in a fresh outfit on a day when I've been missing you, anyway. Your timing is perfect."

"I'm on my way, Miles. Goodbye."

What I had just told her was true. I had been missing her. Lawyers always had a lot in common with other lawyers. More than that, even, was that I missed her closeness in bed. There, I said it. Whatever else, I was lonely, and I missed Inga.

But that wasn't why I wanted to see her. I couldn't stop thinking about what I had learned about Inga from Paul Worthington at the CIA. According to Paul, she had been turning over documents to the Russians, and she had still been actively doing that until Roman Challis terminated her at Gray.

Keep your enemies close. I reminded myself. Even those you had feelings for.

It was twisted, but I needed to see her, and I wanted to see her.

I had to ask, right?

Chapter Fifty-Two

MILES STANDISH

But I didn't get to see Inga that day. Instead, Frank Hemet came bursting into my office. He had to take me to see something for myself right then.

He drove to my house and went back behind, to the alley. A CSI van was there, and criminologists crawled the area with magnification devices and blue lights.

"What?" I asked. Behind my own house?

"I'll send you the video. We set cameras in the trees and started monitoring your fence line. Two Special Agents encountered a young woman there, and she fled in her van and lost them. But inside the van she abandoned, we found a very high-powered rifle with the best scope money can buy. Plus, there were other items to indicate she had been standing watches in the van."

"So who is she? Is she still loose?"

"The video at the mall she ran into gave us good close-ups of her face. We have her face broadcast everywhere. We're quite convinced she's Russian, and we're cross-referencing video nationwide to see where else she might have been. But for now, we're about to hang black plastic walls on this alley-facing greenhouse wall."

"My God."

"Are you carrying the Sig pistol you were issued?"

"No, I'm not. PTSD."

"Well, suck it up and start carrying, brother. You have a big target on your back, and these people have a bottomless budget. We'll keep you alive, but you have to be ready with your gun for those moments when we're away for fifteen seconds and someone steps between us. It happens."

"I know it does. I'm in."

Chapter Fifty-Three

MILES STANDISH

"Now try this *Jeopardy* question, Miles. 'Just 37 words, it's in the article on the executive branch and is the only part of the Constitution that is in quote marks.' What is it, Miles?"

I looked longingly at the dessert menu, but first, I had to play my round of *Jeopardy* with Renz Aldrich the following day at lunch. The answer was an easy one. "The Presidential oath of office. 'I do solemnly swear (or affirm) that I will faithfully execute the Office of President of the United States, and will to the best of my ability, preserve, protect and defend the Constitution of the United States.'"

"Ai yi yi yi you nailed that one, Miles! I sort of thought you might. Okay, here's the next—"

"Hold on, please, Renz. We need to talk first."

"Your topic, friend. I think it's your turn to choose. What will it be? Fifth Avenue fashion? The Washington press roast? American nuclear policy in Eastern Europe? Can you pressure-cook roast? Or what else you have, Miles?"

"None of the above. This is a little more serious. I want

to ask you whether you are distributing secret documents to the Russians, Renz. And I want you to consider the answer you give me. You must keep in mind that I am asking this as a federal officer and that if you lie to me, that is a felony that will send you to prison."

"Whoa! That was a huge jump from the dessert menu to the federal agent. Let me catch my breath here. And you are asking whether I am giving documents to the Russians, is that correct?"

"That is exactly correct. A federal agency is on to you and knows everything about what you've turned over and the money you receive at Gardiner's books. There is more, but I'm going to ask you first to do yourself a favor and tell me the truth. Are you or have you been distributing American secrets to the Russians?"

"I don't believe I have any wiggle room to play here, Miles. So I'm going to have to say yes. Yes, I have been secretly sending American documents to Western Energy Reserves for some time now. In return, they pay me money. This year alone, I have been paid over $500,000. And right now, it feels great to tell you about it. It's been a secret I couldn't live much longer with Miles."

That was too damned easy. Now I had my eyes wide open.

"Thank you for that, Renz," I said. "You've done a very smart thing in confessing to me because I am the one who will decide your fate. First off, will you be willing to continue playing the game with the Russians?"

"What?"

"Will you be willing to pass them phony records and reports? I want to entrap that person on the other end, and it will go a long way toward what happens to you."

"Absolutely, I could do that. I have my contact there,

and I see no reason for anything to change at all. But just let me say this. If you prosecute me in court, the Russians will immediately know, and I will be persona non grata with them. They will immediately distance themselves from me and end all dealings with me. Or they might even send someone after me. Either way, I will be useless to you."

"I have already talked to one magistrate. I will prosecute you behind closed doors in front of people with top-secret clearance. I want a single plea of guilty to one count of giving up national secrets, and in return, I want your continued cooperation with me. There will be no jail time. There will be no prison time. Your name will not be in the papers. You will not lose your license to practice law. You will wear an ankle bracelet and surrender your passport. So that's the sum and substance of where we are. You will go to court with me on Monday at 7 a.m., and we will transact these things with the judge in his chambers. After that, you will be free to leave."

"How long will I be required to cooperate with you?"

"What, are you plea-bargaining already? You will be required to cooperate with me until I say otherwise. Or until the Department of Justice says otherwise. I assume you're in?"

"Oh definitely. And thank you, Miles, sincerely. A lesser man would've seen me doing time in Lewisburg, but not Miles Standish. Miles is big enough and smart enough to know I'm of more value to the nation, free and doing my job and misleading the Russians than I would ever wash dishes at Lewisburg. I cannot tell you, Miles, what a huge relief this is."

"If we keep the Russians thinking you are still a sovereign source, then they will have no reason to nurture a replacement source inside of Gray."

"Which means you will have to be looking over your shoulder wondering who is going to be stealing documents off the Gray servers. I admire your thinking, Miles. It's no wonder you have led Gray previously, and you will lead Gray again in the future. At least that's my prediction for you."

"Renz, it's crucial that you never get into trouble again. But some things won't change. You will still pick up your payoffs at Gardiner's Books. We have to maintain that illusion you're still playing."

"Loud and clear."

"You pay the bill this time. You still owe for the purchase of the book last time, or at least some of it. You pay the tabs today, and we will call it even. Have a good rest of your day, Renz. And don't do anything stupid. Especially this: do not go to the Russians for help. If you do that, I will have you hunted down and shot for being a traitor, and I will throw your body off a cliff and watch the Atlantic swallow you up. Do I make myself clear?"

"No such thoughts, Miles. My rambling days are over. Enjoy the rest of your day."

"Then we'll see each other next week, Renz. Keep your seven o'clock calendar free all week."

I then stood and left the dining area, wondering whether Renz was under surveillance by the Russians, and I decided he probably was and that they had overheard our conversation. Renz might be targeted for it or, if the Russians were wise as I thought they were, they would keep receiving false documents and let the US think they had been fooled.

I shot a last look around the restaurant just before I stepped outside, looking for a Russian face looking for me.

Instead, I found the FBI, and for once, that felt right.

Chapter Fifty-Four

MILES STANDISH

Inga dropped by after work that night. Our chance to discuss why she hadn't come clean with me about the evidence she had on Hemet. We talked at my front door and then hugged, and then we kissed. I was sure the FBI got its pictures from down the street—or wherever they were watching my door.

Later that night, at about 10 p.m., my doorbell rang again. Inga was upstairs in bed, reading, exhausted, like me, from our lovemaking. I hated myself for my weakness for her, but I was the best I had just then. Recriminations could wait until my sleuthing was finished.

Benji had hit the hay early, 8:30, because he'd joined the school's cross-country team and was exhausted from practice.

The bell rang again.

I came out of my home office wearing blue jeans and a T-shirt and soled moccasins. I peeked through the security hole and was astounded at what I saw. I immediately unlocked and yanked the door wide open.

"Franklin Hemet. You can't be here. I'm investigating you."

Hemet pushed past me, stepped inside, and casually looked around. "You've done well, Miles. I approve. Hey, relax. I'm here on official FBI business."

"You're the subject of a murder investigation I'm running. Please leave now."

"That's why I'm here. I'm going to clear my name tonight."

"Now you have a video located that shows someone else breaking into Tommy's office, right? Tell me I'm wrong, Frank."

All right," said Frank, "I'm going on a mission tonight and thought you'd want to go along with me as part of your investigation. We go back, Miles, as I was the one who picked you up that snowy day and took you to that first meeting. Well, tonight, I'm going to prove my innocence to you. I'm going to reveal the real traitor."

"Tell me what you're doing."

"Miles, grab your parka."

"Tell me."

"We're calling on Renz Aldrich. I know what happened in court with him, the secret plea of guilty, and the deal you cut. I need to talk to him, and you're going to help me."

I didn't like that. Middle of the night stuff? It sounded clandestine as hell, and I didn't do clandestine. Besides this, I no longer trusted Frank Hemet. That video might actually amount to something more than I believed.

"I can't do that."

"I'm here by order of Marshall Lakin. You have no choice, Miles. This is part of what you do."

"Lakin didn't tell me about this."

"Get your stuff, and let's go."

The risk I felt from the Hemet video compared to what I might learn about the complicated murder case turned me around. I headed to the closet for my parka. Then I walked into my office, where my winter boots were lying just under my desk, where I had kicked them off after work. I slipped the boots back on, sat up, and shrugged at Hemet.

"Well, all right then. Away we go."

"Is my protection detail following me?"

"What do you think?"

He was right. They had their orders. They would be back there somewhere, which provided just enough sense of safety that I went.

I followed him outside to a black SUV with blacked-out windows. Hemet backed us out of my drive and headed down the street to the main intersection. "He usually leaves work at five-thirty on the button. He drives alone to Georgetown to a townhouse he shares with another man."

"This is Renz Aldrich. I don't like it," I said. I needed to discuss this with Marshall Lakin. "I want to talk to Lakin about this first."

"We're here tonight at Marshall Lakin's request. Today is the day Renz Aldrich never saw coming."

"That's ominous as hell. Are we going to kill him? That's way outside of my job description, and I'm getting out of the car right now."

"We're going to question him. He has a confession to make about Tommy's murder."

"You know this how?"

"Wiretaps and surveillance and computer hacks. I have it all at the office."

"This scares the shit out of me," I said.

He looked across the seats. "Hey, you're gasping for air, Miles."

"You better believe it. This scares me, Frank. I'm not a cop."

"Try to shallow out your breathing. Gasping for air gets more gunfighters killed than any other one thing. It throws your angle off by two or three feet at thirty yards. Please don't quote me about that, but it's somewhere near that bad. So, shallow out."

"Why? Am I going to be shooting?"

"Only if I go down. Take this Glock and stick it in your pocket. You never know."

"No guns."

"He might be armed. You don't know everything about this guy you think you know. Now take the damn gun."

"All right." I stuck the gun in my front pocket. It was small and slipped in easily.

We drove in silence for the next fifteen minutes. Hemet drove a straight route to Georgetown and Aldrich's townhouse. We jumped out of our vehicle in front, leaving it running and the hazard lights blinking. We kicked the snow off our feet on the lobby rug then rode the elevator to the second floor. Hemet wasted no time, me following him around a corner, down the hallway next to condo 215. There we waited.

When we were sure the hallway was clear, Hemet knocked. Renz spoke to him through the intercom. Hemet said he had emergency news for the law firm partner. Renz opened the door, and Hemet was upon Renz, gun in hand, pressing it against the man's skull right behind his ear.

"You will come with me, and you will not struggle," said Hemet. "If you struggle, I will shoot you. I have shot many of your kind. I hate moles, and I hate you, and I will not hesitate to shoot you. Is there anything about that you don't understand?"

"I understand. No need to shoot me."

We went back down to the ground floor, where we passed through the lobby unnoticed. Then we were inside the SUV, and Hemet was handcuffing Aldrich's wrists and ankles.

"It hurts my ankles," complained the white-faced lawyer.

"It won't be long now until you get them off," said Hemet. "Try sitting back and closing your eyes and counting FBI agents. It works."

"I know it's a joke, but I'm sorry, I can't laugh."

I was now riding in the backseat behind our prisoner. Our leader turned and called back to me, "Take out your gun and shoot this man if he tries anything. If he even twitches his lip wrong, shoot him."

"I will do that," I said, not meaning a word of it. I had my agreement with Aldrich, and Hemet was unaware. Which told me I was closer to what Lakin wanted for Aldrich than Hemet was. Aldrich wanted him to pass fake documents while Hemet wanted him dead.

We parked at a boat rental on the river. We climbed out, and Hemet led us onto the gangway where we proceeded down maybe thirty yards, where he stopped at a boat and indicated we should climb on board. The boat was a Grand Banks Eastbay 44 cabin cruiser with an enclosed helm and an outside seating area.

"I can't do it," said Aldrich. "Not with my ankles handcuffed."

"Oh, but you can," said Hemet. "Sit your butt down on the edge of the boat and swing your legs over. Miles will hold you from the back, and I have your hands. That's right, come on now, okay, now stand up."

The white-faced lawyer stood in the bow until Hemet seized him by the collar and walked him to the captain's chair. Hemet sat him down next to the captain's chair, removed the handcuffs from his right wrist, and placed that handcuff around a stanchion supporting the roof above the boat. Now he had his man within view, captured by the handcuffs, so he could not escape. I took a seat behind Hemet and zipped my parka tight against the icy winds that I knew lay just ahead.

We backed out of the slip slowly, and then Hemet switched into drive, and we left the slow water without creating a wake. Once we were free of it, our bow came out of the water as 300 Evinrude horses took control. I was thrown back against my seat, and I saw Aldrich shoot out his free hand and grab a stanchion for support. Hemet turned his head to me and cried out, "Ain't this great? Who would've thought we would be on the Potomac River in the dead of night in the middle of an ice storm?"

For the next thirty minutes, we ran straight downriver in -30-degree air. By the time we arrived at Hemet's target spot, I was frozen from head to toe and wishing I had never left the warmth of my bedroom that morning. Yet, there we were, and Hemet suddenly cut the engine. The boat rocked back and then forward into a deep swell as the trailing water rushed up against the stern. This happened several more times, the boat gentling itself each time.

"Now," said Hemet, "it is time for you to get dumb. You know how to get dumb, Renz?"

"I do not know what you're talking about. But it's cold out here, and you will do nothing to me that would violate my rights. I am a member of the bar of the US Supreme Court. You would be smart to return me to my home right now and quit this nonsense. There are rules about lawyers and law firms and their employees. Those rules protect me, as you well know!"

At that point, Hemet stood and unlocked the handcuff that kept Aldrich in place. He captured the man's loose hand, drew it behind his back, and handcuffed it to the other hand. Now, Aldrich was handcuffed at his ankles and with his hands behind his back. He walked Renz out from under the roof and back to the unprotected seating area.

Then I heard Hemet say, "We have a witness tonight. His name is Miles Standish. He has been looking for you."

"Witness to what?" asked Renz.

"Witness to what you are, of course. Tell us what you find so terrible about the United States you would actively try to destroy her physical beauty?"

"I love America. I didn't hurt America. I'm "cooperating now. Ask Miles!"

He turned to me. I could see the pale disk of his face in the running lights. "Miles? What's he saying about cooperating?"

"Absolutely true. He's working with me now." It was all I felt comfortable saying. I withheld letting him know about our disinformation campaign, where Renz passed false documents.

"Then you're making a huge mistake, Miles. We have us a real traitor right here. I'm finished with him." He turned away and pointed his gun at Renz.

"Renz is a good soldier," I hurried to say to Hemet's back. "Whenever I've needed someone in the past, Renz has always been there. I'm feeling shaky about this. I gave him my word that I'd give him the chance to spread disinformation to the Russians in a plea agreement. He's already agreed to do that. What changed it into this—murder?" I said on a rising note. My voice was loud and carried across the water. And it got Hemet's attention, too, because he turned around and looked at me.

"You, too?" he said to me. "Weak in the knees, are we tonight?"

"Let's stop all this and return to shore."

I heard a struggle as Hemet moved Renz to the rear of the boat, and then there were no words said as he pushed the lawyer overboard.

It stunned me how he didn't hesitate to kill. Then he looked at me with a mad look in his eye. "Do I sense weakness in you, Miles?"

"Enough killing."

Without thinking, I headed for the stern. There was a paddle there and a net. I knew what had to be done.

"He'll be dead in five minutes," said Hemet. "I think we should wait and make sure that an ocean liner does not come along and save his sorry ass."

"We are going to get him out. Hold that paddle out to him, Hemet. I'm in charge now."

"You're in charge?" Suddenly, he went for his gun. I wasn't even thinking now. My hand went into my pocket and grabbed the gun Hemet had given me. I knew it was a Glock and had no external safety. It was ready to fire. In a split second, I had the gun pointed at him through my pants, and I pulled the trigger. The gun exploded, and the bullet found Hemet, knocking him back over the stern and into the water. Without hesitation, I grabbed the paddle and held it out to Renz, who was floating on his back but disappearing under with each second.

"Grab the paddle," I shouted. "It's on your left."

"Can't—hands are cuffed."

Before leaping from the stern toward Aldrich, the last thing I confirmed was a ladder and a platform. The boat had both, but it didn't matter anyway because I hit the water like a pancake. But I'm a strong swimmer, even with my titanium right side. I wouldn't let the man die. It was two sweeps of my arms over to Aldrich.

I saw his situation and let go of the paddle. Then I seized his upper arm and dragged him back to the boat. I pulled myself up onto the platform, which stretched across the stern. Right behind me came Aldrich, who I rolled up onto the platform.

I swung my leg over and down into the boat and reached Aldrich. "I'm going to pull, and you're going to stand. One, two, three!"

I pulled his upper arms with all my strength, and Aldrich got his feet under him. Now he was half-standing, so I could grab him around the waist and drag him into the boat.

"I—I—"

"You're freezing. Got it."

I was, too, but he was in shock, and I wasn't. So I covered him with my parka and bundled him as best I could.

I was standing right above Aldrich, my face just above his. "Of course, you saw none of this," I demanded.

"I saw nothing," Renz choked out. "Free—freezing, Miles."

I dragged Renz up into the cabin and arranged him in a captain's chair in front of a vent. Then I turned the heater on high and brought the boat around. Seconds later, we were up on plane and racing back to the anchorage. I checked the heat vents in the captain's pod and found them wide open. They helped somewhat after my dip in the water, but I still shivered.

At the slip, I tied up the boat, all the time shouting for the night watchman. He came and helped me get Aldrich into the warmth of his watch station. He poured two cups of hot coffee into Styrofoam cups and passed them to us. My FBI escorts were just outside the station, sitting in their SUV and watching my every movement. I knocked on their window and asked them to bring a handcuff key. Then I returned to the watch station and turned my attention to the night watchman. So far, he had said nothing about the handcuffs. But that wasn't good enough.

"I have one thousand dollars that say you saw nothing here tonight," I told him. "Am I right?"

"No need. You'd be amazed by all I see. I keep my job because I don't see."

"One thousand in twenty-four hours. I'll have it here. And I'll be watching you. Never breathe a word of this, or I'm coming after you myself. Do you understand?"

"There's no need for that, mister. I haven't seen nothing."

"Me and you," I said. "I'm watching the night watchman."

My driver and I took Aldrich to my house. Inga and I nursed him the rest of that weekend. By Monday, he was ready to go to work.

But I took him to court.

And an FBI agent took $1000 down to the Potomac River.

Chapter Fifty-Five

MILES STANDISH

The next day, at 9 a.m., District Court Judge Enzo Perini told the bailiffs to lock the doors to his courtroom. I then walked up to the lectern, and a US marshal brought Renz Aldrich, still in handcuffs, to stand beside me. Judge Perini looked down from the bench, then said, "You are Miles Standish and next to you today is Renz Aldrich. Is that correct?"

"It is, Your Honor."

"Mr. Aldrich is here to enter his plea of guilty according to negotiations he has had with your office, Mr. Standish. Is Mr. Aldrich represented by counsel today?"

"I am not, Your Honor. I am a lawyer, and I know what I am doing, and I want to do it without the necessity of hiring a lawyer."

"Very well. It's unusual, but it's been done before. Mr. Standish, I have received a copy of the plea agreement signed by you and Mr. Aldrich. Are there any other matters pertaining to the plea of guilty not included in the written plea agreement?"

"No, Your Honor. It is complete and contained on the paper you have before you."

Judge Perini took a few more minutes as he again looked over the plea agreement. Then he finally looked up and directed his remarks to Aldrich. "Renz Aldrich, for the record, you are forty-four years old, unmarried, and live in the greater DC area. Is this correct?"

"It is, Your Honor."

"And you're presently employed at Gray?"

"I am. My area of practice is environmental law. I am one of the two-hundred attorneys practicing in that area at Gray. I am not in litigation but in the office practice where I help prepare everything and anything my trial colleagues need."

"This plea agreement contains your signature, is that correct?" Judge Perini held up the copy of the plea agreement for Aldrich to see as he asked his question.

"That is my signature on the plea agreement, Your Honor."

"According to the terms of the plea agreement, you will plead guilty to one count of violation of the US Secrets Act. Is that correct?"

"It is, Your Honor."

"And in return, you will be placed on ten years' probation. Is that your understanding?"

"That is my understanding, Your Honor. Along with other obligations, I will now have to perform."

"Besides the ten years' probation, you will cooperate with the special counsel's request regarding the delivery of Gray documents to Western Energy Reserves. Is this correct?"

"It is, Your Honor."

"And should you fail or refuse to perform your obligations, then this agreement is null and void, and you will be returned to court for sentencing. You understand that?"

"I understand that, Your Honor. I intend to perform every action I am asked to perform by the special counsel or his successor."

"And you understand that your serving this plea agreement might put you at high risk of great bodily harm or death?"

"I understand that Your Honor, and I find those risks acceptable."

"Regarding the plea itself, your bio with this court will be sequestered and will not appear on any official case list promulgated by this court. Your case will be top secret and a matter of national security. You are ordered never to reveal this case or what happened here this morning. You understand that?"

"I do."

"And you further understand that if you violate these terms and reveal this case to anyone, this agreement shall be null and void, and you will be returned to my court for sentencing?"

"I understand that, Your Honor. I intend to tell no one."

"Finally, no referral will be made of this case to the Bar Association because the agreement calls for you to continue in your present job as a lawyer. You understand that?"

"I do, Your Honor, and I am extremely grateful for this."

"Mr. Standish, have I left anything out?"

"I think not, Your Honor," I said.

"I will not put into the record the factual basis for the plea in case someone obtains access to this file illegally. The defendant understands that the court does not require the special attorney to proffer facts upon which to base your plea, Mr. Aldrich?"

"I do, Your Honor. And I also agree that, as a matter of law, there exists a factual basis for my plea."

"That was going to be my next question. Thank you for volunteering that. Gentlemen, the court accepts the plea agreement and enters judgment accordingly. I am now going to call this session of court ended. I wish you well."

"Thank you, Your Honor," I said.

"Same for me, Your Honor," said Aldrich. "Thank you sincerely."

At 9:30, we walked out of the courtroom and went our separate ways--him to Gray law and me to Potomac River Runners, where Benji and I kept our boat. I called his school along the way and asked to speak to the principal. When she came on the line, I gave her the full truth. "I'm his Big Brother ten years and his stepfather after a full court hearing and investigation by social services. Well, it's incumbent on me to close any gap between my son and me. Today, I'm going fishing on our boat. I want him to be excused from school for the rest of the day and join me. It's all about bonding, and right now, we need it, as I work such long hours. What do you think?"

"I think it's unusual, and we have no place in our policies for such an absence. But I also think I have enough power to override policy when the facts require it. It sounds to me like this is one of those times. You may collect Benji from the office in fifteen minutes. And have a wonderful day with your son, Mr. Standish."

"Oh, thank you! We're going to have a beautiful time. The sun is shining, the water is the perfect temperature for the fish to feed, and our boat is gassed and chomping at the bit to go. Thank you!"

"Enjoy, Mr. Standish. I agree with what you're doing and give my full buy-in."

We ended the call, and I set the GPS for Benji's school. Twenty minutes later, he was beside me in my car, smiling ear to ear, astonished at his great good fortune.

"How would you feel about being captain today? I think it's time you learned to operate and drive the boat."

"Oh my--you mean it, Dad? I get to start it and back it out and drive it by myself? No one is gonna believe this. My answer is hell yes."

"Just yes, will do, Benj."

After a day on the water--with Benji safely operating the boat the entire time, we docked in our slip at 4:30. We drove home, talking about our boat as we went along. It had been incredible, and I realized again just how much I loved my boy. And I was starting to believe it was reciprocal. We went through a drive-through and picked up Subway sandwiches, salads, and root beer.

At home, the first thing was settling in front of the TV to watch baseball and chomp on subways. But before I broke the news to Benji, I still had the sound off.

"Okay," I said, "when we finish eating, you're going to first take a shower and wash off the river. Next, you're going to check your email and get your teachers' assignments for tomorrow. I arranged that. You'll work these through, and let me go over them with you when you're done. Then you get an hour of free computer time. Questions?"

"It has been a cool day. I'm glad to do my schoolwork. I want a great college and job and a chance to buy my son a boat, too. I'm off to the showers, Dad."

My mind drifted watching the baseball players come and go at home plate. I was thinking about Renz Aldrich and Benji. The only answer was to start young and stay with them every step.

Benji and I were in lockstep, and it was going to stay that way.

I got up, stuffed the sandwich wrappers in the trash compactor, and hit the shower. I had work to do before tomorrow because I'd played hooky, too.

Chapter Fifty-Six

MILES STANDISH

Marshall Lakin wasted no time calling me that noon.

"Miles, I'm in something of a panic," he began, "and the FBI doesn't have panics. We can't find Franklin Hemet. Were you with him Friday night?"

"Me? Not at all."

"Well, we can't locate Frank Hemet, and now I find out you've snuck Renz Aldrich into court and cut a deal with the judge. Now Aldrich is untouchable. And I have no plans to use him to provide disinformation to WER. You've wasted your time."

"Not to worry," I said. "I have enough plans for him that'll take years. I'm going to turn the Russians upside-down for you, Lakin. I don't need the feds."

"I can have you removed as Special Assistant U.S. Attorney."

"Have at it. I'm going rogue. The Russians are mine, too, not yours, if that's how you want to play it. It would be best if you were meeting with your DOJ friends to figure out how to sweet-talk me out of all the Russian intelligence

I'm going to be collecting out of this. Right now, I'm not feeling very cooperative, Lakin, with your threatening and more threatening."

"What have you done with Frank Hemet?"

"Why would you think I had anything to do with Hemet?"

I already knew the answer to that one. Lakin had known Hemet was coming for Aldrich to murder him. He might even have ordered the hit. But I also knew he could never admit that. No one wants to admit to conspiracy to murder.

So we quickly ran out of things to talk about. We hung up. No goodbyes, no talk-laters, nothing,

I had been telling the truth: Aldrich belonged to me now. It was like I had a loaded gun pointing right at the Russian oligarchs. Would I pull the trigger?

Ask Frank Hemet.

Chapter Fifty-Seven

ROMAN CHALLIS

Monday 7:45 a.m., just as the neighborhood kids were getting off to school and the neighborhood parents were getting off to work, an FBI van rolled into the driveway of Roman Challis. The doors flew open as six special agents surrounded all entrances. Special Agent Jimmy Zumwalt stood at the front door, rang the bell twice, and then rapped his knuckles hard five times on the hardStandish door. A fully dressed man holding a coffee cup answered the door and stepped onto the porch ten seconds later.

"You Roman Challis?" said Special Agent Zumwalt, who knew he was Challis because Zumwalt had worked the case since the first assignment. He had been to St. Petersburg, Russia, and Zürich, Switzerland. From St. Petersburg, he had traced the transfer of the $100,000, which Challis had then placed in a numbered account in Zürich, in the name of Inga Kopovsky. The FBI has been all over it like a cheap suit. They knew exactly why it had been done, which was not a crime. But they also knew the required foreign bank account disclosures had not been filed with the government of the United States, which was a crime. Max Jennings had already been arrested that morning. Only Roman Challis remained.

Challis, trying to appear unflustered, crossed arms and said to Zumwalt, "You're trespassing. Get off of my property immediately."

"Mr. Challis, please face away from me and put your hands behind your back. You are under arrest for violation of the foreign bank accounts laws."

Challis hesitated but then set his coffee mug on the cement porch stoop and turned away from Jimmy Zumwalt. He put his hands behind his back, and now his heart was racing as he realized this was the real thing, and he was totally without power. He was Mirandized, then stuck into the 3rd-row seat of the FBI van, which contained a thick metal screen to separate it from the 2nd-row seating. Without a word to his wife, without a farewell, Challis rolled away, headed for jail.

Charges had already been filed—multi-count indictments against both Challis and Jennings. They were taken for an initial appearance at ten o'clock that morning before Judge Basil Johnstone. Johnstone was a thirty-year veteran of the US District Court and hated nothing more than lawyers brought before him in chains. He was very slow to accept any lawyer's set of facts, excuses, or affirmative defenses. He had never once found a lawyer mentally incompetent to stand trial in thirty years of hearing all about incompetency and why this or that lawyer should not have to stand trial.

Johnstone confirmed that counsel represented both attorneys and had received a copy of the indictments against them. He then went into the problem of getting out on bail, calendaring the trial, and finally set the bail at $5 million for each defendant. Their attorneys then lapsed into wailing and crying about the amount of the bonds and why they should be reduced, but Johnstone heard none of it.

"These are lawyers of thirty years," he said to the defense attorneys. "If they can't make bail on this amount by now, then they've done a damn poor job of making careers. The amount will remain unchanged. The defendants are remanded to the custody of the United States marshals and returned to jail unless they post bail. Please do not bother me with further motions to reduce their bail because they will be rejected out of hand. There will be no hearings, and there will be no opportunity for evidence presentation. The motions will be rejected. If you don't like this, you know the way to the appellate courts. But even that takes time." He smiled, and with that, the arraignments were concluded.

The handcuffed defendants tried to hide their faces from the press as they left the courtroom, but it just couldn't be done. Their photographs and video were all over the news in America that day.

It never occurred to Roman Challis or Max Jennings that morning that the partners at Gray would take such fast action.

But by one o'clock that afternoon, the partners were ready to vote.

Chapter Fifty-Eight

MILES STANDISH

The main conference room of Gray was on the seventh floor, which was the floor where the ten senior-most partners were officed. The conference room itself was smack dab in the middle of the hallway. It separated two offices to the north and two offices to the south. The second office to the north had been Tommy Gray's office and was now occupied by Roman Challis.

After the arraignment of Challis and Jennings, Inga Kopovsky, who had heard about the arraignment early enough to make it there in person, met with five others of the senior-most partners beginning at noon. Lunch was brought into the conference room, where the talk was subdued, and the faces strained and stressed. But amidst it sat Inga, who was all smiles and passing out barbs against the two indicted partners left and right. They had tried to smear her and send her to jail; they had succeeded only in sending themselves to prison while she had walked free of their accusations.

The acting chairman was Inga Kopovsky, and she called

the meeting to order at 12:05 p.m. Someone took roll. The partners present at the meeting were Inga, Arnie Truckee, Alice Mendelssohn, Alfred Falsgraf, Isabel Kipling, Dutch Higgelsford, and Denny Walsh. With Inga in the mix, they made up the new Board of Directors; their job was to select the new chairman and managing partner.

After calling the meeting to order and waiting for the others to settle, Inga spoke but was interrupted by the lunch delivery. They had ordered Chinese. Small boxes and chopsticks passed along the line and across the table. When everyone was satisfied they had their order, Inga began.

"No lawyer has had more to do with cleaning house at our law firm than Miles Standish. You all know this. And by now, you all know what he has done by solving Tommy's murder, catching Renz Aldrich, and prosecuting Challis and Jennings for their mess. My nomination for the chairman of Gray law is Miles Standish. Anyone else?"

Alfred Falsgraf spoke up. "Standish it is. Things were very smooth here under his leadership, and I think it's going to take a man of his stature to put us back upright. So, I second the nomination. Can we vote?"

There were nods all around the table. It had gone as Inga thought it would go with just one nomination.

"All those in favor of bringing Miles Standish back into the law firm as chairman, please say, 'aye.'"

Arnie Truckee: "Aye."

Alice Mendelssohn: "Aye."

Denny Walsh: "Aye."

Alfred Falsgraf: "Aye times ten. We wouldn't exist anymore without Miles."

Isabel Kipling: "Aye."

Dutch Higgelsford: "Aye. There's no doubt about this one."

"And I, Inga Kopovsky, also vote, aye."

Arnie Truckee piped up, "I say Inga has to carry Miles the bad news that he is again a Gray man. All in favor?"

There were five more 'ayes' with Arnie. Then Inga relented and cast her vote, too: "Aye."

She stood and abruptly left the room with a smile. "Ta, all. I'm off to Miles's remote office with the good news. Meeting adjourned."

Chapter Fifty-Nine

NADIA AND BENJI

She came quietly up the other side of Standish's housing block, slid out of her truck, came up through the neighbor's yard to the alley, and stopped behind the six-foot Standish fence. Holding her breath, she acclimated herself, listened for FBI sounds, and watched for FBI movements.

She returned to her van and pulled out a painting ladder, which she took up the driveway, around the house on the right, then across to the porch overhang, where she placed the ladder up against the drain gutter and immediately began climbing. Within seconds, she was on the rooftop and removing the sniper rifle carried inside the rifle bag she wore on her back. She had already assembled the gun. Withdrawing its black length, she uncapped the Leupold scope, pressed her eye near the small end of the scope, and looked for the greenhouse and a shadow inside.

Across the alley, inside Standish's house, stood Benji, seen through his bedroom window. Nadia swept the scope across the house when she saw a flash of movement as Benji changed his clothes after school. She found his window in her scope, and then she found him.

Her rifle's laser dot danced on his chest. He saw it there and stepped back out of his room, into the hallway. So, he thought, this is how she's coming for Miles. Now he knew her plan. He went into the kitchen and peered out the backyard windows through a green fern growing in the window. His face was masked; hers was not. He took several pictures of her with his phone, getting the best close-up he could manage.

He sat at the kitchen table and studied her picture. The phone's software enhanced her image, and he studied her features until they jumped fully into focus. Now he knew what she looked like.

Now he knew the face of the enemy.

Benji crept back down the hall and opened the door to Miles's room.

He rummaged through boxes and drawers for the gun the FBI had given Miles--Benji knew everything that came and went in his new home. If Miles wouldn't carry the gun for protection, Benji would. The gangsters taught the kids how to shoot in first grade in his old neighborhood. Age made no difference. If you were going to grow into adulthood there, you'd better know how to shoot.

And Benji had paid close attention. The Sig pistol was no stranger to him. He ejected the magazine, pulled back the slide, and locked it open as the bullet in the chamber popped out. He studied the bolt and studied the chamber. It was as recognizable as any other semi he'd shot. He popped the magazine back into the pistol grip, slapped it in place with his palm, and released the slide. Now there was one in the chamber and a full magazine.

The gun went back into its Kydex holster, then Benji left

the room with the holstered Sig 9 mm. He went into his room, found his heaviest pants belt, and slipped it into the blue jeans loops. The Kydex holster fit easily inside his waistband at nine o'clock, the Sig snug inside of that. Benji pulled a flannel shirt from his closet and slipped it on, unbuttoned and untucked. Now he was concealed, and he was ready.

Chapter Sixty

MILES STANDISH

Inga came into my office at 1:15 p.m. that afternoon as I was in the middle of drawing up interrogatory questions for the WER attorneys. They were difficult questions and complex, and I hoped they drove the Russians batty trying to answer.

"Inga," I said with a lilt in my voice. "It is so great to see you. Have you recovered yet from our barhopping after Challis and Jennings were indicted?"

She sat in a chair and crossed her legs with her purse on her lap. "Recovered, but I swear I'll never do it again. I am just too old for that kind of bullshit. Leave it to the fifties, forties, thirties, and twenties. I'm done. But that's not why I'm here. I'm here to bring you some great news."

I had an inkling what she might be there to tell me. It couldn't possibly happen, given all that had gone before.

"Let's see. You heard from Publishers' Clearinghouse to tell me I receive my choice of ten magazines every month for the next year free with no strings attached?"

"I'll buy you those magazines myself if you return to

Gray to read them in the spare time you'll never have. What say, are you up to it?"

"I think I heard that the new Board of Directors has met and voted. Is this true?"

"As true as the sky is blue. All that remains is for you to move back into your new office on the corner of the seventh floor of Gray. The staff are ready to assist you in bringing all the suits you want against WER. They are poised and waiting for you to give your instructions. Plus, we have made accommodations to enfold your staff in this building into Gray. They will receive commensurate work titles and responsibilities plus a 10% raise. Everyone wins."

"Speaking of raises, do I get one?" I asked. "And the only reason I ask is that it looks like Deonna is about to make off with seventy-five percent of my property. I need to be very careful about my next employment. It will have to be made up in the next five years for me to be happy. Is that going to be possible?"

"You know with you back at the helm, DOJ is going to be dumping more and more environmental cases in our lap. There will be money galore, and the board will see that you are handsomely taken care of."

"I've never decided before in my life based on salary. But this time I'm going to. Would you mind telling the others to have my office ready for me by eight tomorrow morning? And as far as the other people here, the FBI will want to move their property and our computer server system back to Gray. There are some serious top-secret documents and other matters on our servers. They won't allow anything other than moving it themselves. I'll call Marshall Lakin, and he can get right on that with his people."

"Please call him, then. That's one more item off my to-do list."

Chapter Sixty-One

MILES STANDISH

Three days later, I sat in the courtroom of Helena Johnson, family law judge. I was seated at counsel table with my attorney, Bertrand Ames. Deonna sat at the other counsel table with her attorney. It was the date the court had set for the trial of our dissolution of marriage many months ago.

But there would not be a trial. Deonna and I had decided upon a complete property settlement agreement. Now it was just a matter of going through the motions of having the court approve the property settlement agreement and signing off. We were there in person because Deonna had requested it be an in-person hearing. I did not know why she had done that, but there I was.

Judge Johnson asked us whether there was any other matter that needed to be brought up other than her signing the agreement, the order of dissolution of marriage, and fielding questions we might have.

Both sides were quiet.

Said Judge Johnson, "Before I sign these documents and

declare this marriage dissolved, do either of you have any last-minute questions?"

Deonna's attorney stood and told the court that Deonna would like to have a final discussion with the respondent, which was me.

The judge told her to go right ahead and called a recess in the case for fifteen minutes. She turned to other cases on her calendar while I followed Deonna out of the courtroom and into a private discussion office next door.

We went inside without our attorneys and sat down face-to-face across a small conference table.

Deonna went first. "Miles, I have to try one more time. I can't help it. I've just had a total change of heart. I no longer want this divorce. I want us to go to counseling and make every attempt to pull our marriage back together. I know you have feelings for me and hope you will join me in this."

"A month ago, I would have, Deonna. But I have met someone else, and I want to be with her, not you. I'm sorry your time with Max Jennings ended with his arrest, but you will be the better for it. Max is a conniving, deceitful son of a bitch, and he used his looks and your dissatisfaction to complete his scheme. You allowed that to happen, but you want to undo the damage that's been done? Afraid that's impossible. You broke my heart, Deonna, and I could never trust you with my heart again. You are a good person and a beautiful woman, and you will do well without me in your life. So let's go back into the courtroom and complete what we came here for. I am so, so ready for this to be over. I'm sorry to have to say that, but the last good feelings I had for you flew out the window when you moved Max into our home and flaunted your affair in my face. That killed me, so you were successful if that's what you meant to do. But now that's all yesterday, so let's go back in and get to it."

"All right, Miles. I appreciate your honesty."

Fifteen minutes later, the court had gone through all of its responsibilities and queried us regarding our commitment to the dissolution agreement. Once it was satisfied, the court declared our marriage dissolved and signed the dissolution agreement and divorce order.

Then it was done. I let Deonna exit the courtroom before me and purposely waited another ten minutes after that so that I would not run into her again.

My movers came that afternoon to move me into a condo I had rented and would now purchase in my name only. The place had four bedrooms and three baths, giving me plenty of room for visitors, hobbies, and the usual junk I hauled around wherever I went. Benji had a special room, a turret room overlooking Lake Demming, and a swimming pool. He immediately began ordering new posters.

Our marriage was over, and I was free.

I did not feel elated, and I did not feel depressed.

I only felt that it was time to return to my office and get back to work.

Chapter Sixty-Two

BENJI

My secretary had set up the meeting for the entire Environmental team at the Washington, DC, Hilton because Gray's conference rooms couldn't accommodate all 200 lawyers and staff together in one room. So we had made a weekend of it, starting Saturday noon and ending Sunday noon. The FBI swept the place, checked the waitstaff and their backgrounds, and watched the kitchen preparations up close.

Saturday's opening address was mine to do. I wasted no time, as this would be my most notable talk of the year.

"Hello, friends. I must bring you the history of the Russian oligarchs versus Putin versus the United States. The oligarchs are the people we've been suing, and they are who we are about to launch a massive new attack of lawsuits against from one end of America to the other.

"As far back as when Putin took over from Boris Yeltsin as Russian president, the oligarchs were the toughest nut for Putin to crack. These were Russian men who had risen to great financial prominence through their efforts, vision, and thievery. They were extremely powerful and frightened Putin; any of them could make a play for the presidency of Russia if he were angry enough about something Putin did. So it was incumbent upon Putin to keep them happy, but for his own welfare, it also meant he would have to keep them in place.

"A few months into his new regime in 2000, President Putin called the strongest oligarchs, including one named Mikhail Khodorkovsky, to a meeting at Joseph Stalin's old dacha just outside Moscow. The place was still furnished with the desk and daybed from where Stalin dreamed up his great purge of enemies. Millions were murdered from that desk and daybed. With that unsubtle statement, Putin laid down the new law or, more precisely, the new balance of power.

"He would allow the oligarchs to hang onto their ill-gotten gains, and he would allow them to keep operating as they had for the last ten years. But the condition was this: they would offer no opposition to the new regime in the Kremlin. If anybody in the room was unclear about the meaning of Putin's message that day or how strongly he meant what he said, what happened next to Mikhail Khodorkovsky soon ended all doubt.

"Khodorkovsky, who owned one-hundred percent of Yukos Oil, didn't know the limits, and he boldly crossed the ocean to America and cut a deal with Exxon-Mobil that would make him the wealthiest man in Russia. Remember that.

"Under Putin, the oligarchs increased their wealth tenfold in just a matter of years. Then the oligarchs came West. The United States became their most significant and most potentially lucrative hunting ground in their history. From the Western vantage point, Khodorkovsky's success was proof that free-market capitalism was still the bomb, so powerful it could grow blue-ribbon winners. Khodorkovsky then merged his oil company with another Russian oligarch, and he now owned the world's second-largest oil company. Putin and his Moscow clan were already wary of Khodorkovsky, and this new oil company proved an enormous threat.

"So, Putin did Putin.

"Putin's henchmen arrested Khodorkovsky. Putin took control of Yukos. Now he owned it.

"Western Energy Reserves replaced Yukos' oil grubbing in the United States. Remember, Putin secretly owns it. WER immediately got the lay of the land, and its Saudi-trained engineers decided the cheapest and most productive way of mining was by fracking. Fracking was only done in the US before as onetime experimentation by minor nobodies. But now, here came the biggest whale in the Russian oligarchy, ready to drill horizontally clear across Oklahoma if that's what it took to turn a profit.

"And so they did."

I paused and drank down half a bottle of water. Then I carefully plunged ahead, wanting to get it correct before my new group of lawyers—as I saw it. This was a new beginning for all of us. We were one team, and we would defeat the Russians.

"It wasn't six months before the Environmental Protection Agency was drowning in complaints, all associated with WER fracking activities, mainly in Oklahoma at that point. The EPA turned to the Department of Justice for legal muscle. The Department of Justice jumped right to it and quickly found itself outgunned on all sides. The oligarchs had too much money and could hire too many lawyers for the DOJ alone to enforce EPA laws and rules. So the

Department of Justice did what it usually did and hired outside law firms to do its fighting. Gray received most of those fracking cases against WER in place of the DOJ itself.

"Today, we stand at a crossroads. "Our law firm—your law firm—has just undergone a total reclamation project headed by me and supported by the Federal Bureau of Investigation. We all understand that the FBI *is* the Department of Justice carrying a gun. DOJ/FBI could not have a mole in Gray continually sabotaging its cases and losing them. Because I was on the outs with Gray, having been fired by Tommy Gray, the FBI came to me, thinking I knew as much about Gray as anyone they would find on the outside. My mandate was to find Tommy's killer and to find the person leaking documents to WER. Not necessarily the same person. By a series of rather fortunate occurrences, I could put the finger on the guilty party. I can't say any more about that.

"So, where does that leave us? I propose it leaves us in better shape than ever. We are strong, and we are hungry. But most of all, we are bright—no—we are brilliant. We have the best petroleum engineers on earth trained as lawyers, the same people in our litigation team. We have key petroleum engineers as our expert witnesses, along with geologists, cartographers, biologists, and wilderness people. Never has the United States launched such an attack from the inside on the inside. The time has come to drive these crazy sons of bitches off our land and reclaim it for our country.

"I am pleased to be back at Gray. In all truth, I have missed it greatly. Most of all, I missed the people of Gray. I know each one of you. I have been in your homes and at your parties, and even at your graduations as you collected degrees. I am proud to call you my friends; I am even prouder to call you my colleagues."

I could sense feet shuffling, and attention spans dropping off. So I made a point of closing up my remarks rather quickly.

"So just let me welcome you to the new Gray. May we live long and prosper."

I nodded, smiled, and stepped away from the podium.

I saw her, then, a shadow closing from my right side. She wore the hotel serving staff's white shirt and black skirt and carried a large silver tray of donuts and Danish. She approached and held out the tray. As if I was dreaming, I saw the tray fall away from her hands and saw her shake the linen cloth from her wrist. She raised a large black gun in her right hand; then, I saw the laser dot dance up my body. Just before she fired, I ducked and grabbed my head.

Then it was pandemonium, as I felt the single bullet enter just below my right eye socket. The bullet's foot-pounds slammed me backward against the wall. I slid down to the floor in a sitting position, fighting to remain conscious.

Through watery, bloody tears, I saw Benji come in from the wings, holding something. It was a gun—I knew it was the Sig pistol I'd been told to carry. Then the girl who shot me took aim to finish me, but Benji raised the Sig pistol and scored a perfect hit on the side of her head. She flew sideways as Benji raised both hands and shouted, he was my son, don't shoot! The feds didn't shoot him by some miracle, and I passed out.

My secretary told me the EMTs were there within minutes. They came to me and took me away on a gurney. Benji followed the gurney as one hulking FBI agent walked beside him, his arm draped over Benji's shoulders.

Chapter Sixty-Three

MILES STANDISH

The following days in the hospital were taken up with physicians and X-ray techs coming and going, nurses talking to me and doing vitals, and visits from Gray staff, including Inga, who refused to leave my side. Benji was in school during the days, but he stayed every second until Inga took him to my house. She slept there, monitoring my boy. It turned out he needed counseling twice a week to help him work through shooting and killing someone. He attended religiously every day he had a session. When I came home, he was already faring well.

My trauma surgeon came on the second day and told me I had suffered a gunshot wound from a small-caliber gun. The bullet entered my face from the side below my right eye and was still lodged in the socket. They were afraid to remove it until they had the swelling under control and could visualize the nerves and bony structures at the wound site.

Drugs were plentiful, as it was an excruciating wound. The drip narcotic kept me on the borderline of sleep.

Lawyers in Gray

Coming awake and falling back asleep every few minutes left me stranded in a dream. Poor Inga couldn't reach me through my fog. But I felt her presence and knew she held my hand in hers many times.

It was a three-day hospital stay. Then I was released home in her care—more sleep but tapering off the pain meds until I was on OTC Tylenol. A week after the shooting, I re-entered the hospital, and they removed the bullet. It was not a painful surgery, and I was released to return home the same day.

My shooter's name was Nadia Karamov. Nadia was a full-fledged member of the Russian spy service, the FSB. She had devoted her life to the service, was unmarried, and had no children. When in Russia, she lived with her mother in the country north of St. Petersburg, where, Lakin told me, they subsisted on eggs laid by their dozen chickens and meat from their pigs. That was the sum and substance of what they knew about my assassin, and they expected to learn little more. By way of payback to the Russians, the State Department ejected six Russian Embassy workers with the accusation of spying. It was a half-hearted response by State, Lakin admitted. I wasn't worth all that much on the State Department's list of important personalities.

Chapter Sixty-Four

MILES STANDISH

Two weeks after the surgery, I still suffered double vision in the injured eye. It affected my ability to walk evenly, even on flat surfaces—as if my artificial lower leg wasn't enough of a problem already. It caused unremitting dizziness and headaches that required dark glasses, even in my office.

I made it to the end of the third week and was happily surprised to finally experience a lessening of the double vision. My FBI bodyguards helped me out to my Mercedes and arranged me in the passenger's seat.

We stopped at my favorite coffee shop on the way home that evening. My head was throbbing with a migraine, and I just needed time to figure out the next part of the dance called my life.

Roman Challis and Max Jennings were transported to federal prison and were serving ten-year terms. Challis's wife had immediately sued him for divorce, and, as the grapevine had it, she had already sold all marital property and was moving to California. Max Jennings's lawyer told Gray that

Max would be out much sooner than anyone expected since he was waiting for the court to reconsider its sentence as too harsh. The reasoning went like this: Max had been following an employer's directions when he committed the crime of offshore banking and failure to comply with government regulations and registration. However, we had also found out that he was suffering from hepatitis C not long after he arrived in prison. What would happen to him from then on was anyone's guess.

Inga Kopovsky now stood next in line as chairman after me. It had crossed my mind that I wanted to step aside and put Gray behind me. But I still hadn't settled on that and knew I wouldn't for some time yet.

I ordered a refill on my coffee and a stack of apple pancakes when I received a phone call from Deonna. She lived in a long-term-stay hotel, went to therapy, did yoga, and was again involved in her psychology practice. We talked about some financial chores we had to do but did not talk about us.

But then I allowed myself one margin of error and asked her one question. "Can you tell me, in a sentence or two, what it was about me that turned you off to me? Why you ran to Max instead of me?"

"It just didn't work anymore."

I got up to leave the coffee shop but then sat back down. There was one more call I needed to make. It had been nagging me all day. I had the guy's cell number, so I pressed the call button.

"Devon Bradley? Miles Standish calling. Hey, I want to see where we stand on the Heinlein law firm's attempted takeover of Gray. Gerry Heinlein has said he has the DOJ's backing to do just that. True or false?"

"False. Absolutely, undeniably false. We are contracted

with Gray, and we plan on staying right there, Miles. So what else can I do for you?"

"I guess that's it. Thanks."

"Sure."

Now I could leave the coffee shop. By the time I got home, I was tired and just wanted to be alone. Inga was working late, and I needed to collapse in a corner and tell the world to move along without me.

Benji arrived home from school and sensed my condition. He kept it quiet but made me coffee and served toast with it, heavily buttered and slathered with fig jam. We talked little, but we didn't have to, as two guys totally comfortable with each other now.

Chapter Sixty-Five

MILES STANDISH

While shopping at an antique store in Maryland, I saw something that would change the course of my life. I decided I loved Inga and thought seriously about spending the rest of my life with her. But I wasn't feeling it. Then, as I watched her that morning while she talked to the salesman helping us, I wondered. He was a man in his forties, like me, but he smiled and gesticulated wildly over each item of antiquity he told her about as she shopped. She responded with smiles and laughter, and, for just a moment, I saw them as a couple. She seemed thrilled with him, and he was very easygoing, the type of man who attracted Inga. Of course, I compared myself to him, and I realized I came up way short. I was never that excited about what she liked, and I never got into such happy discussions about something she liked in some store, theater, or restaurant. I was non-talkative. Maybe, it occurred to me, she would be better off with a man like him rather than a man like me. I'm not sure what I was feeling; it was just a flash where I saw her truly happy with that man, and I couldn't think of such a moment with me where she was ever as free.

But I didn't speak up.

On the first spring day, we decided we would go to Las Vegas and get married. We would leave Benji for a week with his mother's sister, a kind woman married to a pastor in Pennsylvania. She would be glad to spend a week with Benji and told us to bring him right then.

Marriage for us was a spur-of-the-moment decision, yet it wasn't. The topic had been under discussion for some time, but she proposed to me that morning, and I said yes. We stopped whatever we were doing, grabbed some clothes, jumped in the car, and headed west. It seemed like a great idea, which helped me ignore the pool of reserve I carried in my gut. My little cautionary man inside got beat down, and so off we went.

On the outskirts of Cincinnati, some eight hours after leaving DC, I was close to having a nervous breakdown.

We were weaving through heavy rush hour traffic when I said out of the blue, "I think I'm rushing into this."

"Rushing into getting married?"

"It feels like I'm scared to death. This thing with Deonna has all but ruined me. I don't think I can give you what you need."

"Let me worry about that. I'm not complaining."

It just rolled out of me again as easily as when I shot Frank Hemet without softening the load. "I'm too newly divorced to be jumping right back into another marriage. I should wait at least two years and give myself time to assess and reassess who I am and who might make me happiest."

"Oh."

We found a hotel on the outskirts of Memphis and checked in. A college-age young man helped us with our luggage, and I tipped him and closed the door behind him. Then I went over and sat down on one of the queen-size beds and stared morosely at the floor. Inga immediately sat down across from me. She had been humming and had taken her makeup and beauty Ziploc bags into the bathroom and gotten herself arranged. I could see the fear in her eyes when she said to me, "Uh-oh, more second thoughts?"

"I'm not right."

She folded her hands in her lap. "You know, I have to say I've had the same thoughts about you. I didn't want you to be rushed by me. That's the last thing I wanted. And it was wrong of me to propose to you. It should have been the other way around, and I should've waited."

"We need to talk."

"I'm exhausted. Let's go down to the bar and have a glass of wine first. Please?"

We changed and went down. We carefully chose our wine, and I was halfway down the glass when Inga languidly looked over at me. "Would you be a sweetheart and grab my phone upstairs? It's in my purse. I need to make a call to check on my mother."

"Sure." I climbed off the lounge and headed upstairs. I found her purse on the bed where she'd left it. I've always hated opening women's purses, but I did it anyway and found the phone on top. I closed the purse and stood.

A nagging thought returned to my brain. Without hesitating, I logged into her phone—INGA11—with the login I knew. Then I went into her email account and read through her junk folder just for the hell of it. Sometimes people forget to delete those emails. And then I found it.

A confirmation email from Sportsman's Paradise in Arlington. The email confirmed her purchase of a brand-new Mossberg Shockwave shotgun two weeks before Tommy was murdered. I quickly forwarded the email to my email. My hands were shaking by now because I knew. The shotgun that had killed Tommy Gray was a Mossberg Shockwave. Inga had purchased a Mossberg Shockwave.

I went downstairs and handed her the phone. She immediately called her mother and lapsed into the nightly checkup I'd heard so many times. I jiggled my wine against its glass and tried to think.

When we went back upstairs, I went into the bathroom and locked the door. I sat there thinking. Then I flushed the toilet, waited several minutes, then flushed it again. Still, I didn't come out. Then I flushed again and opened the door.

"I'm sick," I said. "Too much stress."

"That doesn't surprise me. You've been through way too much. Let me get you some chicken noodle soup and get you into bed. You should also have some 7-Up with that. Take your clothes off."

We slept in separate beds that night. My sudden illness had worked. When we were awake, I told her I was still feeling awful. I told her I was confused and stretched to the point of breaking. I told her I needed time alone to unwind and sort through my feelings. She immediately agreed and said she'd fly back to DC alone. She wanted me to have the space I needed.

Chapter Sixty-Six

MILES STANDISH

We said goodbye at the hotel without a kiss or touch. Inga took an Uber to the airport in Indianapolis at noon. She had called and planned to fly back to DC and was eager to get going.

Then I was back on the freeway, headed for Vegas and my first real alone time in many, many years. *Alone* as in no one in the car with me. Somewhere behind, the FBI was still along.

I didn't know if I even liked myself anymore; that's how out of touch I was. But I was game, and being game counted for a lot. On I drove.

An hour later, I liked myself a lot more. And an hour after that, I was crazy for Miles Standish. Just that fast, I had myself back.

At around one o'clock that afternoon, I stopped at a Burger King and went inside to relieve myself. Then I came out and queued up. This was an easy one. I was really into the Whopper with fries and a chocolate shake. Original, no? Anyway, I found an empty table, sat down, turned off my mind, and tried to turn off the compulsion that wanted me to drive straight through to Las Vegas without stopping or seeing anything or quitting the road early enough to get a swim in a hotel pool.

Then I was back on the road again until I eventually stopped around five in the morning in Albuquerque. I checked into my room at a Best Western, called room service, and ordered a carafe of coffee. When it arrived, I pulled open the blinds and saw that the pool was just below. It was early in the day, and the only person there was a gentleman shirtless but wearing cargo shorts. He was leaned back on a chaise lounge and had spread a book across his eyes to avoid the sun while he napped. Two young girls arrived, maybe thirteen or fourteen, slathering themselves in sunblock while they arranged their seating and table, gabbed at each other, and laughed.

I needed a dog to help me through. It just came to me like unexpected grace.

I did some browsing on my smartphone and found the local dog pound. It was two miles beyond the other side of town, but I went anyway despite the rush-hour traffic.

I could see the place from the freeway, so I took the next off-ramp, turned right on the frontage road, and followed a sign that read No-Kill Animal House.

Parking my Mercedes and opening the door, I could see a chained-off area behind and to the side of the building. Dozens of dogs were walking around the chain-link fence in a repetitive swirl of canine angst as they waited to be adopted. Inside, I went up to the counter.

"Yes, sir, may I help you?" asked a young girl, who was probably a volunteer.

"I need companionship on my trip. A smaller animal who loves people and loves its owner."

"Wow, we have lots of those here. Is there any breed you prefer?"

"I know I like Lhasa apsos and cocker spaniels, and a friend of mine has a dog that is part Chihuahua and part Yorkie. He's a cute little thing and wants to live in my friend's lap. So there is plenty of companionship there. Do you have someplace we could walk and look at some of them?"

"Sure, just follow me, and we'll take a walk to the kennel."

And so I followed her through the door that led to a world of barking. Cages almost as far as the eye could see. Beautiful little animals, all of them wanting to get out of that cage and go home with someone. We began the walk. But it didn't take long. Three pens in, and I found one of those small pups that looked just like my friend's lapdog.

"Is this one up for adoption?"

"Sure. Do you want to hold him?"

"I do."

The puppy named Hank fit the crook of my arm perfectly. Then the face-licking began, and for the first time in months, I smiled a real smile. Hank had touched me just like that.

"Let's go to the paperwork. This guy is mine."

"Are you sure? There are fifty more dogs in here. You might find one you like even more."

"Like more than Hank? That's not gonna happen. Hank and I are already bonded. Let's pay his fees and let me get going. I have a long drive ahead of me."

"Really? Where are you going?"

"I'm going to Las Vegas to play the slot machines and stare at my belly button."

"Stare at your belly button? Is this a new thing?"

"It means that I'm going to practice being alone. And my friend Hank is going to help me do that."

"Wow, I wouldn't mind going to Las Vegas myself."

"Save your money. It can be expensive there."

We went back into the main lobby and did the paperwork, and I paid the $350 fee, which included room and board and all shots. Hank was ecstatic during the process. His tail wouldn't stop wagging. I knew I needed to find out what he was so happy about. He had a secret, and I wanted it, too.

"All right, thank you, Mr. Standish," the girl said. "You wouldn't have room in your car for one more, would you?"

"Sorry, I don't. There will be room for Hank and me alone."

Hank and I exited the front door and headed for my car. It first looked like he might sit in the passenger seat, but as soon as I got going, I found him in my lap, pressing his body against my chest as I drove. And it was a great feeling.

We drove back to the Best Western, and I napped for three or four hours while Hank sniffed every inch of the room nonstop.

Then we were on the road again, driving into the high sun.

We rolled in Sin City just before 3 p.m., and I checked into the Bellagio. No, I didn't get the suite, but I wanted a good room and amenities if I would find myself again.

Las Vegas was a zoo, but a fun zoo. I found that my favorite activity was finding a bench outside the hotel's casino and sitting there with Hank, watching the people go by. By now, I had purchased a kennel for Hank, a circular bed that fit inside the kennel, two kinds of dog food—bagged and canned—a half dozen chewy toys, and a white leash with rhinestones. Hank was all about the glitz and glamour of Las Vegas. I realized how lonely I must have looked based on the number of prostitutes who offered me their services. Then it hit me that if I entered a bar smiling and acknowledging other people I passed by, I didn't look so lonely. That seemed to moderate the number of drive-by flesh dealers.

On the night of the third day, I was tired of the casinos and did not go downstairs. Instead, I climbed up on my bed with my book of the day and patted the bed beside me for Hank. He came up immediately and crawled onto my lap. I could see there would be none of that "beside me" business. It was on top of me where he thought he belonged. I did not fight him off. I gave him full rein to make the rules about the two of us. So far, those rules were quite simple: hold him at all times, feed him Greenie treats, and take him outside to potty at least once an hour, which was usually nonproductive and turned into a bush-smelling venture for Hank.

Anyway, it was six o'clock that evening when I began my reading that would go on for hours. Hank shut his eyes and was asleep within minutes.

I soon followed, with a call to Benji, just checking in, then off to bed for me.

The next day, we turned around and headed home.

Chapter Sixty-Seven

MILES STANDISH

It took me three months to decide.

Three months to decide about Inga and her shotgun. She had bought the exact model of the gun that had killed him. She admitted being there the morning he died; she admitted to horrible fights—it was an open and shut case of first-degree murder.

She had killed Tommy Gray. Tommy Gray was a traitor, turning over top-secret documents to the Russians. But I wasn't sure that's why Inga killed him. It was almost a cliche that she had killed him because of a romance gone bad, so I discarded that. Put another way, when he died, she had Tommy, and she had her ex-husband, the Russian. The man selling top-secret documents and the man buying them. Did she fear them because she had become a witness and killed Tommy before he killed her?

In the third month, I called her into my office and confronted her. She sat down across from me, and I tossed a printed copy of the shotgun receipt to her. She picked it up and read. She couldn't stop reading. Finally, she looked up at me, and her eyes were full of tears.

"I need to know. What was your motive in killing Tommy Gray?"

She wiped away her tears and cleared her throat. "He was selling American secrets and wouldn't stop."

"You knew he was doing it?"

"Of course. He was selling them to my ex-husband. I had introduced them at a dinner party."

"What brought it to a head? Why did you pick that morning to shoot him?"

"The report from the Petroleum Engineering Institute. He was hours away from selling it."

I knew the report. It was the most damning piece of evidence we'd ever had against fracking—the most extensive study done of fracking and its aftermath. Had the Russians grabbed it, they could prepare an answer. But we were going to catch them off-guard and get a federal ruling that stopped them for good.

"He turned that over?"

"He was turning it over that day. So I shot him."

"Why didn't you ever tell me this before?"

"That's easy. You've been refusing all my calls."

"What evidence do you have he was turning over the PEI report?"

"You've seen his bank statements. You've seen the million-dollar deposit. You just didn't know what it was. The Russians couldn't do enough for Tommy."

"What else do you have? Just your word won't cut it."

"How about this statement from Dimitry Kopovsky admitting to the deal with Tommy?"

She played a recording on her phone. It was the recording she'd made the day she went to Oklahoma to tell

Dimitry goodbye. The speaker identified himself as her ex-husband, then admitted to the deal with Tommy Gray.

"This puts your case in a whole new light."

"What are you going to do?" she asked.

"What do you see me doing? Knowing me as you do?"

"I'm guessing you have two FBI agents outside waiting to arrest me."

I punched the call button on my phone. "Send them in."

The FBI agents quickly went about their work. Little was said. Just as they took her out the door, she turned to me.

"Are you sure, Miles? I know you love me."

I turned away.

Then she was gone. I had dismissed the indictment against Max two months ago. There had been no need for that to proceed, not once I had the purchase receipt from Inga's phone.

Inga called me from the jail the next morning.

"I know you hate this," she said. "Are you going to act as the prosecutor? Or will you give that to someone else because of us?"

"I have to go now, Inga. No, I won't be prosecuting. I'm blocking all calls from you, so your case isn't compromised."

I hung up.

Inga and her attorney convinced the US Attorney that the killing of Tommy Gray was a patriotic deed that saved America's efforts against the Russians. A sympathetic judge agreed and handed down a period of probation.

She was free again.

And I was glad.

Chapter Sixty-Eight

MILES STANDISH

Lakin and I hadn't talked since he lost Hemet, whose body never did wash ashore. I don't know why. But even if it had, they couldn't hang it on me. There was zero connection there.

Renz Aldrich and I kept slipping papers to Arkady Rezlof and the Russians in the best spirit of American patriotism. Papers containing false information about the lawsuits I managed against them. And it was working. We were winning again.

We had a large trial coming up. Our theory of liability was based on national defense laws, an approach we had taken to using. The Russians thought they knew the names of all our rebuttal witnesses. They had names, all right, thanks to what we gave them through Renz. But none of them were the names of actual witnesses. It was a trap, and they would fall right into it. That's how we planned to win North Dakota. Then Colorado. Then a new trial in Oklahoma. It wouldn't be Renz after North Dakota because the

Russians would know he was a double agent. There would be others. Renz, I would then leave alone. He had a decent future.

Until Christmas Eve. Arkady Rezlof got the bright idea it would be a great publicity stunt for Renz to take him to the Department of Justice Christmas Eve dinner and take his picture among the Americans. Aldrich refused at first, but Rezlof knew his trigger points. He threatened this or that; I am sure. Even more, Renz knew we needed Rezlof at the other end of the document funnel. So, last night, Renz Aldrich attended the DOJ Christmas Eve dinner with his guest, Arkady Rezlof, a very dangerous Russian spy.

Just before the main course was served, Aldrich excused himself (restroom) and dashed off to a quiet corner where he called me. I was in the middle of a fierce Canadian hockey game on ESPN.

He was breathless. "I'm here at the DOJ Christmas Party. Arkady Rezlof threatened me unless I took him along as my guest. He was adamant that I would memorialize his attendance with a series of photographs of him shaking high-and-mighty DOJ hands during the evening. Maybe even the attorney general, Miles. Long story short, it's propaganda they're after, Miles. Pictures of the Russians openly dining among the Department of Justice."

"Tell him--"

A loud slamming door, and then the phone went dead. My pulse raced, and I thought of who I might contact for help.

I called Marshall Lakin and reported.

"Thank you," he said. "Be out front in fifteen minutes." He hung up.

Christmas Eve, on my circular drive, the snow fell in

clumps. I wore hiking boots, khakis, two polypro tops, a windbreaker, and gloves. Tight and ready.

Sure enough, ten minutes later, a car came snaking up my drive. Its lights were on low, and the interior was dark. It stopped beside me, and the rear passenger door opened. I climbed inside.

"Miles," Marshall Lakin said from the passenger seat. "Russians just couldn't leave it alone, eh?"

"No, sir."

He sighed and stretched his arms as best he could in the cramped space. I couldn't get a look at the driver's face, but I had a feeling it didn't matter.

The trip was twenty minutes from my house to the banquet. We took 6th Street NW down to F Street, waited for a snowplow to move back into the right lane for all of a block while we followed, then stepped it up and took the last light on a stale yellow. We parked in front, and the driver didn't move. He turned off his lights.

"Well?" Marshall said with a look at me. "Shall we?"

"What are we doing?"

"What do you think we're doing?"

"I don't know. I'm terrified to find out about Renz Aldrich."

"Renz Aldrich is already dead. Let him go."

"Then what else?"

"We have a Russian spy inside the Department of Justice. We are going to remove him from the party. Follow me."

I did. I followed Lakin inside, into the vaulted lobby, where, instead of passing on into the banquet hall, we made a left. We passed through an electronic door with a keypad, which Lakin keyed to let us pass through. Then we traveled a second hall and made a right. We entered a second keypad room and looked at four men gathered around a steel table. Three of them wore dark business suits. The fourth was in formal wear. His eyes were clenched shut, and his face tilted to the ceiling. His lips were moving.

"He's all yours," said the closest business suit. He had a quart of Old Turkey on the table, and there were water glasses, dark liquid in each one, including Mr. Formal Attire.

"ID?" Lakin said.

"Fingerprints. Arkady Rezlof. Won't speak English. We don't know if he's praying or having an out-of-body experience. Hasn't touched his Christmas Eve toddy."

"Anything else?"

"Sig 365 in appendix carry, empty chamber. Don't they teach these shits anything?"

Lakin went to the man and, in a blink, had removed his own concealed weapon and pressed the muzzle against Rezlof's head. "Did you get your party pictures, Arkady?"

The lips stopped moving. He came upright in his chair. "I am with the Russian Embassy. You have no authority over me. I demand you deliver me there."

"All right," Lakin said, nodding for the man to see. "Let's go there."

Another drive through the dark, late Christmas Eve city. The streets were empty, and traffic lights flashed yellow. A few cops parked here and there, probably asleep in their prowl cars waiting for the night shift to end. Rezlof rode next to me in the backseat, sitting on his handcuffs. He didn't make a sound as we sloshed along through the melting snow. Eyes straight ahead, lips moving again, in another world.

Twenty minutes later, we pulled down a gravel lane that looked familiar. Then I got it—the plantation mansion where all this had begun. We stopped at the main door.

Only then did Rezlof look up. It wasn't the Russian Embassy. He turned to me. "Why are we here?"

I adopted the Bureau's stock response. "Why do you think we're here?"

Lakin swung open the front passenger door and jumped to his feet. "Gentlemen?" he said with a sweep of his arm. "Coming?"

The driver stepped out and turned and opened Rezlof's door. He pulled him to his feet and moved him around to Lakin. I climbed out and felt the skin crawling on my neck, for we were at the end, and I knew it.

Lakin opened the door to the mansion with his key, and the four of us filed inside. We went into the main room where we had first met. Lakin produced handcuffs and passed them to his driver. The driver pulled handcuffs off his belt and roughly moved Rezlof backward to a heat radiator. Using handcuffs from his belt to lengthen Lakin's cuffs, he secured the Russian to the radiator. Not to burn him or mistreat him, just to keep him in place.

Then Lakin came to me. He held out a small pistol. "Here. It's the one you murdered Frank Hemet with. Your prints were everywhere."

My knees buckled; I was in instant shock. How in God's name had they found it? I had tossed it into the Potomac. And my fingerprints? How on earth had they got useable fingerprints off a river gun? My mind was racing, looking for deniability, a story, an explanation, but nothing came. He had me. I would be prosecuted for the murder of an FBI agent.

His face was set, and his eyes were cold, hollow, in the black room. I had never known this Marshall Lakin.

I didn't know what he had in mind. But I took the gun from him.

"Mr. Standish, you have played the spy game, but now it's done. Your over-exuberance at tricking the Russians caused the death of Renz Aldrich. One of my best men."

I had no words. Renz? The Renz I knew? It all made sense about Renz just then. I understood why they had allowed him to stay free and a member of Gray. Renz, a double-agent. Renz wasn't really Renz. The Renz I knew was a made-up personality, a character some gifted agent had played. Stanislavsky, eat your heart out.

My head went spinning away; I had to slump into an upholstered chair. I had been living in a dream world. These people were way out of my league. I wanted no more of it, ever. "I want to go home."

Lakin turned as if to leave, then stopped. "When I return in the morning, one of you better be dead." He came back to me. "Here is the key to the handcuffs. Let's see if you are clever."

"Wait!" cried Rezlof. "This man is crazy! I can see it in his eyes!"

Lakin pursed his lips as if in thought. "Then he just might make it beyond six a.m."

With that, Lakin turned and placed his hand on the driver's back, who was walking ahead, and the next thing I heard was the SUV starting up.

The radiator hissed and ticked. I turned to Rezlof.

"I have to get angry at you," I said. "Did you kill Renz Aldrich?"

"No."

"See? You're lying to me already."

"Nonsense. We were fast friends for ten years. We served each other."

I casually pointed the gun at him. "Tell me about Russian spies in my law firm. I want names."

He tossed his head back and laughed. "Really? Or what? You'll shoot me? We both know you will do that, anyway. No, you must use a threat more imminent. Like maybe gouging out an eye. I have a feeling that would make me talk." He strained forward against his handcuffs. "Here's an eye. Here are two eyes. Take one out and you get the names of all Russian spies in your law firm." He had just called my bluff. He was a professional, and I was a weak civilian. That's what the FSB/KGB taught him.

I wanted those names. Gray belonged to me, and I wanted an exorcism. An eye for names? I felt the knife in my pocket, the razor-sharp blade I used for pruning Deonna's flowers. It would be enough.

The next part was a dream. I stood and rushed him, forcing him back against the radiator and the wall behind. I had my left arm across his throat as he twisted his head from side to side, avoiding the knife in my right. Then I caught his jaw with my elbow, and I had him.

The image of the moment still comes to me as the red-haired teen at 31 Flavors scooping a chocolate marshmallow out of its quart container and holding it for me to taste.

I had his eye on the end of my knife blade, and I staggered away from him. He was screaming, straining away from the radiator.

"Names," I said. "Speak names into my phone." I made myself move back and held the phone. "Speak."

He reeled off two quick names. I held up the eyeball I had speared on my blade. "More," I demanded."

"You already know Inga Kopovsky. There are no others I run."

"Fine." I switched off my phone.

He dropped his chin on his chest, exhausted from our

struggle, held upright by the handcuffs. He was alternating between low animal howls and cursing me in Russian—maybe it was cursing.

"Now, you must kill me," he said. "There are no one-eyed spies. They will return me to Moscow, and I will live under a bridge a month later when my separation pay runs out. Spare me that. Shoot me, please!"

I had shot Hemet to save Renz, but I couldn't shoot Rezlof to save myself. It just didn't work that way. So I ran the scenarios. If I just handed him the gun, he would shoot me. If I didn't shoot him, Lakin would shoot me. If I ran, they would hunt me down.

Wait. What had Lakin said about the handcuff key? See if I am clever enough? The clouds in my over-taxed brain parted, and I caught a glimmer.

"I won't shoot you, Rezlof. But I will let you shoot yourself."

I sprung the magazine from the Glock pistol. Next, I removed a cartridge from the magazine, inserted it into the chamber, and racked the gun.

"How will I ever shoot myself?" he cried. "I'm bound like a pig."

"I am giving you five minutes alone with the gun. If you have the courage I think you have, you will destroy yourself. If you don't, I will return for the second eye. Then I will see to it you're returned to Russia, and we will make it known you are cooperating with the United States. Here we are. I'm freeing your right hand."

Using the tiny handcuff key, I sprung the right handcuff, and his right arm swung free. He squeezed and released his fist several times. Then he swung his arm up and back, up and back.

"Look at me."

"I'm blind! You damn fool!"

"Look."

He fastened his remaining eye on mine. "I am not your enemy. I am your answer. I will move back to the door and slide the gun to you. You'll know what to do from there."

I stepped back to the doorway and positioned myself so I could duck behind the plaster wall. Then I slid the gun across the Standish floor, watching it slide up to the toes of his dress shoes and stop. He bent down.

Behind the wall, I moved several steps down the hall, fighting the second-guesses now pouring into my mind. How stupid was I? What would have been so wrong about shooting a soldier, an enemy of the United States? What the hell had I done? I put my face into the wall and held my breath.

It wasn't long. I heard him weakly cry out a single Russian word; then, I heard the roar of the gun. It was several minutes before I peered around the corner. Seeing him slumped against his handcuffs, his free hand dangling almost to the floor, almost down to the gun that lay just out of reach, I breathed out all my air.

I checked my watch—dead body time. 12:15 a.m. So be it. I punched up the Uber app on my phone. I was taking myself home. I keyed in the request at my geo-location and pocketed the phone. A driver was seven minutes away here in Maryland.

I refused to approach the body. But then the clouds parted, and I saw a golden opportunity.

Lakin had left me with the only connection to the murder of Frank Hemet, which was Hemet's gun. I was certain they had retrieved it and already had run the ballistics tests against Hemet's known sidearms and found this Glock to be the one that fired the single bullet that killed him. Now, all I had to do was take it away, and I was free because they couldn't take me to court and say they'd lost the gun. I scrambled up to the dead body and walked straight out of the room, the warm Glock inside my right front pants pocket.

Lakin had paid me back by giving me a chance.

Chapter Sixty-Nine

MILES STANDISH

Ninety minutes later, I lay in my bed at home, hopelessly awake and fighting off wracking chills that shook me like a leaf.

Just before dawn, I stumbled from my bedroom and retrieved the *Post* from the front porch. Maybe there would be news about Renz. Most likely not.

Hank pawed my ankle to remind me. Of course, Hank food.

Feeling not the least bit hopeful, I first made coffee and checked the squirrel feeder. I added corn nuts. Next, Hank got a bowl of Dr. Marty's. Then I sat down in my chair and read the report of the DOJ Christmas party last night.

Nothing after three paragraphs, two to go.

Then there it was. In the final paragraph, the *Post* reported a DOJ contract lawyer in attendance at the banquet was found dead in the restroom after suffering a fall on a wet floor. Identification withheld pending etcetera.

I immediately called Lakin, who, perhaps knowing I

wouldn't stop calling, took my call even before the sun was up.

He listened without comment. He said nothing when I finished reading aloud to him.

"Well?" I asked. "What do you have to say about it?"

"Damn poor reporting. It wasn't in the restroom where Rezlof broke Aldrich's neck. But he put him there and dumped a massive overflow from the sink onto the tile floor to make it look like poor Renz had slipped and broken his neck."

"And?"

"And you have a law firm to run. I've made sure of that. Get back to it, please, and no more lost documents."

"I think we're done with all that."

"Be very sure of that. And lose this number."

That was two years ago, and that's the last I heard about Lakin until tonight when Reggie Theobald called me at home. He began slowly.

"New Year's Eve two years ago, Lakin passed me a note at the firm party. I was just elected chair of the hiring committee. The note said, 'Michigan law alumni. Number 2 in class. 7th Circuit Clerkship. Mother nursing home. Greenhouse hobbyist. Immediate hire. No questions.'"

"What was that about?"

"I caught up to him at the bar. He said you had signed off on it."

"Never heard of it until right now. What did you do?"

"I just hired them. No problem. Until now."

"What is it?"

"We had two new applicants this week for the litigation team—identical resumes. Michigan, second in class, Seventh Circuit clerkships, mothers in DC nursing homes. One raises Rocky Mountain wildflowers in his greenhouse;

the other is into plains grasses, for fuck's sake. My second in command, Jan Stage, noticed the identical resumes, of course. She's raising hell about it and threatening to take this outside the firm. She says the government is behind it."

"Let me get back to you."

I hung up and even though it was past nine, and even though it was New Year's Eve, I headed straight for the office, my FBI driver and escort vehicle providing security and transport. Four other agents watched my house—and Benji—as I set off.

It took us twenty minutes to navigate the salted roads to my office. We made all the lights and parked in my slot, where I hit the ground doing the best hurry-up I could manage.

Into the elevator, I hurried and pressed 7. I wasn't in a great rush, but I felt the nerves.

My computer was always on. Even as I unzipped my parka, I opened the firm's personnel files. Oddly enough, I had never even bothered to look at my personnel file before, but something was making me very nervous.

I found my resume from my first job application in 1999 —University of Michigan, second in class. I had clerked for Henry Armstrong, Chief Judge of the Seventh Circuit. My mother lived in a DC nursing home. What the hell?

My fingers wouldn't type fast enough as I retrieved the Frank Hemet resume next. University of Michigan, second in law class, Seventh Circuit Court of Appeals, mom in Daylight Manor in Virginia. Greenhouse specialist in Andean wildflowers. Right, and my name is Abraham Lincoln.

Now I searched all 750 Gray lawyers by alma mater and came up with eleven from University of Michigan, second in class, 7th Circuit clerkships, mothers in DC care centers, greenhouse hobbyists.

Okay, got it. But what was their purpose at Gray? I read further in the file of Noel Hardesty (Michigan, 2015). There was a portion titled Projects, which contained dated entries. Noel had been busy leading the charge to implement new methods for controlling top-secret documents. He now had those attorneys handling sensitive materials working in twos, never alone. Reading on, Donald M. Chase (Michigan 2012) had taken over disinformation. Thanks to Donald, we now ginned up a thousand disinformation pages to dump on the Russian lawyers every time we sued a Russian fracker. And it was all different. Our adversaries no longer knew what was real versus what was the work of the technical writers who'd taken over two offices on the third floor, ripped out the wall between them, and shoved their desks together. They dreamed up new reports, studies, and university experiments we weaponized and delivered to the Russians. Gray law had no pity.

So that was it. Lakin's FBI agents had infiltrated my firm right under my nose. How much trouble were we in? I began with Gray's numbers. We had won twenty-three EPA lawsuits in the last twelve months and had lost none. Our documents were no longer walking off. That was all sunshine and roses.

Eleven FBI agents were loose in the firm. It was a government takeover of a private law firm. If Congress ever found out, someone might go to prison. I could hear the congressional committee asking where the hell I'd been while all this was going on.

I pulled on my gloves, then decided I'd have a quick drink for Auld Lang Syne—I wasn't driving. My bottom right drawer held the scotch I lifted and set on my desk—

two fingers in a water glass. Just as I raised the bottle to pour, my eyes went to the very bottom of the open drawer. There it was. I hadn't even thrown the gun back into the river. I had known Lakin would only find it again.

I had a drink for Deonna. Goodbye and best of luck. I had a drink for Inga. I'm so sorry you sent me back to the room for your phone that day at the pool. I had a drink for Frank Hemet, who I shot to save Renz Aldrich. Then a swallow of whiskey for Arkady Rezlof, who shot himself rather than return to Russia blind and accused of cooperating with the West.

Here was my New Year's Eve gut check just as I was about to leave. The Russians had sent an assassin to murder me. The FBI had investigated. We knew who she was and why she came after me. I knew all about her preparations to shoot a bullet into my greenhouse and my head. She hadn't counted on anyone knowing what she looked like; Benji proved her mistaken and shot her dead. My PTSD had worsened, and it took twice as long to talk myself down. The FBI had ordered me to appear at the Bureau's gun range twice a week. The instructor told me, "Put a target on your wall at home. Draw your gun and dry-fire 100 times a day. If they send another assassin, we don't want a fair fight —we want you to shoot first. That's the preferred order of things when the guns come out."

My PTSD fed off that combat preparation. My hands shook, and desert scenes of blown-up legs returned to sweep me away. I resisted because I knew there was a safe place for me at home. Benji would wait up with a movie ready to roll after we'd made popcorn and hot apple cider.

I swallowed down the rest of my scotch and shut off the lights with thoughts of a certain dog named Hank sitting atop the living room couch, fixated on the circular drive and the headlights that would come sweeping home at any moment. Since I bought out Deonna's half in the divorce, I owned the house.

Including the flowers.

Riding home that night, it pissed me off about the flowers. It was the scotch that brought the flowers and the ex- to mind. I found myself thinking I might just toss the flowers.

Then I'd put in a dog kennel and adopt friends for Hank.

"Happy New Year, Miles," said the driver up front, cutting through my mental routine.

"Happy New Year's to you too, Special Agent Tichenor."

I looked out the window. I could see no enemies out there.

I decided to see how smart the kennel and dead flowers looked tomorrow. That would be after the scotch had worn off and the PTSD was on simmer, and the sun was shining.

I was back and knew I would sleep all night without the dream.

It could happen.

Also by John Ellsworth

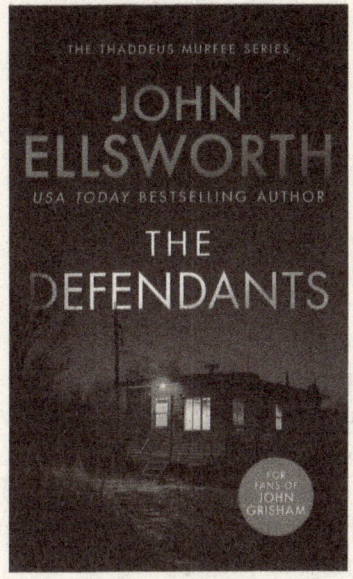

vinci-books.com/thedefendants

A killer client. A deadly case. A lawyer in over his head.

Young attorney Thaddeus Murfee lands his first big murder trial—but his greatest threat isn't the prosecution, it's his own client. As he navigates a treacherous web of secrets and lies, he must uncover the truth… before it buries him.

Turn the page for a free preview…

The Defendants: Chapter One

She was standing at the ancient desk in his law office when she unbuttoned her blouse. She was wearing a white button-down Ralph Lauren, paisley tie, khaki slacks, penny loafers, and a red barrette to keep the pageboy cut off her face.

Ermeline Ransom was thirty-two, the mother of Jaime, authentic blond, pale blue eyes. Like most cocktail waitresses she was a little taller than average, had clear skin and full lips, and was proud of her work and proud of her ability to support her little boy by honest work. Until last night she had no tattoos, but now she had a mess.

Ermeline began by loosening the tie and raising it over her head like a noose. Next, the blouse was unbuttoned, top to bottom. She was wearing what could only be a Victoria's Secret bra, with its trademark structural engineering, icy red, that featured a green butterfly where the bra clasped in front. The butterfly held everything together and it separated, wings to the left, thorax to the right. The girl clicked the butterfly and her breasts spilled forward, freed at last, and pointed at Attorney Thaddeus Murfee like two pears, separate but equal. She shivered and looked away.

Thaddeus Murfee's eyes bulged. "Good grief—who did this to you! Let me grab our camera!"

Thaddeus Murfee was twenty-five, unmarried, a member of Orbit's Rotary and Moose, and a lawyer of eighteen months. He was tall enough to play point guard— which he had, on the Arizona Wildcats team that went to the Sweet Sixteen. A bowl cut kept his dark brown hair naturally in place, and the wire spectacles with their round frames gave him the look of a friendly owl. Or so his last girlfriend had said. They had broken up after he chose the Midwest over Los Angeles. She had opted for L.A., where her visual arts career could take root.

Thaddeus couldn't believe his own eyes. Someone had taken a ballpoint and tattooed V-I-C-T-O-R into her breasts. Three letters per breast, each letter maybe two inches tall. The ballpoint had broken the skin and the cuts were deep and angry. There was matted blood around the wounds.

Thaddeus was stunned. "Who did this?"

"Victor Harrow did this. While I was passed out."

"You're certain it was Victor?"

"That's who I was drinking with. We were at his portable office."

"The purple bus."

"That's the one."

He knew it well. The bus said *"Harrow and Sons"* along the side. If Victor Harrow was in fact the one who had mutilated Ermeline Ransom, then Victor was going to end up owing the woman a busload of money. The County would erupt over news like this. He would finally become known. A twinge of excitement thumped through his chest.

"Why would Victor do this?" Thaddeus said, coming back to reality.

"I think he did it because he knew he could get away with it. Some men are like that."

Thaddeus frowned. It was more than a little difficult imagining Victor carving his name in anyone's breasts. After all, Victor was a deacon at First Christian, the president of Orbit Rotary, and a Silver Star from Vietnam. He was a lot of things, but an assailant of women? Thaddeus' frown deepened. It was all very hard to imagine.

"I don't know any men like that."

"Then you don't know men. Trust me. Victor Harrow *is* like that, especially when he's three sheets."

"Wait right here." Thaddeus went around to the office door and swung it wide open. "Come in here, please," he called to Christine, "and bring the firm camera with you."

Christine complied, and in minutes had made her way to Thaddeus' side. She was unclicking the camera case when she looked up. "Damn!" she cried. "What happened to you, girl?"

"Victor Harrow happened to me. Isn't it lovely?" She wiggled her breasts side to side.

Against his will, Thaddeus found himself growing aroused. "Now Christine, I'm going to go in the other room and get some coffee while you take a dozen pictures of Ermeline's breasts. Shoot from across the desk, then side view, and then close ups. When I come back let's everyone be buttoned up and ready to talk. Okay?"

"Got it," said Christine.

Thaddeus was passing through Christine's office/waiting room when the phone beeped. He quickly retraced his steps and picked up. "Thaddeus Murfee here. How can I help?"

"Thad, did she come over?" said Quentin Erwin, Jr., the Hickam County District Attorney and Thaddeus Murfee's best friend. "I sent her to see you because I sure as hell didn't know what to do with her. Great tits, though, huh?" Quentin loved raunchy cases like Ermeline's.

"She came over. Thanks, I guess. Christine's getting pictures right now."

"Are you watching the show?"

"No, I'm here in Christine's office, talking to you."

"Oh, man, you should be in on taking the pictures."

"No, chain-of-evidence. I want to be able to put Christine on the stand and ask her about the photos and establish chain-of-evidence."

"So you're thinking court?"

"I guess. Any ideas?"

"File suit against Victor Harrow, I guess. He's got the bucks."

"Are you going to prosecute him?"

"For what? He'll just say she consented to it. How else does he get his whole damn name there? I mean if she was resisting he wouldn't have gotten anywhere."

"She says she was passed out."

"That's what she told me too. I've been to a lot of parties with Ermeline. That girl can hold her booze. I can't see her passed out. My guess is it was Vic who was passed out and Ermeline did it to herself to get into his bank account."

"Damn, you're sick."

"Why?"

"I'll be over at the Dome for coffee around ten-fifteen. We can talk then. I don't want them to hear me, out here. Bye."

Thaddeus hung up and peeked into his office. From the

backside, Ermeline Ransom looked like a bat about to take flight. Her hands and arms were outstretched and her shirt was held wide open while the camera clicked and whirred. He poured a cup of coffee. He slowly counted to 200 and noisily went back inside. By now, Christine and Ermeline were seated in the two client chairs side by side.

"Okay, Chris, you got them?"

Christine nodded. "I hope they're okay. Front, side, top-down."

Ermeline pulled a tissue from the box on Thaddeus' desk. She dabbed at her eyes. "I showed Dr. Ahmad this morning. He tried alcohol but he said it's too deep. Alcohol didn't touch it."

"Did he have any other suggestions?"

"Not really. He had a mom call in for labor and had to leave anyway. But his nurse gave me a tetanus shot. He left a prescription for pain pills. I haven't filled it yet."

Thaddeus gulped his coffee. "Did Christine offer you coffee or a drink when you came in?"

"I told her I was too upset to have anything. Look at my hands shake!"

"I can see that. You should be upset. But we'll find someone who can do something about this. A dermatology doctor. Maybe it's just a matter of some kind of skin peel or dermabrasion."

"Dr. Ahmad said it's too deep for that. I already asked." Ermeline's eyes welled up with tears again. She instinctively placed her hand across her breasts, which were protected once again by bra and shirt.

The young lawyer knew Ermeline Ransom was a good soul, a hard worker and a dedicated single mom. But, just now, her look was of grave confusion. Something had gone terribly wrong in her life, and she didn't know where to start to unravel it. She dabbed at the tears.

"Look, Ermeline, why don't you take us through what happened. What was it Saturday night or last night?"

"Last night. Amateur night. I worked from two until ten at the Silver Dome. Lounge side." Thaddeus nodded and scribbled a mental note. "You got off at ten on Sunday night?"

"Right. Bronco Groski comes on duty then, because Bruce wants someone there who's tough enough to handle the rowdies. I'm only five-seven and 120 pounds, so I don't scare anyone."

"Got it." Thaddeus pulled out a yellow pad and scribbled his first notes.

"Ermeline, here's a thought. I'm pretty new at lawyering. Which you know. You might want to have someone with more experience than me handle this. Like Jeremy down the street, or his partner Elvin, although Elvin really only wants to do estates. Jeremy used to be District Attorney and might really have a feel for this kind of case, where I'm still learning how to patty-cake."

"I thought of that already. Trouble with everyone in town is they're all in bed with Victor Harrow. Or they want to be. I bet having him for a client is every lawyer's dream. He's always getting someone hurt on a highway job, or not paying his subs, like he did to my dad, or making new investments and needing more legal papers drawn up. I'm even surprised you're talking to me. You must want him for a client too."

"I might at that. But he would never come to me, I'm too green."

Victor Harrow was the richest, and thus the most

respected, man in town. He did *this*? To this poor girl? Thaddeus felt the indignation rising.

"Now, let's back up. What time did you get to work yesterday?"

"1:45 in the afternoon. Bruce was changing out the till and making a deposit before the bank deposit box closed."

"What were you wearing?"

"What I always wear. Black mini and white peasant blouse. My hair was blown dry, held by a barrette, and I was wearing pretty heavy lip gloss. Smiles mean tips."

"How'd you wind up at Vic Harrow's office?"

She turned to the window. "Vic had been buying rounds for everyone. He always does. Some of the guys from his crews were there, and they were kidding around, and Vic was getting them drunk. A benefit of working for him."

"Sure."

"So, around nine o'clock, he's in the hallway by the restrooms. I came out of the Ladies', and he's hitting the cigarette machine. He's cursing. I told him I'd get Bruce to unlock it. He said okay. Then he said, Ermeline, I need your help tonight. I asked how. He said he had just heard his bid was accepted on a new State job, and he was going to become a millionaire—again."

"So he was trying to impress you. Was he trying to get in your pants?"

"That's just Vic. He's always saying what's on his mind, and he doesn't mind who he's saying it to. Maybe, maybe not."

"But you left with him after you got off?"

"Over the next little while he kept buying rounds and asking me would I tag along to his office. He wanted to share a glass of champagne. He got pretty insistent. He said

Betty Anne Harrow was out of town, so he had no one to share the good news with. Honestly, he sounded very lonely."

"So you volunteered."

"Color me stupid. I guess you could say I volunteered. Vic leaves huge tips for all the girls. What's not to love about Vic and his money? We want him to keep coming back."

"So you volunteered, but you were also feathering your nest a little?"

"A little, yes. I call my babysitter, and she calls her folks to ask if it's okay for her to stay an extra half hour. She's fifteen and it's past curfew, but her parents have no objection. So I tell Victor I'll follow him out to the bus but only for a half hour, one drink, and then I was off."

"Was that okay with him?"

"His eyes lit up. He smiled that huge smile of his. I felt like I had made his night."

"You followed him in your car?"

She turned away from the window and looked Thaddeus in the eye. "I followed in my car. I had no intention of staying a minute past ten-thirty, and I wanted my own ride out of there. Swear to God."

"I'm sure that's true. So what happened once you got to the bus?"

"We went inside. He turned on some lights. He had me wait on the sofa while he poured us a tumbler of champagne. He brought it to me, we toasted. That's when someone knocked on the door. It sounded like the rear door of the bus. Vic went over to the window and looked out. 'Be right back,' he said. He disappeared down the hall.

"I heard talking but muffled. Then there was brief shouting, angry sounding. Then a man I've never seen before. He came in with Vic close behind. 'Meet Johnny Bladanni,' Vic says, and I stand up and stick out my hand. He takes my hand. Then—of all things—he kisses my hand. I was mortified, that's not how we do things in Orbit."

"What did you find out about Johnny Bladanni?"

"He was down from Chicago on business with Victor. He was only staying ten or fifteen minutes. Victor told him to help himself to some champagne. Mr. Bladanni asked if I needed a refill, I said 'No,' but he insisted and almost yanked it out of my hand. Still smiling all the time. He was very smooth, very oily, very Chicago."

"Got it. So he got you a drink?"

"He did. Then we had a three-way toast to Victor's new business."

Thaddeus looked up from his scribbling. His notes covered two pages of the yellow pad. "What happened next? Give all the details you can remember."

"Next? I woke up, it was black outside, and my breasts were, like, on fire."

"And you did what?"

"I switched on the light over the couch. My blouse was pulled down and my bra was around my neck all tangled up. I saw my chest and screamed."

"Did Vic come when you screamed?"

"No. In fact, I never did see Vic again. He might have left me there alone, for all I know."

"How do you know it was Vic who did this to you and not Johnny Oily Guy?"

"Why would anyone carve someone else's name in a girl's breasts? Just doesn't make sense, does it?"

"Not that I have that kind of experience, but no, I guess it doesn't. So we're pretty sure it was Vic."

"When I left there were no other cars. Just Vic's truck and my car. Johnny Bladanni wasn't around. Besides, I was too terrified to pay much attention. All I wanted to do was get the hell out of there and get home and check on Jaime."

"You needed to see Jaime."

"That was my only thought. I wasn't thinking about what had happened to me or why. I could only think about my little boy who I'd abandoned. My watch said a little after four a.m. As soon as I got on Washington, I tore home."

"You had been there maybe six and a half hours."

"Something like that."

"What happened next?"

"Got home, found the babysitter asleep on the couch—with her mom, God bless her. Went tearing into Jaime's room. Sound asleep, hugging his teddy bear. I felt horrible and couldn't explain what had happened. The mom was insanely angry with me and thought I'd been out on an all-night hoot. I started crying and trying to explain, but she wasn't listening by then. She shoved her daughter out the door. 'Never again,' she said as the door slammed. 'Never again.'"

"Which only made you feel worse."

She nodded and tears rolled down her cheeks. "I felt like the world's worst mother! I had no idea what happened to me."

"What did you do next?"

"I found some cigarettes in the back of the kitchen drawer. Salems. I don't smoke, but that didn't stop me. I lit up and stood at the kitchen sink. I was smoking and crying. I had to keep it soft for Jaime's sake."

"Did you call anyone?"

"Who's there to call?"

"The cops?"

"No."

"Why not."

"My first idea, once I put out the cigarette, was get in the shower and see if the ink would come off. I also needed to see if I had been raped."

"Were you?"

"I don't think so. If I was, he used a condom. The ink didn't come off."

"What did you do?"

"Believe it or not, I took my tooth brush in the shower with me. I scraped some soap on it and scrubbed the letters on my breasts."

"Did it help?"

"Not a bit. It just made it hurt more. Some of the scratches were so deep they started bleeding."

"Just a minute. Christine," she was still sitting beside Ermeline, "how about some more coffee? I'll bet Ermeline would like one now."

"Ermeline?"

"Black," said Ermeline. She put a hand on her chest and held it there.

"Okay, so you probably weren't raped, and you took a shower."

"Then I went to bed and couldn't sleep. Around seven I called my mom, and she came over. I left her with Jaime, and I went up to my doctor's, then to the Sheriff's office. I talked to Sheriff Altiman, and he said I should come see District Attorney Quentin Erwin. I drove back home, got Jaime off to school, and drove back to the courthouse and parked next to Quentin's space. I sat out front until Quentin arrived."

Christine returned with two coffees and set one on the

desk before Ermeline. She passed the second one to Thaddeus and excused herself. "I'm going back out to get the phones. Don't want to miss any exciting calls."

"Thanks," said Thaddeus.

"So what comes next?" Ermeline asked after swallowing a gulp of coffee. "Can you help me?"

"I think so. I need to talk to Quentin and Sheriff Altiman and see whether they plan to prosecute. Then I'll call you, and we'll make some plans, is that okay?"

"Did you want to get any more pictures?"

"I think we've got enough," he said. "Chris was trained to take pictures in the Army and does a very fine job for me."

"I'm going to go call a skin doctor in Quincy. I want to know if they can get this stuff off."

"Unknown. It might depend on the type of ink, but I'm just guessing, and I don't like to guess," he said.

"No more peasant blouses at work, not for a while anyway."

"It would show?"

"Yes, I already tried. Sad to say. Thaddeus, can I ask one thing?"

"Sure."

"Would you sue Victor Harrow for me?"

"I would, if the facts pan out. Right now, it looks very promising. But I still need to talk to some people and read some law."

She placed her coffee cup back in its saucer. "Well, then, I guess we're done here?"

"For now. Remember the rule: don't discuss this matter with anyone. Not even your mom. Everyone is a potential witness if you discuss the case with them."

"I'll be quiet."

They shook hands and their eyes met like conspirators. Thaddeus walked Ermeline to the front door. They said their goodbyes, and Thaddeus returned to his office and checked his watch. 10:15. Time to catch Quentin at the Silver Dome. They had a lot to discuss.

That morning, Thaddeus had begun his day at 5:45 a.m. like he did every day except for Sunday. He flew out of bed wearing nothing but boxers, and mounted the Lifecycle, which he pedaled like a jackhammer for the next thirty minutes, working up a glistening sweat and matted hair.

He dismounted the Lifecycle and went to the junior fridge in his studio. A new gallon of OJ awaited him. He spun the cap and drank half straight down and topped it off with a protein bar, the wrapper of which guaranteed increased muscle mass.

At 6:25 he was in the shower, listening to Sirius on the waterproof pink radio, and flossing.

Dressed in his gray pinstripes and black wingtips and fresh from the shower, Thaddeus had checked his briefcase that morning and counted files. Everything looked fine. Satisfied that the previous night's work was accounted for, he stepped onto the small porch outside his front door. Thaddeus lived only four blocks off the Orbit County Square, where all the lawyers spun their webs.

His porch faced Madison Street, to the south. The sun was still hiding behind the buildings on the town square off to his left, but its orange glow could be seen above the rooflines and trees. As quickly as the sun was coming up, the clouds from last night's rainstorm were burning off, and large patches of blue sky could be seen. The air was clear, the mourning doves were calling, and two small boys came blasting by on skateboards, probably headed uptown to the best skating around the courthouse.

He paused on the red brick porch, flipped the Oakley's over his eyes, inhaled a huge breath of the clear Illinois morning air, and reached the southwest corner of the square at exactly 7 a.m.

He strolled past a few stores and took a right into the Silver Dome Inn, part of Bruce Blongeir's spread. Here, Thaddeus drank his morning coffee and caught up with the latest.

His coffee group consisted mostly of Orbit County farmers who came to town and had coffee with their gossip every day just like Thaddeus. And there was also one other lawyer in attendance, 89-year-old D.B. Leinager.

Cece Seymour, came around with coffee, cup, and saucer for Thaddeus. She presided over the room, filling cups and taking breakfast orders, laughing and back-slapping and keeping the place happy and loud.

One farmer, Jonas Meiling, was offering his two cents worth when Thaddeus' coffee was poured.

"From what I hear, some very funny business went down in Victor Harrow's bus last night," Meiling said. He raised a white eyebrow and waited to see if anyone else wanted to chime in. Not a nibble. "Harrow's funny business involved a certain young lady we all know, I might add."

"Vic Harrow throws some wild parties in that bus," Thaddeus offered.

"Pure hearsay," interjected D.B. Leinager, the emeritus lawyer in his loud, boisterous, German voice. "Victor Harrow is my client and a good and decent man. I don't know where you people come up with such rubbish as that.

No such thing as wild parties at his bus. For your information, that bus is his office. I've been there, and I've never seen a single bottle of beer or jug of whiskey."

"Which means old Vic didn't care enough to offer you a drink," laughed Jonas Meiling. Both white eyebrows shot up in anticipation of D.B.'s comeback. But D.B. only snorted and forked a glob of scrambled eggs in his mouth.

"So what did you hear, Jonas," Thaddeus asked. "What kind of funny business went down last night in the bus?"

Jonas Meiling snidely remarked, "Sheriff Altiman was paid a visit early this a.m. by a very distraught young woman who our fine sheriff referred over to the District Attorney. Seems she had been attacked by Victor Harrow—now this is just gossip, and I'm the first to admit it. But I heard this from a deputy sheriff who shall remain anonymous."

"That wouldn't be your son-in-law Deputy Mike Hermes, would it?" D.B. Leinager shot down the table. "This anonymous source a close family member?"

Jonas Meiling spread his hands and shook his head, a smile playing around his mouth. "Can't say."

"What about you, Thaddeus," Frances Dorman asked, moving all eyes to Thaddeus. "Tell us what you've heard about last night."

Thaddeus took a sip of his coffee and shook his head. "Last night I watched my two shows on HBO and was fast asleep by eleven. I haven't heard jack."

"Isn't Harrow a client of yours?" Dorman persisted.

Thaddeus smiled. "You know I couldn't confess to that even if it was true. A lawyer can't tell who his clients are and aren't."

Dorman looked around the table. He cut off a half sausage and poked it in his mouth, which didn't stop him from coming after Thaddeus. "From what I hear, you're the one lawyer in town he doesn't do business with. At least not yet. Victor Harrow likes to keep all you lawyers busy so none of you is free to sue him ever. Conflict of interest or some such thing." Dorman smirked, letting everyone know he knew more than they might think.

Thaddeus knew Vic Harrow's money came from the strategic relationships he maintained with politicos in Springfield, people who helped him file lowball bids on state highway jobs, especially the never-ending saga of the freeway between Springfield and Chicago. Like all Illinois highway boondoggles, this particular freeway had been under construction for forty years, and no less than eight general contractors had made enough to retire forever, thanks to this concrete plum. In return for getting hired as the general contractor on the freeway, Victor kicked back to the pols and the mob in Chicago. This way everyone remained happy—with the exception of the traveling public, who, in planning to journey between Springfield and Chicago, always allowed extra time for the twenty miles of construction zone that perpetually plagued the four-lane, like a flesh-eating pox that was always tearing-down and hauling away truckloads of dirt and concrete, which it later replaced with dirt and concrete that looked remarkably like what had just been removed.

"You might be right about Victor's choice in lawyers," Thaddeus finally said. "But I don't know enough to be much help there, sorry."

Cece came wheeling around with the coffee pots and a tray of desserts. "Anyone?" she asked the table.

Thaddeus covered his cup with his hand. "Nothing more for me, Cece. Gotta go make a buck."

"Knowing the lawyers in this town, you'll make more

today than most farmers make in a month!" Jonas Meiling shot at Thaddeus as he climbed to his feet.

"That's because I'm such a hard worker, Jonas," Thaddeus replied, resting a hand on Jonas' shoulder. "Unlike you, I don't have hours to burn in the coffee shops around our little town. Later, Gents."

They all nodded goodbye, and he paid his check at 7:50 and left the Silver Dome.

The sky was flaming red in the east as the early morning yawned over the City of Orbit. Last night's rain was gone, and the air was clear and cool.

As he did every weekday, Thaddeus scampered across Washington Street when he saw a break, and jumped up on the sidewalk on the east side of the square along Monroe Street.

He was headed toward his office and kept a brisk step in his stride as if he had important business waiting at the office. In fact, he knew he had no appointments this morning, and the best he could hope for was a DWI from Saturday night or a domestic dispute over the weekend that was continuing today with divorce lawyers.

On his left, was the courthouse, a magnificent structure built in 1890, according to its inscribed cornerstone, when so much of the rest of America was built in what must have been a gigantic building boom.

Thaddeus crossed the street on the north side of the square, edged left two doors, and inserted his key. His office was directly above a Western Auto catalog store.

At 8 a.m., on schedule, he sat behind his wide oak table and took a sip of coffee. He looked at his calendar for the day and sighed. He admitted to himself that it looked neither promising nor profitable. Yet, here he was, ahead of the crowd, and ready to rule it all across the street. Just biding my time, he thought. It will happen, sooner or later, the great case will walk in that door, and I'll be on my way.

Paralegal Christine Susmann had received her professional training in the U.S. Army. Following Basic Training, she had begun her career working as an M.P. and had served two years at a Black Ops detention center in Baghdad. She was under lifetime orders to never discuss what she had seen or done on that post, which was fine, she never wanted to discuss it anyway. Following two successful years working hand-in-glove with the CIA field officers, she had her choice of Army schools and selected paralegal school. She had seen all she ever wanted to see of detention centers, prisons, jails, or any other institution where people were held against their will. Paralegal training had dragged on for almost a year, but when she finished she was assigned to a JAG unit of busy lawyers in Germany.

Christine was five-five and average weight, but that's where "average" ended for her. For one thing, she was beautiful and had won Miss Hickam County in the summer of her senior year, right before enlisting. For another thing she was built like an NFL safety: broad, heavily muscled shoulders and upper arms, muscular thighs and calves, and she could still press 275 while she only weighed 135. She worked out religiously at the East Orbit Athletic Club with her husband, Sonny. Christine found working for Thaddeus to be pleasant yet difficult, mainly because Thaddeus knew so little about the practicalities of law practice, which drove Christine to the phones, where she was constantly calling her friends in other law offices with questions about how to do this and that, the nuts and bolts that pay the bills.

Chris's day began at 8:30. At 8:25 she came up the stairs two-at-a-time and bounced into the office. She called out good morning, made sure Thaddeus had coffee, checked the voice mails, and went over the day's diary.

Today, she was wearing the outfit that always made it to the office at least one day a week: long gray skirt, embroidered top, and navy blazer with gold buttons. She kept the nails short and clear of polish; they would only be traumatized at the athletic club anyway.

Following the scan of the calendar, Christine called into Thaddeus, "Got another hot chick for you next Saturday night!"

Thaddeus winced. He answered her over their intercom system which consisted of the two of them shouting back and forth from their desks, down the short hallway separating them. "No thanks. I'll do my own recruiting. Besides, my ideal woman is getting her Ph.D. in English lit. I doubt you know her."

"No, this is different. Her name's Lila and she went through Basic with me. She's coming for a visit."

"She's too old for me if she went through Basic with you. I don't date older women, I told you that."

"Thad, I'm five years older than you. So's Lila. That's not an 'older woman,' as you so hatefully put it."

"Not hatefully, not scornfully, just cautiously."

"We need to get you matched up with someone."

"Why is that again?"

"So you can be truly happy. Like Sonny."

He knew better than to say anything about her husband.

"Quentin Erwin, Junior just called from the DA's office. He's sending over a young woman for you to talk to."

"Probably a divorce client. Here's hoping she's got fifteen hundred bucks."

"I'll second that!"

While Christine was busy in her office, Thaddeus went back to updating his Facebook page. Status: Single. But looking.

Ten minutes later Ermeline Ransom was standing on the other side of his desk, unbuttoning her blouse, while Thaddeus, for once, was speechless.

The Defendants: Chapter Two

The governor's mansion was located in Springfield. But, because of the huge number of state employees—not to mention registered voters—in Chicago, most governors maintained a residence there, too. On the taxpayers' dime, of course. And Governor Cleman L. Walker was no different. He kept a beautiful 1920 tri-level on the Gold Coast.

The Governor himself was short in stature but long on mythology: it was said, while he was a Chicago precinct committeeman, he had seen more than one uncooperative political crony chained and dumped in nearby Lake Michigan, and that, while he was quick to pull the trigger on politicians of the opposite political party, he was equally as quick to head up a dozen charitable drives a year.

His favorite charities were the ones that got the big headlines: veterans and orphans and dying children without insurance. He was known to have a huge heart, it was true, but he was just as well known for having a heavy hand when it came to running his state. He was red-faced from his booze and cigars and high stress levels.

A week before the Ermeline Ransom incident, the governor was in his private study, reclined in a leather chair, whiskey and water in hand, a Cuban cigar burning nearby, enjoying the trouncing the Bears were handing to the Cowboys.

Occasionally, he would check his Rolex. Bang Bang Moltinari was already a half hour late and Cleman L. Walker was beginning to wonder if the man was late simply because something unexpected had come up, or was his late arrival aimed at proving a point about his sovereignty from the Governor?

He took another deep drag off the rolled Cuban tobacco leaves. "The best," he murmured and rolled the cigar in his fingers admiringly. He closed his pale blue eyes, savoring what few Americans got to savor anymore, Cuban smoke. Within two minutes, one of his three cellphones rang. It was Robert K. Amistaggio, the Illinois Attorney General.

"Bob?" the Governor said. "I'm going to need to talk to you for about ten minutes tomorrow. Confidential, my office."

"Done. What time?"

"Noon. We'll have lunch brought in. You still like the oysters?"

"I do. Should I bring any files along?"

"Bring what you have on Victor Harrow."

"Who?"

"Victor Harrow of Harrow and Sons. He's a two-bit contractor out of Orbit. He has the contract on the Springfield-Chicago run."

"Name doesn't ring a bell. We need to control him?"

"We do. And if we can't do it through your office I'll have to go to the mat with him."

"Anything I should look for?" said the AG.

"We need to figure out where he's vulnerable. He's stiffing us."

"How far behind?"

"The contract is seventy-five percent paid out. We're in for half. He's paid us less than one-fourth. Word is, he's done and refuses to pay another dime. This cannot continue. Either the AG's office or Bang Bang is going to have to enforce."

"Another cowboy."

"Yes, he's got a wild hair from somewhere; you know what I always say."

"A wild hair from somewhere."

"See you at noon, then."

Ricardo "Bang Bang" Moltinari was the namesake and head of the Moltinari mob. This was the mob that controlled Chicago, operating primarily out of Skokie, where the key labor unions and building trades offices were located.

Like the Governor, Bang Bang also lived on the Gold Coast, except while the Governor's residence was English Countryside and consisted of a home and attached three-car, Moltinari's spread was a Historic Register enclave walled in by indigenous rock and mortar, and consisted of a 10,000 square foot home and four outbuildings, including a guest house where his bodyguards passed their off-time with high-stakes poker, craps, and a steady stream of Michigan Avenue hookers whose arrivals and departures spanned about one hour apiece.

Bang Bang left home that day handcuffed to a

Halliburton aluminum briefcase. He exited the gates in a bullet-proof Cadillac sedan. He was backed up by a Cadillac SUV bristling with guns behind black-out windows. The windows were illegal, but the cops knew better than to hassle one of the Governor's key friends. In short, Bang Bang was immune. He enforced the Governor's state contracts. In return, the Governor protected Bang Bang's crime syndicate. That's the way it had been done for 100 years in Chicago, and it wasn't ever going to change. Not as long as the Chicago politicians and the Chicago mob were in charge and running things.

Bang Bang's entourage headed southeast, toward Lake Michigan. As they clipped along at twenty over and careened around corners, a lookout was kept for other cars that might try to cut them off or follow too close. Those idiots were menaced with a gun barrel or a killer stare-down from one of the vehicles. Mostly, though, the people of Chicago knew that there were certain cars and certain neighbors one simply did not approach. To do so was to risk life and limb.

At 3:45 Bang Bang's procession screeched into the Governor's lot and proceeded to park. A small army of Illinois State Policemen, all burly and scowling, peered inside the cars and cautiously allowed the visitors to exit their vehicles. They were prudently searched but allowed to retain their firearms unless going inside to meet with the governor.

Bang Bang was first out. The briefcase dangled from his wrist while his hands went on top of the car. He was frisked by an angry looking sergeant. A state trooper escorted him to a side door of the Governor's house, and knocked twice. An interior state trooper took him from there. The leftover police and mobsters lolled around the two black vehicles. They smoked. They engaged in stare-downs. Nobody minded; everybody stared right back. Here were nature's natural enemies come together on solemn ground, where the outside rules didn't apply, where the lions let the lions alone. There was a high degree of mutual respect and mutual distaste. Each group had its orders. You better damn well get along with the other side if you want to keep working this easy duty. Everyone obeyed. At the end of the day, it was easy and safe duty. No one would ever be insane enough to make an attempt on either the Governor or on Bang Bang.

Bang Bang Moltinari followed the state trooper into the Governor's office. "Morning, Your Honor," he snarled at the Governor, upset that he had been called away from family on a Sunday. His son was home for mid-term break from Harvard where he was pre-law, and his twin daughters were home from the University of Illinois in Urbana.

"You're looking old today," the Governor said, and choked on laughter.

Bang Bang was in his early fifties and had come up in the mob the hard way. He had started out running numbers and girls on Chicago's West Side, and then he caught the eye of Jimmy Novalici, a Lieutenant in the mob who was expert at cargo hijacking from O'Hare International.

Bang Bang had become wealthy exploiting interstate freight and gunning down those who interfered. He was tall, wore his black hair combed straight back and his teeth were perfect. His smile stopped the ladies cold. He had never had a love problem; they all adored and worshipped him and he was very generous with the gifts ladies like. Cartier, Australian Pink Diamonds (a lady's best friend), Rolex—all of the good names found their ways onto his ladies' fingers, necks, and wrists.

"Hello, Bangman," the Governor said, using his pet name for the mob boss.

"We got problems to get me out this cold Sunday?"

"We do. We got some customers who are neglecting their payments to our little fund."

"What, we couldn't do this Monday?"

"I'm leaving for a governors' conference in San Francisco after lunch tomorrow. Too late. Don't worry, I've only got three names for you."

"I'm listening. Who's first?"

The Governor pulled a page from the back of the legal pad on his desk. "Great Lakes Underpass and Overpass, LLC. Late as always."

"GLUO again? I warned that son of a bitch to keep up with his contracts. How much?"

"Well, I'm down $150K for the month, and GLUO's portion is thirty-five."

"Got it," said Bang Bang. "A call from me will jar this guy loose. Next."

"Midland Freeway and Secondary. They have four paving jobs open east of Springfield, and the management has changed due to a shareholders' restructure. The new owner is playing dumb, like he's never heard of us."

"We'll visit him first thing in the morning. We'll make sure he understands the program. How much we light?"

"Fifty grand, give or take, five. Fifty makes me happy at this point."

"Done. Who's the third?"

"A nobody out of Orbit. Name of Victor Harrow, Harrow and Sons Construction."

"Poor Victor. He picked a damn poor time to stop paying if he's the reason I'm over here on Sunday."

"He's a large part of the reason. He's into me for one-ten."

"110 G's?"

"That's right."

Bang Bang spread his hands. "Look, you gotta tell me these things right away. This guy's way over on the skim. He'll cry like a pig when we demand the whole play up front."

"Let him cry. My people tell me he's been paid three-fourths on his bid contract, there's only about a fourth left, and he says 'Enough,' he says 'he's done with us.' We're in for half, he's paid less than a fourth."

"Stupid SOB. What do you want from me here?"

"Just put the fear in him. He's a nobody. But he's high profile in his crapola little town."

"Johnny Blades?"

"Johnny's perfect. Just don't break anything on the guy. We only need him scared. And tell Johnny not to come back without at least fifty grand on him. Persistence is what this is going to take. Johnny might be down there a couple days."

Bang Bang smiled. "You don't know Johnny. He can say more to a man in thirty seconds than anyone I've ever known. And I've known plenty."

"I don't doubt that, Bangman. I don't doubt that."

"So what else we got?"

"Like I say, I'm $150K light this month. Make it a happy holiday for me, yes?"

"Done. Until next time."

The Governor's eyes narrowed. He gave Bang Bang his coldest look. "Aren't you forgetting something," he said, holding up his hand while his face glowed red. "Don't you have a little something for me?"

Bang Bang smiled and opened the briefcase. He pulled

out a stack of banded $100 bills and bounced them against his knee. "It's all there. $75K, all from yesterday, all from Michigan Avenue."

"Bless those merchants. They are going to be very happy when we allow them to open for Black Friday on Thanksgiving Day. They deserve no less."

"Black Friday, Pink Tuesday, who gives a big damn?"

"I do, Bangman, I do."

Grab your copy…
vinci-books.com/thedefendants

About the Author

John Ellsworth is a attorney turned author. His legal thrillers have sold more than three million copies, achieving bestseller status.

He lives on the west coast of the United States, where he continues to thrill readers with his edge-of-your seat courtroom dramas.